PENHALIGON'S ROCK

To escape from a devastating experience in
connection with her job in London,
Rachel Hayward goes to stay in the little
Cornish village of St Morwenna's Bay. At
first, it seems to be a place where nothing
much ever happens, but things are not
quite what they seem. Rachel's fascination
with a rocky island out in the bay,
reputedly the haunt of the long-dead
smuggler Penhaligon, leads to danger and
the discovery of a shocking secret
— shared with a man who is also escaping
his past.

Books by Betty O'Rourke
Published by The House of Ulverscroft:

MISTS OF REMEMBRANCE
ISLAND OF THE GODS
NIGHTINGALE SUMMER

BETTY O'ROURKE

◆

PENHALIGON'S ROCK

Complete and Unabridged

ULVERSCROFT
Leicester

First Large Print Edition
published 2000

The moral right of the author has been asserted

Copyright © 2000 by Betty O'Rourke
All rights reserved

British Library CIP Data

O'Rourke, Betty
    Penhaligon's rock.—Large print ed.—
Ulverscroft large print series: romance
1. Love stories
2. Large type books
I. Title
823.9'14 [F]

ISBN 0–7089–4208–3

Published by
F. A. Thorpe (Publishing) Ltd.
Anstey, Leicestershire

Set by Words & Graphics Ltd.
Anstey, Leicestershire
Printed and bound in Great Britain by
T. J. International Ltd., Padstow, Cornwall

This book is printed on acid-free paper

into the wind, adding, 'I suppose you've something else lined up. You wouldn't give up a good job otherwise.' He leaned forward and began moving aside some ropes that lay coiled on the deck near his feet. He didn't appear to need any answer, so Rachel didn't offer one. She leant back against the rail, closed her eyes and lifted her face towards the sun and began to day dream.

Her job had been a good one, enjoyable and fulfilling. She'd been lucky to be taken on, straight from University and that had been one of the reasons she had said no when her mother had invited her to come and live with her and her new husband in Canada. There were other reasons as well; much as she liked Phillip, she didn't want to share a home with two newly-weds. She'd fly out and visit instead, once they'd settled in, she told herself. It was five years now, yet somehow she still hadn't found time to make the trip.

When Roger Yateley joined the company in January, life had seemed as if it couldn't be better. She had a job she loved, a nice flat in a good area, a generous salary, and a great social life. Then, without warning, her world had collapsed around her. It was still too painful, the memory still too raw to dwell on. It became imperative that she left London, which had become a lonely, hostile place, no longer the place where she had friends and was happy, but now full of people who distrusted her, who looked at her as if it was she who had committed the crime, she who was responsible for the terrible disruption at work.

In her misery and despair, Rachel thought of Cornwall. She had never been there, but had always imagined it to be a place of warm, sparkling seas, little villages offering cream teas and Cornish pasties, and comfortable, non-judgemental Aunt Freda and Uncle George in their farm at the top of the cliff. It seemed an ideal solution for a temporary escape.

She had telephoned Aunt Freda that evening, and been encouraged by her aunt's eager response. The visit had been intended only as a few days' respite, a brief break while the chaotic situation at work resolved itself, but then Claire, the Director's secretary and her loyal friend, who had been the only one to stand by her, declaring that she would never believe any of the lies being bandied about, had warned her that there were rumours that the situation, and Rachel's defiant attitude to it, were threatening to make her an embarrassment to the company. There seemed little alternative to immediate resignation. The visit to Cornwall looked like becoming considerably longer than she had envisaged. Claire helped her find a temporary tenant for the flat — Rachel couldn't bear the thought of giving it up entirely — and within a week she was on the train to Truro.

Uncle George met her at the station. It was a relief not to have to think about her problems or her future plans for a while. She had sat, silent, in the car, watching the narrow lanes and high hedges go by. Aunt Freda made much of her, welcoming her like a daughter of her own, and Uncle George, with little conversation or interest except what concerned farming matters, was kind and rather touchingly proud of his niece by marriage, who had an impressive-sounding job in London. She had spent the weekend in Cornwall, doing little except let the warm weather relax her, letting Aunt Freda encourage her to sit reading in a deck chair in the garden, but by Monday morning she had had enough, and, glad of something useful to do, had set off to fetch some urgently needed groceries and explore the surrounding countryside. St Morwenna's Bay had been the first Cornish village she had seen, and it had lived up to all her imaginings.

Rachel opened her eyes. The boat had all but stopped, and Stephen had lowered the sails. She saw he was manoeuvring them towards a bright red float, bobbing on the waves some hundred yards from the shore. As she watched, he deftly caught it with a boat hook and brought the Sea Pie alongside.

'I hope you're not squeamish about creepy crawlies,' he remarked, beginning to haul on a rope.

'What? Why, of course not!' Rachel had been so deep in thought she had almost forgotten where she was.

'Some people find live lobsters a bit scary, that's all.' Stephen lifted a wicker basket from the sea and tipped the contents on to the deck.

In spite of her disclaimer, Rachel tucked her feet hurriedly away from the waving claws of a pair of large lobsters. One by one, Stephen raised a series of baskets over the side and tipped their contents on to the deck. Some of the baskets contained nothing but sand and a few strands of seaweed, but by the time he had lifted eight baskets and emptied them, there were six large lobsters staggering pathetically on the wet and slippery deck.

'What will you do with them?' Rachel asked.

'There's a hotel in Launceston which will take them. There aren't enough to offer to the big places, like in Penzance, but there'll be more tomorrow.' He replaced the baskets over the side, tipped the lobsters into a bucket and unfastened the boat from the float. 'Have you back at the harbour before you know it,' he said, letting the sails fill again. 'The wind's with us, what there is of it. I thought you'd gone to sleep earlier.'

'I'm sorry. I was thinking,' Rachel said shyly. 'About leaving my job. It's rather complicated but I'm not sure I want to go back to work in London, anyway.'

'There's not much work available in Cornwall,' Stephen said. 'Seasonal work in hotels and some of the beach shops and cafes, but I doubt that's the kind of work you'd want.'

'I wouldn't mind. After the London rat race, it sounds restful.'

Stephen laughed, a little contemptuously, Rachel thought. 'Others might mind! There are few enough jobs for the locals, without outsiders taking some of them! Enjoy a holiday here, then go back to London and keep your illusions about Cornwall. It isn't blue skies and sparkling seas all year round, you know.'

Rachel flushed. 'I realise that. I'm not completely stupid. But why shouldn't I work here? I've met Cornish people who work in London.'

Stephen shrugged. 'Whatever your plans, I

wish you luck. If you want to come out again in Sea Pie, you'll usually find me in the same place by the harbour wall, or you can leave a message with Mrs Blamey.'

They were passing the bay below High Topp farm now, having made good speed on the return journey. Rachel felt uneasy that she had somehow offended Stephen, though she didn't know how. Perhaps he thought of her as a city dweller patronising the local country people, which was sad because that was the last thing she had intended. In an attempt to remedy things, she said, 'Yes, I'd love to come out again. And I promise I won't fall asleep in the sun next time. Look, what's that out in the mouth of the bay? Is it an island? It looks a wonderful place to picnic or sunbathe.'

'That's Penhaligon's Rock,' Stephen replied. His face looked surprisingly stern. 'And don't even think of trying to reach it, either by boat or swimming out from the shore. There are currents round it that make it terribly dangerous, and there are rocks all round at sea level, sharp as needles. No one can get near it, let alone land on it. Leave it to the seagulls; they're the only creatures that can use it.'

Rachel studied the huge rock as they passed. It looked hardly more than twenty yards across and was some forty or fifty feet high. Perhaps it had once been part of the headland, becoming detached from it in prehistoric times. Its summit was flat and grassy, looking ideal for sunbathing, but she could see for herself there was no way a boat could put in and land anyone, for the rock sides rose sheer out of the sea.

'Why is it called Penhaligon's Rock?' she asked.

'He was a local smuggler, hundreds of years ago,' Stephen said, without interest. 'And a wrecker, too, probably, since the Cornish went in for that sort of thing a lot, round this coast. They used to shine lights to confuse a ship into thinking it could sail into the bay safely, whereas it would crash on the rocks and then the wreckers would row out and plunder it.'

Rachel shuddered. 'How horrible!'

'They were desperate men, and very poor. Stealing from wrecks and outwitting the Revenue men was a way of life, two hundred and fifty years ago. Only way a good many Cornishmen could keep from starvation.'

They were about to enter the harbour again and Stephen skilfully manoeuvred the Sea Pie through the narrow gap. In seconds they were through the rows of other moored boats and he was tying up to the same ring in the harbour wall. He reached out a hand and helped her over the rail on to the lowest step above the water. As he passed her her shopping basket, he said, 'Thanks for your company, Rachel. Be seeing you around, I expect.'

Slowly she walked back up the hill towards High Topp farm. At the bend in the road she looked back and saw Stephen, his bucket of lobsters in one hand, cross the street to a van and put the bucket in the back of it. Then he got into the driver's seat and a moment later the van drove off, out of sight round the corner towards the main road.

Rachel arrived back at the farm in time to join her aunt in mid-morning coffee.

'Enjoy your walk to the village?' Freda asked, her comfortably ample form settled at the kitchen table.

'Yes, thank you. I met Stephen Tresillian and he took me for a sail in his boat, round the bay.' Rachel sipped her coffee.

Jennifer, the girl who helped Freda in the house, looked sharply at her. 'Stephen takes parties out shark fishing in the summer,' she said. 'I hope you're not thinking of hiring him for that. It's no sport for a woman.'

'No, I wasn't. Stephen invited me to come with him to check his lobster pots, that's all. We didn't go far.'

Jennifer gave her an odd, almost wary look.

She was in her early twenties, small, plump and dark and was, as she had proudly informed Rachel the previous evening, Cornish born and bred. Her manner towards Rachel was cool, polite but not friendly. Rachel suspected she resented her presence on the farm, but if so, why?

'Lunch will be at one o'clock. We eat in the kitchen during the week and some of the farmhands join us. You won't mind that, will you, dear?' Freda said anxiously.

'Heavens, no! I'll enjoy meeting them! Do let me help you prepare things.' It was beginning to be embarrassing, the way Aunt Freda seemed to want to treat her like a formal guest.

'You take a deck chair out in the garden, dear. Jennifer and I do the men's lunches,' Freda said firmly. Not wanting to be difficult, Rachel went out into the little flower-filled garden at the back of the farmhouse after coffee, and found herself a deck chair, but she disliked the feeling of being idle and waited upon while everyone else at the farm seemed to be working hard. She wandered round the side of the house and found Jennifer pegging washing on a line.

'Isn't there anything I can do to help? I'd like to,' Rachel asked.

'Help? You're here on holiday, aren't you?' Jennifer's tone was clearly intended to discourage.

'I wasn't thinking of my staying here as holiday,' Rachel said patiently. 'I'd like to pull my weight.'

'How long are you intending to stay, then?' Jennifer stared at her, a peg gripped between her teeth.

'I thought possibly for the rest of the summer; longer if I find a job, though I know the job market isn't very good here. But I was hoping to help around the farm in the meantime. Aunt Freda takes in paying guests, doesn't she?'

Jennifer glowered. 'She did, but she won't be taking many more of them now, will she?'

'What do you mean?' Rachel was taken aback by the girl's aggressive manner.

'Mrs Prescott has one large and two small singles to let. You've got the large one, and there's not much call for singles, so while you're here she won't be able to take bookings, will she?' Jennifer spoke as if she was explaining to a rather slow child.

'Oh, my goodness! I never realised! Oh, I can't let her lose business like that!' Rachel was horrified. 'I'll say something to her at once! Why did nobody explain to me?'

'She won't let you change your room.

You're family, after all,' Jennifer said with a touch of scorn.

Rachel hurried back to the farm kitchen at once.

'Aunt Freda! Why on earth didn't you say I had the room you normally let out? I'll move out straight away. Isn't there an attic room I could use, so you can still have all your usual spare ones?'

Freda, as Jennifer had prophesied, was firmly against Rachel moving out of her room, even to one of the smaller, single ones. 'You're family, dear,' she said 'and those single rooms are poky. I only let them out to children if a family books in.'

'I know there must be another room in the attic, where Jennifer sleeps,' Rachel said firmly. 'And I want to work for my keep, since you refused to take anything for my board and lodging.'

'I should think not indeed! Charging my own sister's child to stay with me! The very idea!' Freda tut-tutted indignantly.

'Aunt, the situation isn't quite what you may have thought. I hadn't merely intended coming to Cornwall for a week or so's holiday. I've left my job, and I'd like to stay here at least until I decide what direction my future is going to take. I can't stay here like a guest under those circumstances, can I? I'll look for a local job in town as soon as I can, something to tide me over, and a flat or a room nearby. But, in the meantime — '

'I wouldn't hear of such a thing!' Freda raised her hands in horror. 'Of course you must stay with us, dear, for as long as you care to.'

'Only if I may have a room that won't be used for your bed and breakfast customers, and if I may help around the house. And the farm, too, if Uncle George would let me.'

Freda took a great deal of persuading, but Rachel was insistent, and, realising that her aunt hadn't actually expected her to be staying the whole summer, a bargain was struck. Rachel would move into the smaller of the single rooms and look after any paying guests who booked in during the summer. She would go into Truro the following day and see the people at the Information office, tell them what rooms were available at the farm and ask them to send along any suitable people who enquired for accommodation.

'I only reckon to do bed and breakfast,' Freda said. 'Usually they're on their way somewhere and it's just for the one night, but occasionally they stay longer, up to a week at most. They're no trouble; they're always anxious to be out exploring as soon as

26

breakfast is over, and we don't usually see them again until bedtime.'

Once everything was sorted out to the satisfaction of them both, Rachel stayed in the kitchen to help prepare lunch. At half past twelve, Jennifer appeared, raised her eyebrows at the sight of the table already laid, but said nothing. Rachel had an uneasy feeling that perhaps it had been the Cornish girl's job to look after the paying guests, and that she would give offence by taking it over, but it was difficult to approach her on the subject; Jennifer's manner towards her was frosty, to say the least.

George Prescott and three farmhands appeared at the kitchen door promptly at five minutes to one. All of them were in their stockinged feet, their boots ranged beside the back door. The farm hands were shy, rather bashful young lads, eyeing Rachel covertly and blushing whenever she glanced at them.

'This is my niece Rachel, come from London,' George announced in his booming voice. 'And these lads are Ted, Bill and Darren. Now, don't be shy, lads, you'll be seeing Rachel often enough. My wife tells me she'll be staying here all summer at least.'

News gets passed on fast, Rachel thought, wondering when Aunt Freda could have spoken to Uncle George about her intentions.

Jennifer looked up sharply at George's words. Clearly, she hadn't expected Rachel's plans to have been confirmed so soon.

'I've discussed things with Aunt Freda,' Rachel, taking her place beside Jennifer, said quietly. 'I'm moving my things into the smallest room this afternoon. And I'm seeing the Tourist Office about bookings tomorrow, so hopefully we'll soon be having plenty of enquiries for paying guests.'

Jennifer said nothing, so, after a moment, under cover of the general conversation, Rachel added 'I told Aunt Freda I'd like to help with them, but I don't want to take over if it was your job. Was it?'

Jennifer shrugged. 'I used to help look after 'em, but if that's what you want to do, go ahead. I'm not bothered either way.'

'If you're sure you don't mind.'

Jennifer said off-handedly, 'There's enough to do around the farm as it is. You look after them if you've a mind to, I sha'n't care. Happen you'll get tired of it soon enough.'

'I'm no stranger to hard work,' Rachel said. 'I may not have done this kind of work in London but I assure you I'm perfectly capable of doing whatever's needful.'

Jennifer gave her a long stare. 'I'll bet you

are,' she whispered meaningfully, then turned her attention fully to Freda's excellent stew and ignored Rachel for the rest of the meal.

When she went upstairs to change her room after lunch, Rachel considered asking her aunt if she knew why Jennifer appeared so unfriendly, but it seemed like complaining about the girl, so she said nothing, vowing that at least she'd never give Jennifer cause to think she felt herself above any kind of domestic work.

That evening, after supper, which they took without the farmhands, who had left for home, George settled himself in his favourite arm chair with a copy of Farmer's Weekly, and Freda brought out her knitting and sat in the matching chair on the other side of the fireplace.

'There's television if you like, dear,' she said to Rachel, who was wondering what she would do with herself until bedtime.

'Some books on the shelf on the landing, if you like reading.' George clearly didn't, unless it was a newspaper or the Farmer's Weekly. 'We leave 'em for any of the guests but you're welcome to help yourself.'

Jennifer came into the room and for a moment Rachel thought that perhaps she could begin to get to know the Cornish girl better with an evening's chat, but Jennifer had her jacket on and her handbag slung on one shoulder.

'I'm off to the cinema now. Goodnight, Mrs Prescott,' she announced.

'Goodnight, dear. I'll leave the back door open. Lock up when you come in.' Freda barely looked up, she had been counting stitches.

Rachel opened her mouth to suggest that she'd like to come along as well. Surely Jennifer couldn't remain unfriendly for a whole evening if they went out together? She was relieved, though, that she had not actually spoken, when Jennifer added, 'Must dash — Alan's waiting for me at the end of the lane with his motor bike.'

She could hardly intrude after that. Rejecting television, Rachel wandered upstairs to find herself something to read amongst the row of dog-eared paperbacks left behind by previous guests. When she returned, Aunt Freda was knitting energetically in what appeared to be a complicated pattern, and Uncle George was dozing, his paper propped against his chest.

What have I done? Rachel thought, in a moment of sudden panic. I've given up my flat in London and broken contact with everyone I knew there. I still knew people who weren't work colleagues; they would have stayed friends. I might have found another interesting job. Instead, I've given it all up — for this? Is this going to be the pattern of my life now? Have I made a terrible mistake by running away to Cornwall so impulsively?

2

As it happened, Rachel didn't go into Truro the following day. There was a telephone enquiry shortly after breakfast, asking for accommodation for a week, starting that evening, for a couple and their small son, a boy of eight.

'I'll prepare the rooms, Aunt Freda,' Rachel said eagerly, glad of something to do.

'The rooms are already prepared. The beds are always made up with fresh sheets,' Jennifer informed her sourly.

Rachel ignored her. She went into the garden and cut a few flowers for a welcoming vase for the dressing table, then dusted and polished the furniture, conscious that it had already been recently dusted by Jennifer.

She checked the larder for all they might need for breakfast, and decided that it might be a good idea to buy some ground coffee, as an alternative to offering tea or instant coffee.

'I'll walk down to the village and buy some before lunch,' she said. 'We could do with brown sugar, too. And perhaps a wider choice of cereals.'

'You won't find Ida Blamey stocking fancy

stuff like that,' Jennifer said, sniffing her scorn. 'She doesn't have the call for it, and she doesn't have the room to stock much beyond basic foodstuffs.'

'That's right,' Freda confirmed. 'Ida's all right for any emergency groceries, but if you think these people will expect anything more, best to get it when George takes me in to do the monthly shop at the supermarket.'

'But I'll need these things for tomorrow morning,' Rachel said. 'I'll hardly have time to go into Truro by bus now. Isn't there anywhere else which might have a bigger stock?'

'Well, there's Pengorran,' Freda said doubtfully. 'It's the village over the headland; much bigger than St Morwenna's Bay. It has a supermarket and several other stores. You'd find everything you needed, there, but there's no bus. I'd ask George to drive you, but he's gone over to Arthur Pengelly's farm to see about some heifers. He won't be back before supper-time.'

'How far is it to walk?' Rachel asked.

'A goodish way by road, but it's not more than two miles if you walk over the headland. Keep to the path at the cliff edge until you're the far side of the bay, then turn inland. The lane's signposted from there.'

'That shouldn't take me too long, and I

33

could do with a walk.' It was a good opportunity to escape from the farm and Jennifer, for a couple of hours. Rachel ran to fetch her jacket and a shopping basket.

'It's a long walk if you're not used to it,' Jennifer warned. 'Sure you're up to it? Best part of five miles it'll be, all told.'

'It may surprise you, but we do manage to walk in London, too,' Rachel snapped tartly. Jennifer's manner was annoying, but Aunt Freda didn't appear to be aware of the friction.

She set off, striding over the fields at the back of the farmhouse. At the edge of Prescott land a stile led to a lane which opened out to a path along the top of the cliff.

Rachel stopped to look out over the water. There were a couple of small sailing boats, far out to sea, and, below her, on the beach, she could hear the sounds of children shouting as they played. It must be low tide now, uncovering a wide expanse of rock and pool strewn sand, an exciting playground for children. To reach the beach, they must have climbed down a steep and winding path from just a little further along the cliff top. Up here, Rachel could see a few cars parked on a flat, gravelled area. The path was the only way of reaching the beach, she had been told.

Rachel continued round the cliff top, and, at its further end, looked out again at the sea. Now, she could see clearly the large mass of rock jutting out of the waves just outside the curve of the bay. Penhaligon's Rock, once owned by a notorious wrecker, as Stephen had told her. From here, she could see now that the rock was further out from the land than she had first thought, and rose sheer out of the sea some fifty feet to its flat, grassy top. She could see the white tips of the waves breaking round the base of it, and it certainly looked dangerously inaccessible from the bay.

And yet, if Penhaligon lit lanterns to lure ships on to the rock to be wrecked, he must have found a way to land on it. I suppose the tides and rocks might have been different in those days, she thought, it was, after all, at least two hundred and fifty years ago.

The cliff path ended in another stile which led into a sunken lane with high hedges on either side. A leaning wooden signpost pointed away to the right, with half obliterated letters stating 'Pengarron, 1½ miles'.

The lane finally led onto a metalled road, with neat bungalows lining it on either side. Within five minutes Rachel was at the outskirts of a sizeable village, boasting shops, cafes, pubs and a small public library. It looked almost as big as a small town.

She found the supermarket, which stocked everything she needed. There was also a small specialist delicatessen which sold a rather exotic brand of ground coffee. She bought some, feeling with a sense of proprietorial pride, that these people who came to stay at the farm shouldn't be left with the impression that the country couldn't provide a breakfast to satisfy any city dweller. She hoped they would be the kind of people who appreciated good coffee for breakfast.

Rachel wandered round the village for a while, glancing in shop windows, into the entrances of intriguing passageways which seemed to lead to mysterious, secret homes tucked away behind the main street. There were a fair number of people about, but from the way they greeted each other, or scurried past with shopping bags, she guessed they were mostly locals. It would seem that the summer tourists hadn't discovered Pengarron, either. Perhaps there were fewer attractions in an inland village.

Time was getting on. After a cup of coffee in a cosy, old-fashioned tea shop full of middle-aged ladies, Rachel started for home. She reached the first stile before she noticed that the temperature seemed to have dropped by several degrees. As she crossed the first field a cloud of mist rolled towards her from the direction of the sea, enveloping her in a thick, moisture-filled fog. It happened so suddenly that she was, at first, disorientated by it, and stopped to take her bearings. To her right she could hear the roar and rattle of the tide on the shingle, and moved towards it. She felt relief when she came up against a hedge, and followed it until she came to the beginning of the clifftop path.

The sea mist was thick, not soot laden like a city fog but as impenetrable. Sudden fear struck Rachel. Was it wise to walk along this path, at places right up to the edge of the cliff, and unfenced along its length, when she could see nothing, hear nothing except the muffled sounds of the sea below?

I could walk across the fields inland. I'm sure I'm near enough to the farm not to get lost, she thought. The clifftop path, though a shorter route, held no appeal when there was no longer any view out to sea.

Rachel turned left, clambered over a gate into a field and set a course slightly to her right in an attempt to cross the field at right angles. According to her calculations, the far side of this field should be next to a field belonging to the Prescotts and she should be able to follow a path from there to the farm itself.

Either the field was much larger than she had thought, or her route had wavered, for, half an hour later she was still in the middle of the field, with nothing on which to take a bearing; she'd passed no bush, tree or hedge and the sea mist was an thick as ever.

Rachel was experiencing the beginnings of panic, half convinced that she would wander forever in this enclosed world without ever finding a way back to the farm. She had never known anything quite like this before. Aunt Freda had talked of the sudden sea mists which could blow in off the coast with the incoming tide, but Rachel had never imagined it could be as dense as this.

When she had almost convinced herself that she should begin shouting for help, a hedge loomed up in front of her and she almost cried out in relief. She didn't recognise it, but surely, she reasoned, if she followed alongside this one it would be bound to bring her to a gate or stile that was familiar.

Rachel turned in the direction she thought the farm was, and, keeping the hedge as close beside her as practical, walked on. She was convinced that Prescott land must be on the other side, and, if she once reached that, there would be a path or at least a track of churned earth leading to the farm, made by the cows coming in for milking.

There wasn't a stile or gate, but so convinced was she that she needed to reach the other side of the hedge, that when she found a gap made by a dead tree which had fallen sideways, she scrambled through into the next field.

This one was very similar to the field she'd left, but then, she told herself, cows didn't keep near the hedge; she'd find their path nearer the centre. All she had to do was walk straight ahead, looking for signs of a track made by cattle.

The mist seemed slightly thinner here and after a few moments she thought she saw something ahead that looked like the side of a barn or a hayrick. She began walking towards it when she unexpectedly came up against a fence made of strands of barbed wire. Fastened to the fence was a wooden board which had on it in red lettering: DANGER. KEEP OUT.

What on earth would something like that be doing in Uncle George's fields, Rachel thought, stopping in bewilderment. I must be somewhere quite different from where I thought — not near the farm at all.

She really was frightened now. She had visions of wandering endless fields in an everlasting mist until she was exhausted and

39

darkness came. She had heard of the dangers of wandering on Bodmin Moor but it hadn't occurred to her that an ordinary field could prove just as hazardous.

As quickly as it had rolled in from the sea, the mist suddenly lifted and in front of her Rachel saw a crumbling brick building, the size of a large shed, with a chimney and piles of loose stones lying on an expanse of cracked concrete.

What on earth is this place, she wondered. She was sure there was nothing like it on Uncle George's farm, but then, she hadn't explored all his land yet and perhaps this was some long disused outbuilding or part of an older farmhouse, crumbled into decay. Glancing along the length of barbed wire, she saw a wooden gate some yards to her left, standing slightly open. Disregarding the Keep Out board, she stepped through the gate and walked towards the ruined building. The mist still hung here in patches, thicker near the wall. She was half way across the broken, weed-strewn ground when she saw some movement beside the wall. A figure in oilskins came from round one corner, walking towards her.

At first Rachel was startled, almost convinced it was some ghostly apparition, then common-sense and relief asserted themselves. Here was another human being, someone who could tell her where she was, put her in the right direction for High Topp farm.

'Help! Stop, please! Stop!' Rachel called.

The figure hesitated. For a moment she thought he was going to go back again behind the wall, then he strode briskly towards her and a moment later she was almost sobbing out her relief.

'Stephen! Thank goodness it's you! Please help me!' She ran towards him, stumbling on the uneven ground.

'Rachel! What on earth are you doing here?' Stephen's voice sounded sharp, angry even.

'I lost my way in the fog. I've been wandering round these fields for ages.' Now that she felt safe, her voice wobbled tearfully.

'Do you know what this is?' He took her arm, steering her back to the gate. 'Did you not see the notice to keep out?'

'Yes, but —'

'This is one of the old tin mines. Cornwall's littered with them. Most of them are crumbling and dangerous but this one is particularly so because there's an open mine shaft behind the wall. What on earth possessed you to come wandering up here in weather like this?'

'I told you. I lost my way. It was a clear, sunny day when I walked into Pengorran, and then, suddenly, it was all — '

'You walked from Pengorran? But that's miles back; miles away from here,' Stephen exclaimed.

'I didn't fancy walking along the cliff path when I couldn't see, so I tried to come back inland, over the fields.' Really, Stephen seemed to be making very heavy weather of her experience. Surely he didn't think she had deliberately gone for a walk round the mine in the mist?

'You're some miles from High Topp farm,' Stephen said. He saw her face fall and added, 'But don't worry. The road's just the far side of this field and I can take you back in my van. Here, let me take your shopping basket.' He took the basket from her and, holding her arm with his free hand, hurried her towards the gate. Once they were through, he produced a padlock and chain from his pocket and fastened it shut. 'It's too dangerous for people to wander about inside,' he said. 'I'll have you back at the Prescott's farm in ten minutes, providing you don't mind the van smelling of fish.'

'I don't mind anything so long as I get back to the farm,' Rachel said. 'I was really beginning to be scared out there. I didn't know where I was.'

'You should have kept to the cliff path. You can't reach High Topp farm by walking inland,' Stephen said, 'unless you go by the road, and that's twice the distance.' He sounded cross, as though, Rachel thought, he was annoyed that she had been there. Meekly she followed him up the field to the hedge by the corner, where there was a stile. A few yards away, his van was parked pulled off the road under a large oak.

Thankfully, she slipped into the passenger seat. As they drove off, she tried to get her bearings and work out how she could possibly have found herself this far from the farm. She had left the clifftop path with not more than half a mile further to go.

'Surely it would have been just as dangerous to walk along the cliff edge in mist like that?' she asked, trying to justify her actions.

'It isn't dangerous if you're careful.' Stephen kept his eyes on the road and didn't appear disposed to talk.

'Do you often have mists like that?' Rachel wanted to keep the conversation going. For some reason, Stephen seemed to be annoyed with her. She wondered if it was because she had behaved stupidly and he considered she might have put herself in danger.

'Sea mist is a feature of the Cornish coast. It rolls up suddenly, and just as suddenly blows away again. It comes in with the tide, often, and when it's going to be hot. It hangs around over the fields but it doesn't come too far inland. Look!'

They were cresting the brow of a hill and he pointed away to the left, where vestiges of mist hung in patches, some four feet from the ground.

'It's very curious. I haven't seen anything like it before,' Rachel said.

'Wind's rising. It'll be long gone before evening. Fine, hot day tomorrow. You should have left your exploring until then.'

Annoyed, Rachel stayed silent. Surely the evidence of a shopping basket of groceries was enough to indicate she hadn't merely been out exploring? Come to think of it, what was a fisherman doing in a deserted, ruined tin mine? But she didn't have the confidence to ask.

Stephen drove into the farmyard, scattering the few hens that Freda still kept to roam freely and scratch for food. He pulled up at the farmyard door and, out of politeness, Rachel invited him in for a cup of coffee.

'No, thanks. I'd best be off. Take care!'

He helped her out with the shopping basket, then returned to the driver's seat and had turned the van before Rachel had time to reach the door..

The main door of the farmhouse, which everyone used, was the back door and led directly into the big kitchen. Rachel stepped inside and put her purchases on the table.

'You've been a long time, dear. What did you think of Pengarron? Bigger than St Morwenna but still not like the places you're used to, I expect.' Freda was at the stove, prodding the contents of a saucepan with a fork. Jennifer came from the passageway carrying a handful of cutlery and began to lay the table, pointedly moving Rachel's shopping aside on to the dresser.

'I got lost,' Rachel said briefly. She didn't want to go into explanations about the mist and her trek across the fields.

Jennifer gave her a sharp, disbelieving look. 'Was that a car in the yard? You got a lift back, then?'

'Stephen found me. He brought me back.'

Jennifer stopped laying the table and stared at her. 'Stephen? Where did you meet him? Surely not in Pengarron?' Her voice was sharp, almost suspicious.

'I walked back over the fields and lost my way. I came across some kind of ruined building and luckily Stephen was there. He told me it was an old tin mine.'

'You went up by the old tin mine?' Freda turned from the cooker. 'That's a terribly dangerous place. You could easily fall down the shaft or have some of the wall fall on you. I hope you didn't go inside the wire. It's supposed to be fenced off and a notice warning people to keep out.'

'So I saw. I was so relieved to see Stephen. I'd become completely disorientated by the mist.'

'You'd better see you steer clear of that place in future,' Jennifer muttered. She glared at Rachel, and added, in a whisper that did not reach Freda 'and you can leave Stephen alone in future. Do you understand? Don't go chasing after him; he's better things to do with his time than waste it with you. Besides, he's not your type,'

'What! But I wasn't — ' Rachel began indignantly, stung by the unfairness of the remark. She turned away. What was the point of arguing with the girl? She left the kitchen before she was tempted into saying anything more, which could lead to a full blown argument. Jennifer was still glaring after her as she went into the hallway to hang up her jacket.

So that was how things stood. Jennifer evidently considered Stephen her own property, though what Stephen felt was more open

46

to doubt. It was strange he hadn't mentioned her if the attraction was mutual, and Mrs Blamey, the local busybody, would surely have made it her business to see that Rachel knew that Stephen had a girlfriend.

There was something else that was strange, too. When Jennifer had gone out to the cinema the previous evening, hadn't she mentioned that she was meeting someone called Alan? Was she stringing along two boyfriends, or was it that she was being a dog in the manger?

The bed and breakfast family arrived about five o'clock that evening and Rachel showed them up to their rooms, the large double for the husband and wife, the smaller of the singles for their little boy. Mrs Pringle, who told Rachel they'd spent their honeymoon in Cornwall but hadn't been back since, expressed delight at the farm and seemed touched by the vase of mixed flowers that welcomed them.

'We live in a flat in north London,' she said. 'It'll be wonderful for Brian to be able to play here, there's so much space.'

Rachel gave them directions to a good place for their evening meal, ascertained what time they would like breakfast next morning, and left them to unpack. Jennifer seemed to have made herself scarce after her outburst.

The evening began as on all the previous evenings, once supper had been eaten and cleared away, Freda settled with her knitting and George picked up the newspaper. After a few minutes he tossed it aside.

'This is no way for a young girl to be spending her evenings,' he announced. 'Rachel, you must be bored silly, sitting here with us old fogeys, every evening.'

'It's quite all right, really, Uncle. I have my book,' Rachel said hastily, not wanting to admit that he was right, she was bored.

'Nonsense! It's no life for a young woman to be stuck indoors of an evening! Come along, fetch your jacket. I'm taking you to visit our local nightspot.'

Rachel looked up in surprise, and even Freda raised her head from her knitting to look at her husband open-mouthed.

'Look lively, m'dear. I'm taking you to sample the nightlife St Morwenna's Bay has to offer. We're not all fuddy-duddies going to bed at ten, y'know.' He gave her an exaggerated wink. Freda saw it, smiled in understanding and bent her head to her knitting again.

Intrigued, Rachel collected her jacket and handbag and joined her uncle in the farmyard. He opened the passenger door of the Range Rover for her, then climbed into the driver's seat beside her. 'We could walk, I suppose,' he said, 'but it's a long haul, back up the hill, and dark, too. No fancy street lighting like you have in London, m'dear.'

When he drove along the road beside the harbour wall, Rachel finally understood. The only lights came from riding lights on the boats in harbour, and the Anchorage pub, which glowed with welcome from across the road.

'It's all we have here, I'm afraid,' George said, helping her down from the Range Rover. 'But if you come here regularly, you're certain to meet everyone in St Morwenna's Bay, eventually.'

The pub was fairly full, mostly farmworkers or fishermen, Rachel guessed, the latter still in their navy sweaters and heavy seaboots. The farmworkers had smartened themselves up a little, but this was certainly not a place for wearing one's best clothes.

There were a few women, all of them young and all of them either with a man or in a group. In a far corner Rachel saw Bill and Darren, the two younger farmhands who worked for George Prescott. They were with a group of other men of about the same age, and two young girls, who sat together, looking a little left out of things.

George raised his hand to them in a brief

greeting, then turned to the bar.

'Evening, Harry,' he greeted the landlord, who was serving pints to a group of fishermen.

'Hallo, George! Don't often see you in here of an evening,' came the reply. 'Missus kicked you out, has she?'

George steered Rachel forward to the counter. 'I've brought my wife's niece in for a bit of excitement,' he said, 'and to meet some of the locals. Poor lass is staying with us and it's no fun for her, stuck indoors with me and Freda dozing in our armchairs. Here, Rachel, m'dear, meet our landlord, Harry Penrose. Harry, this is Rachel Hayward, come down from London for a bit of a holiday.'

'How do?' Harry finished serving his customers and turned his full attention on Rachel and George. 'What can I get you? Care to sample our scrumpy? You don't often get that in London, I reckon.'

'Aye, she'll have scrumpy,' George decided, before Rachel had time to speak. 'Just a half, mind, that's potent stuff, especially if you're not used to it. Give me a pint of the local brew, Harry.'

Harry pulled the drinks expertly, standing them on the counter. 'If it's excitement you're after,' he said to Rachel in a conspiratorial whisper, 'I reckon you've come to the right place tonight. Place is fair humming with it. Jack Trescoe caught a mighty big shark today when he was out with a bunch of people from the east. He's over there, celebrating with them now, and I reckon that shark gets larger by the minute.' He grinned at Rachel and added 'hope you enjoy your holiday here, miss, and the weather keeps fine for you.'

Rachel smiled her thanks but inwardly sighed. She wasn't going to keep explaining that she wasn't here for a week or two's holiday. If she was still here by the autumn, then maybe they'd accept she wasn't merely a visitor.

She looked across to where Harry had indicated, and saw a group of men sitting round a table, laughing and talking loudly. Only one had the jersey and seaboots of a fisherman; the others, though casually dressed in jeans, had the unmistakable look of town dwellers on holiday. They were all drinking shorts, whereas the fisherman, like most of the locals, nursed a glass of beer.

George moved away from the bar to make room for some fresh customers, and began making his way to the far end of the room, where there were some unoccupied seats. His progress was slow, since he knew everyone in the room and stopped for a word or to introduce Rachel, to most of them.

51

Rachel sipped her scrumpy. It tasted like ordinary cider, but before she was half way through her glass, discovered it was far stronger than she had expected. She was glad to sit down at last and look round the crowded bar.

The pub was genuinely old, with small, diamond-paned windows and horse brasses and pewter tankards adorning much of the wall space. There was a large fireplace at one end, unlit now but piled with logs ready for the first chilly evening of autumn. George watched her looking at everything, and remarked, 'Regular haunt of smugglers in the old days, this place was. It's got cellars in the rock below that have held a deal more than legal barrels of beer, that's for sure.'

'I know Cornwall was famous for smuggling in the old days,' Rachel replied.

'Not just the old days, neither. Fair amount of it still goes on, if truth be told,' George said quietly. ''Course, contraband might be a bit different these days, I reckon.'

Rachel leaned back against the wall, at a place which wasn't covered with horse brasses and decided she rather liked the Anchorage, though it didn't look as if it was the kind of pub that women frequented, at least, not by themselves. She was used to the pubs near her London home where the clientele was more evenly distributed between men and women.

She happened to glance up towards the door and saw a familiar figure enter. Stephen crossed to the bar and chatted with Harry while he bought himself a pint. Mindful of Jennifer's remarks, Rachel didn't try to catch his attention and invite him to join them, though on reflection, she didn't see why she shouldn't, with George here with her, who clearly knew him too.

Stephen didn't see her, and crossed the room to join a group of three fishermen sitting together. Perhaps, Rachel thought, she'd say hallo to him when she passed by his table on her way to fetch George a second pint. A few moments later, the door opened again and Jennifer came in, followed by a young man carrying a motorcycle helmet on his arm. George saw her look, and said, 'That's Alan, Jennifer's young man. Works at Oundle's farm, a few miles inland.'

It was clear at once that Jennifer and Alan were a couple. They laughed and talked together with Harry while waiting to be served, and Rachel noticed that Jennifer, dressed in jeans and a leather jacket, also carried a motorcycle helmet. They didn't notice her or George and, once served, went to join Bill and Darren. To do this, they had to pass the table where Stephen was sitting, and Rachel noticed with interest that Jennifer gave him no more than the briefest of nods as she passed. Once seated with Alan and the other two, she chattered to them animatedly, turning frequently towards Alan as if to confirm something, or draw him into the conversation. She seemed a totally different, far more pleasant and friendly person in this situation. Twice, Rachel saw her rest her hand on his leather jacketed sleeve in a proprietorial gesture. To any onlooker, they must appear to be close.

What was going on? Why should Jennifer want to warn her off Stephen if he wasn't her boyfriend, if she had someone else with whom she was clearly very close? Why should it matter to her who took an interest in Stephen, since she obviously didn't?

Rachel doubted if Uncle George would know what the situation was, but there was no harm in a tactful enquiry.

'Has Jennifer known Alan long?' she asked.

'Oh, aye, they've been going out together for some time now,' George answered readily. 'Don't suppose it will be too long before she announces she wants to get wed. Then she'll be moving to Oundle's, I reckon, and we'll lose a good little worker. Freda will miss her, that's for sure, but the young 'uns never stay long in the same place.' He gave a resigned sigh.

Well, really! Rachel thought crossly. What right had Jennifer to warn her off Stephen if she was practically engaged to someone else? She glanced across at Stephen, whom she could just see through the throng of people between. He really was a striking-looking man, so tail, and that flaming red hair and beard were certainly eye catching. If she were Jennifer, she wouldn't have looked twice at the stocky, nondescript Alan with Stephen around.

At that moment Stephen stood up to go to the bar for some refills. He happened to glance across in Rachel's direction and she deliberately smiled and waved. At once, he turned back and came up to their table.

'Evening, George,' he said. 'Nice to see you again, Rachel. I'm glad you have an escort home tonight so you won't get lost again in any more sea mists.'

George looked puzzled. Rachel smiled back. 'I've learnt my lesson over that,' she said. 'If there's any sign of a sea mist I shall stay put, wherever I am.'

'Don't worry. They're not all that common. Today's was unusually thick. May I get you another drink?'

'Thanks, but I owe you one for the trip on

Sea Pie. I was going to come and invite you to join us, but you were with your friends.' Rachel stood up. 'Another beer, Uncle George? And you, Stephen?'

'Well, thank you. I'll come to the bar with you. Those yokels I'm with have given me complicated orders.' Stephen smiled at her and stepped back to allow her to pass ahead of him. As they passed the table where George's farm workers were, Darren looked up and greeted her.

'Hallo, Rachel! I'm surprised to see you here.'

At once, Jennifer's head swivelled round and she stared at Rachel, with Stephen close behind. The expression on her face was furious, but there was also a look of fear, too.

3

Rachel enjoyed looking after the Pringles and was touched that Mr Pringle, at least, appreciated the brand of coffee she produced at breakfast, though Mrs Pringle preferred tea. They were little trouble, driving off after breakfast for a day's exploring or on the beach, and returning at Brian's bedtime, when Freda invited them to join her and George for coffee. Twice in the week, Rachel offered to look after Brian while the Pringles drove into town for an evening by themselves. The little boy was invariably asleep before they left, exhausted by the day's activities, and never stirred until morning, so there was hardly any effort involved. When they finally left, it was with glowing appreciation of all Rachel's care, a promise of recommendation to all their friends and that they would return the following year for sure.

'They always say that, but you never see 'em again,' Jennifer said sourly, watching the Pringles' car bounce across the muddy farmyard and out of the gate, into the lane.

'They might. If they come to Cornwall again I'm sure they'll want to stay here. They

57

know what they'd be getting,' Rachel replied mildly.

'Hmph! Fancy food! You'll spend all the profit on expensive stuff when all they expect is good, wholesome country fare.'

'They appreciated it.' Rachel's hand closed over the twenty pound note Mr Pringle had pressed on her as they left. She hadn't wanted to take it, embarrassed that they'd already paid a fair price for the accommodation, but he'd insisted. Now, she felt guiltily that Jennifer would have been the recipient, had she not taken over looking after the farm's paying guests.

'But I'm jobless now,' Rachel told herself, in mitigation. 'And I need a real job, not cooking breakfast and making beds. I can't carry on taking advantage of Aunt Freda's hospitality indefinitely.'

There were no more paying guests booked in as yet, so it seemed a good idea to visit the Tourist information Office and put High Topp farm firmly on the list for exceptionally good accommodation.

When they were seated round the kitchen table for coffee mid-morning, Rachel broached the subject to Freda. 'Do you have a photo of High Topp that I could give the tourist office? The farm looks so attractive, just like I imagined a farm ought to look, that I'm sure it would be a good selling point.'

George, who had, for once, joined them for coffee, looked up. 'There's some pictures of the place, taken a couple of years ago. Visitor took 'em; gave us some copies. Two years isn't too long ago, is it? Place can't have changed much.'

'Ideal! I'll take them in this morning. I feel like spending the day in town,' Rachel replied.

'Going to blow your tip on some posh clothes?' Jennifer asked. Rachel heard her, but chose to ignore the remark.

George stirred his coffee thoughtfully. 'Buses aren't that frequent. If you're going into town, best go in by car.'

'Oh, but I couldn't — ' Rachel had visions of being offered the Land Rover or, worse still, having George take time off to drive her in.

'There's a little car in one of the barns, Austin Metro. Don't use her much. I bought it for Freda but she's had no call to use her for months now. You could take that; she's been looked after, she'll start all right, I reckon.'

Freda smiled across at Rachel. 'Of course you must have it! I only ever use it for shopping, but when I go to the supermarket to stock up, George drives me in the Land Rover. There's more room for all the groceries.'

When Rachel still hesitated, Freda added 'to tell you the truth, I've always been nervous of the winding lanes round here, especially in the summer when there are visitors in their big cars trying to drive as if it was a city street. You do drive, don't you, dear?'

''Course she does! All young women know how to drive these days!' George said scornfully.

'Yes, I have a licence. I didn't have a car in London, it was more trouble than it was worth. I had an old banger when I was a student, though.'

'You'll manage this. She's easy to drive. If Freda can do it, anyone can,' George said, with something less than gallantry. He rose from his chair and pulled open a drawer of the big Welsh dresser that stretched along one side of the kitchen. 'Here are the keys.' He tossed a bunch on to the table in front of her. 'I'll get Bill to give her a once-over, make sure she's clean and the battery isn't flat.'

'Thank you so much, Uncle George!' Impulsively, Rachel jumped up and hugged him.

'Look on it as yours while you're here,'

Freda said, smiling. 'It's only going to be mouldering away in the barn, otherwise. Do it good to be used and I can't see myself ever driving it again before winter.'

When she was ready to leave, Rachel found Bill in the barn, brushing bits of straw off the car's roof.

'Battery's fine, Miss Rachel,' he greeted her. 'And she's got half a tank of petrol, plenty to take you into town and back. Nice little car, this.' He patted the bonnet approvingly. 'Get you around very well, and narrow lanes won't be a problem. Slip past anything, I reckon.'

He'd clearly checked the car over, for the engine started at once. Rachel drove out of the farmyard and down the lane, a little nervously at first, then gaining confidence as the skills came back to her. It was a great improvement to have her own transport, to be able to reach Truro in a matter of half an hour without being dependent on buses to restrict her length of stay.

It was still early, and she found a place in a car park easily enough, a patch of rough ground off a back street behind a row of shops. She wandered round the town, half tempted to buy something to wear with the Pringles' money but hesitant because she dreaded Jennifer's inevitable snide remarks.

61

There was also the fact that, as she was now out of work, she ought not to fritter away any money she had.

She bought a local paper and scanned the list of jobs vacant over a cup of coffee in a café in the High Street, but there was nothing that she thought she could do, or would wish to do. Part time waitresses and chambermaids dominated the wanted columns, but Rachel decided that if she wanted to do something like that, it would be better to try to increase the number of guests staying at the farm, and do the same job at home.

Later, she went to the Tourist Information office and had a helpful session with one of the staff, who was only too happy to include High Topp farm among the list of accommodation addresses, particularly with a photo of the farm to include with the details.

'Mrs Prescott registered with us last year and took quite a few visitors,' she said. 'but so far she hasn't had many this year, and she cancelled the registration recently; said she had family staying. The farm hasn't changed hands, has it?'

'No, nothing like that,' Rachel assured her, explaining the situation. 'I'm hoping to increase the business. I want to be fully booked for the whole of the rest of the season. I aim to offer special country breakfasts, home from home comforts, extras that other places might not think of.'

The assistant laughed. 'They all try to do that,' she said. 'There's quite a competition for tourists in the bed and breakfast trade. Fortunately, the county is such a popular holiday venue that there are plenty of visitors to go round. So, you're taking over from Mrs Prescott, are you, Miss Hayward?'

'Not exactly taking over. I've said I'll look after the guests for Aunt Freda. She has enough to do on the farm as it is.'

The woman nodded. She'd often wondered how some of the working farmers found time to run a busy bed and breakfast sideline. They must look forward to winter and some respite, as did some of the local people who were irritated by summer traffic jams and perpetually crowded shops.

Rachel left the tourist office and wondered what she should do next. A whole day off to herself, with her own transport, was a great treat, not to be wasted. She'd been round the shops in the main street and considered taking a drive out into the countryside, find a secluded beach, perhaps, if one still existed at the height of the summer here. Perhaps she'd look for a quiet country pub for lunch, away from these increasingly busy streets.

She looked about her, not entirely sure

which way she'd come since leaving Aunt Freda's car. The car park had been tucked away behind shops, she remembered, but not these shops, in the main street. Rachel turned down a side street, but there were no signs to a car park anywhere.

This is ridiculous, she told herself crossly. I can't lose my way in a town this size. The car MUST be somewhere nearby.

There were two empty shops at the end of a row, with a narrow passageway between them, which seemed to lead into a square where she could see cars parked. This had to be the place where she'd left the Metro, she thought. It must be behind this row of shops.

She set off down the passageway, narrow and rather dank, with weeds sprouting at the sides and a few rusting beer cans lying half hidden by their roots. It didn't look as if the passageway was used much; probably not at all since the shops had closed.

Rachel was halfway along its length when she heard running footsteps behind her. She had no time to stop or move aside before she felt a hand thrust heavily on to the middle of her back, and she was pushed forcefully to the ground.

Startled, she put out a hand to save herself and felt it land on something sharp. There was a stinging pain in her palm and she saw a spurt of blood ooze between her fingers. As she tried to get up, she saw the outline of a man bending over her. She opened her mouth to scream and he calmly bent down and lifted her handbag from her arm, where it had slid from her shoulder in her fall. Clutching it to him, he ran, pounding down the passageway and disappearing at the end, leaving Rachel dazed and with only the vaguest impression of light blue jeans, a dark top, and a man who had done this kind of thing before.

She let the scream come, more from anger than anything else. She screamed at the top of her voice, and went on screaming. After a few moments she vocalised it and began to shout 'Help! Help! Somebody, help!' But it seemed that in this busy town there was suddenly no one around to come to her aid.

Slowly she got to her feet. It seemed pointless to think of running after her assailant; her screams must have encouraged him to get as far away as possible by now. And almost at once she realised she couldn't run in any case, she was bruised and stiff and her whole body was shaking so much with shock that she could barely stand.

Rachel leant against the wall of the passage, and looked down at her cotton trousers. She saw that both knees were muddy and one side was torn and blood-stained. Her hand began to throb and she saw that a jagged piece of glass was embedded in her palm.

Slowly, her mind began functioning again. I must get help. I must find someone. Tottering shakily towards the end of the passage, she felt strangely vulnerable, a feeling of naked-ness, deprived of her handbag.

The passage opened out on to a small square that was used as a car park, but it was not, after all, the car park where she had left Aunt Freda's car. There were shops along one side but most of them had blinds drawn and looked shut. Rachel realised it must be lunch time and these small places had closed for the mid-day break. She walked on slowly, looking round. The square seemed quite deserted and of the man who had stolen her handbag there was no sign at all.

A few yards further on, she came to a shop selling antiques. It, too, looked closed but then, through the window she glimpsed someone moving at the back of the shop. Pushing the door open, she stumbled inside, calling out 'Please — can you help me? I've been mugged.'

A man came briskly from the gloomy recesses at the back of the shop. 'Good Lord, so you have!' he exclaimed, taking her by the arm. 'Here, sit down.'

He drew Rachel towards a long, pew-like

wooden settle that formed part of one of the displays in the window. He moved aside an assortment of bric-a-brac that covered the seat and steered her on to it. 'Where are you hurt?' he asked, dropping on to his knees in front of her.

'I — don't know.' She was still in a state of shock, hardly knowing what she was saying or doing. Deftly the man slid his hands along each leg and then each arm and around her neck. 'Nothing broken,' he announced. 'But that hand looks nasty. I'll bandage it for you. Don't worry, I know what I'm doing. I used to be a paramedic.' He disappeared into the back of the shop and returned a moment later with a mug of water.

'Sip this slowly,' he ordered. 'You'll feel a bit calmer in a minute and then you can come into the office in the back and I'll clean up that hand and your knee. Make you a cup of tea, too, and we can telephone the police. Did the mugger take anything?'

'My handbag,' Rachel said. 'He pushed me over and snatched it off my shoulder.'

'That's rotten,' the man sympathised. 'I suppose he's run off. No point in looking for him in the square?'

'No. He'll be long gone.' Obediently, she sipped at the mug of water and, surprisingly, it did make her feel less shaky.

'Feel able to move into the back, now?' He reached out a hand and took her good arm by the elbow. 'I'll telephone the police. They'll need to know your name. What is it?'

'Rachel Hayward.' She said it automatically, still in a daze.

'My name is Michael Conway.' He reached out to shake her hand, then, realising it was the hand she'd hurt in her fall, said, 'Let's get that glass sorted. I'd suggest the Casualty department at the local hospital, but, frankly, you'd have a long wait and I can do as good a job here.'

The shaking had subsided a little as Rachel rose to follow him into the back office of the shop. Michael pulled out a leather swivel chair from behind the desk that took up most of the room. After settling her in it, he picked up the telephone and punched out a number. While he telephoned, Rachel had time to look properly at her rescuer. He was in his mid to late thirties, she judged, of medium height, dark-haired and with light-brown, almost hazel eyes. He wasn't particularly good looking, but there was an attraction about him that made her feel at once that she could trust him. Perhaps it was the competent way he had dealt with her shock when she'd stumbled into his shop. Paramedic, he'd said. Perhaps that accounted for his combination of sympathy and efficiency. But what on earth was a paramedic doing, working in an antique shop?

She was hardly aware of what he was saying into the receiver, but as he put it down, he said, 'They're sending someone round. I'll put the kettle on and see to that hand of yours.'

He was away only a moment, then Rachel became aware of a bowl of water and an impressive-looking first aid box being put beside her on the desk. Her hand was taken and the fleshy part of her palm probed with gentle, yet skilful fingers.

'No other bits of glass; just this bit sticking out. I'll strap it up firmly, I doubt if it needs stitches. Better off without, if possible; with luck you won't even have a scar, but try to use your hand as little as possible for the next few days.'

Watching him dress and bandage her hand, then clean and cover the graze on her knee, she asked curiously, 'Did I hear you say you were a paramedic?' She hardly believed she could have heard aright.

'That's right. Worked on ambulances in London for years. It got very stressful, especially the motorway accidents involving children. Five years ago I decided I'd had enough, so I packed it all in, came down here and opened this antique shop.'

Rachel's eyes widened in surprise. 'That must have been a huge change. Why antiques? And why here?'

Michael moved across to where the kettle was beginning to boil. He made tea in a pretty, flowery pot and collected two mugs and a carton of milk from a shelf behind him. When he'd finished, he said, 'Antiques wasn't a sudden whim. I'd always been interested, and I'd collected quite a few bits and pieces over the years. It was something I'd hankered after doing for a long time, but London wasn't the place to start. It all came to a head one night when there was a particularly nasty accident — but enough of that. I've kept my hand in. You'd be surprised at the number of times I've been involved in first aid situations since leaving the service.'

'I'm so glad I came to your shop, then,' Rachel said. 'I couldn't have chosen anywhere better, though I suppose I didn't have any choice. Everywhere else seemed shut, and there was no one around.'

'This is a bit of a backwater,' Michael agreed. 'Everyone round here shuts for the lunch hour. I do, normally, but today I was working on my accounts and forgot the time. I had a sandwich while I worked and left the shop open.'

As he spoke, the shop door opened and the bell above it tinkled. A man's voice called, 'Hallo — anyone here?'

Michael went into the shop and returned a moment later, accompanied by a rather young-looking constable and a WPC.

'This the lady you telephoned us about? Miss Hayward?' He had his notebook out as he spoke, pencil poised. The woman police constable crouched down beside Rachel, her face concerned.

'Are you all right, dear? Were you attacked? Can you tell us what happened?'

Rachel told them, between sips of tea. There didn't seem to be much to say, it had all happened so quickly.

'Your first visit to the town?' The constable, who had introduced himself as PC Baker and his companion WPC Hanson, looked sympathetic. 'That's bad luck. You were walking down the alley between the empty shops, just near here? Why was that? It's rather a derelict place.'

'I thought I'd left my car here. I'd lost my bearings and — oh, my God, he's got my car keys too!' Realisation was beginning to dawn on her that it was not just her money that had been stolen, but so many other things that she had stuffed, unthinkingly, in her handbag over the last few days. The more she thought, the more things she remembered putting into her handbag before leaving High Topp farm; her driver's licence, her cheque book, credit cards, diary, lipstick, comb — even things of no use to anyone else, but essential to her.

'Oh, dear! I feel so naked without my handbag!' The reaction was beginning to set in. To her great embarrassment, Rachel felt tears pricking behind her eyelids.

'Can you give us any description of the thief?' the young WPC asked. Discreetly, she slipped a tissue into Rachel's hand.

'I hardly saw him. He came up behind me. All I saw was a glimpse of — jeans, and a dark padded jacket, like an anorak. I suppose most young men dress like that.'

'How old? Young, was he?'

'I barely saw his face, but, yes, I'd say he was young. Sixteen or so. He ran off very fast down the alley and there was no sign of him when I reached the end. That was several minutes later; I took a while to get to my feet again. I couldn't believe what had happened to me.'

The two police constables exchanged glances. Michael saw the look and asked, 'Do you have some idea who it might have been, then? Perhaps you've had this kind of thing happen before?'

'We don't have a name,' PC Baker replied.

'But that alley, and the area just at the end of it, is notorious for drug pushers. We both think the chap who snatched Miss Hayward's bag might well have been loitering nearby, waiting to meet his supplier. He saw her go down between the shops and took the opportunity to acquire some easy money. How much money did you have on you, Miss Hayward?'

'About forty pounds. And he was waiting to buy drugs, you think?'

'Every town has this problem to some extent. Here it isn't as serious as some of the bigger towns, but the holiday trade brings its own problems. We might, of course, be completely off the mark with this one, but from what you've told us, it looks very much like one of our young problem kids who wants a bit of extra cash for his fix.'

'My money going into a drug pusher's pocket!' Rachel shuddered.

'There's nothing more we can do at present. If there are any developments we'll be in touch with you at — ' PC Baker glanced at his notes. 'High Topp farm. And if you remember any further details — anything distinctive about him — '

Rachel shook her head. 'I barely saw him. Look, what am I going to do about my car? I haven't the keys and I haven't even the money for the bus fare home.'

'Don't worry about that now,' Michael said quickly. 'If you can wait another half hour I can drive you home myself. You're in no fit state to travel by yourself.'

'Oh, but I couldn't — '

'I was going to shut up shop early anyway. Today has been so quiet it's hardly worth staying open.'

He saw the two police constables to the door, while Rachel, feeling much better now, began to look with some interest at her surroundings.

'That's a curious map of Cornwall you have,' she indicated a framed picture on the wall behind the desk. She stood up and went over to take a closer look. 'What strange names! Kirrier, Pyder, East Wivel, Lesnowth — they sound so foreign! I've never heard of any of them.'

'Cornish Hundreds,' Michael said, coming to stand beside her. 'Cornwall was divided into nine of them. It goes back more than a thousand years. No one knows who made the divisions, or why, but the names are still in use. This is a very old map; I found it a couple of years ago but it's one thing I'll never sell. It's fascinating, but then, the whole of Cornwall is fascinating. It's quite different from any other part of the British Isles. Don't you think so?'

'Yes, I see what you mean. I've been here only a very short time, but there's something about Cornwall that's different.'

'You're here on holiday, then?' Michael sounded disappointed.

'No, not exactly, though everyone seems to think so. I left my job in London — it was impossible to stay on there — and came here to escape for a while, I suppose. The practical reason was that this was the only place where I knew anyone. I have an aunt living at High Topp farm, but I hadn't thought of coming as a holiday, but a chance to think about my future, decide on a change of direction, I think you could say.'

'Just the same thing happened to me,' Michael said. 'I couldn't go on with the ambulance service, so I came here. I find it a soothing place to live.'

Rachel hadn't meant to tell Michael — or anyone — about the disaster that had led to her resignation from her job, but in him she felt she had found a kindred spirit, someone else who had left London because it was impossible to stay there.

'I worked in experimental research in the field of food manufacture,' she said, confident that he, at least, would not stare blankly or let his eyes glaze over at the thought of such a job. 'It was fascinating work, I loved it. And the work I was doing could have led to a significant improvement in the nutrition of third world populations. Then, last year, a new man, Roger Yateley, joined the staff. He seemed interested in what I was doing, and knowledgeable about it, too. I began discussing my work with him, particularly after he offered to help with some minor experiments.'

'A collaboration?' Michael asked.

'I never intended that. I was working on my own. I should have kept it that way. My old university professor had warned me, years ago, to keep everything to myself until I was ready to publish, but I never gave it a thought. It was so good to have someone to bounce ideas off, and Roger was employed in the same company, after all.'

'And then?'

'I had completed all the work. All that was needed was to write up a detailed report of the whole thing. I never liked that part of it much, the formal part, and I suppose I was putting it off. I'd hardly settled down to sorting out my notes when the whole company seemed suddenly buzzing with excitement. Roger had published a paper in one of the professional journals, detailing research he said he had been working on privately for the past year. And it was on exactly the same subject as my own work; lifted entirely from the experiments I'd been discussing in detail with him over the last months.'

'That's appalling!' Michael looked at her in horror and sympathy. 'What did you do?'

'People at work were sympathetic, but they took the attitude that it was merely unfortunate. Two people working independently might well find they had been thinking along similar lines. If one completed ahead of the other, it would necessarily render the other person's work valueless. I knew better; all Roger's examples, all his experiments, were too similar to mine to have been mere coincidence. And if he had genuinely been working on a similar project, why hadn't he said so, at the beginning? An honest person would have done so, but Roger had stolen my entire project and passed it off as his own.'

'You could have challenged him, surely? Would no one believe you?'

'I did challenge him. He laughed in my face and told me to prove it. The trouble was, I'd told no one else; no one knew anything about what I was doing except Dennis Watson, who was head of the department. I'd told him, as a formality, but he'd discouraged me from discussing it with him until I'd completed, and, in truth, I hadn't wanted to trouble him. He was terminally ill at the time, and died just before the furore blew up. He was the only one who could have spoken up for me, and he wasn't there any more.

'My friend Claire, the Managing Director's secretary, told me in confidence that he'd spoken to the MD, knowing he hadn't long to live, and put my name forward as his successor. What Dennis said usually went, but this time they thought that Roger, with his newly published paper, was better qualified, and I was becoming something of an embarrassment, making a fuss and accusing Roger of plagiarism. To them, it must have sounded like sour grapes. No one believed me, except Claire, and she wasn't in a position to do more than provide a shoulder to cry on. I couldn't have stayed to work under Roger, and the story of my accusation had got round; I wouldn't have been a popular candidate for a job in any similar field. I suppose I reacted impulsively; as soon as I heard about Roger's appointment I telephoned Aunt Freda and invited myself down here. It was the only place I could think of; it's the only place I have any family, apart from my mother in Canada.'

'Have you had time to think what you'll do

next?' Michael asked. 'You were right to leave; a situation like that would have been intolerable. But in the long term?'

'I don't think I want to go back to London. Already I feel as if I'm slowing down, more in tune with the pace of the countryside. I'd like to stay in Cornwall for a while yet, some months at least, but I can't impose on them at the farm for too long. I'll have to look for a job seriously. Looking after bed and breakfast guests is one thing, but it's not really a proper job and it's unlikely to last beyond September.'

'Hmm, not much in your line to be had round here,' Michael remarked thoughtfully.

'So everyone keeps telling me! I don't think I even want another job like mine, now. I'd take anything that's offered, if I could find something. There was precious little in the local paper apart from waitressing or chambermaiding, but they were only for the summer. I want to stay on, see the Cornwall the tourists never see, in the winter.'

'I wish you luck! There'll be something if you're prepared to be flexible and consider anything,' Michael assured her. 'Look, I have these accounts to sort out. You don't happen to have accountancy qualifications, do you?

'Sorry, I'm afraid not. And I'm sorry I've taken up so much of your time already,'

Rachel said guiltily. 'You've been so very kind.'

She lifted her bandaged hand in acknowledgement.

'Not at all! It's good to find I haven't forgotten the old skills. Instinct takes over in accidents. I couldn't have let you go to hospital, knowing I could easily treat you myself. Now, if you care to pretend you're a tourist and browse among my stock for a while, I'll finish off in here and then I'll drive you home.'

Rachel wandered into the shop and began to look at all the goods for sale, ranged haphazardly in front of two large bay windows. Mostly, they consisted of small pieces of furniture; an oak chest, carved on the lid and with an intricate looking lock; a rather nice walnut ladies' desk, probably Victorian, and several chairs, set round a rather worn table, filled one side. On the other, smaller objects, vases, statues, and some china, were displayed. This side was dominated by a large bench with high back and sides. Rachel realised this was what she had sat on when first entering the shop. It looked cumbersome, out of place beside the better quality furniture that surrounded it, but was largely covered by smaller objects, piled on to the seat to display them.

Remembering how she had been bleeding badly, she checked on the arm of the bench and the floor beside it to see if she had left any bloodstains.

'That bench was a mistake,' came Michael's voice from the office doorway. 'It's an old church pew. Don't know how I managed to be so daft as to end up with it. I'll never sell it, that's for sure. It's quite useful for piling things on, though.'

The shop, though small, held a surprising amount of goods, and to Rachel's inexperienced eyes they appeared mostly of good quality, not the contents of an average junk shop, but beautiful, old pieces. There were some lovely carved objects, some clearly damaged, but all had once been good. There was quite an amount of dust over everything, as though Michael hadn't cleaned the shop very often. Rachel would have liked to offer to dust the window displays for him, but it seemed an impertinence to suggest it. Instead, she found some books, stacked in a wicker basket and saw, to her delight, they were old children's books. She was soon absorbed, curled into a large armchair near the back of the shop. Once, an elderly neighbour had entertained her with some of her own children's books. Rachel hadn't been very enthusiastic as a seven year old, but now she found herself delighted to renew the acquaintance of the 'Daisy' books, and 'Christie's Old Organ.'

'You look as if you're miles away.'

Rachel looked up, startled to see Michael standing over her, a bunch of keys in his hand. 'I hadn't the heart to disturb you, you looked so comfortable,' he said, 'but it's time to shut up shop and take you home. It's later than I intended, but you seemed so settled and I finished sorting the accounts with no interruptions from customers. Inconvenient creatures, customers can be, when you want to work, but they do help pay the rent.'

'I'm sorry! I remembered these books from when I was a child and I was reliving some early memories.' Rachel put the book aside, but Michael picked it up, glancing at the title.

'Like old books, do you? But you surely didn't read this sort of thing when you were a child, did you? It's more likely your grandmother did.'

'We had an elderly friend who used to give them to me to look at when I visited with my mother. I hadn't realised how much of them I must have taken in. I thought I'd only looked at the pictures, but the stories came back to me. I've been feeling like a seven year old for the last half hour.'

'It's been more like two hours. The longest

anyone's ever spent in my shop so far. Now it's time to shut and drive you back to St Morwenna's Bay.'

'It's terribly kind of you. I hate to impose, but —'

'Think nothing of it.' Michael went to lock the shop door when someone came up to it and pushed it open.

'Sorry, we're closed. Oh, it's you!' He opened the door wider as the young police constable entered.

'Is Miss Hayward still here? Good, I see she is! This wouldn't be yours by any chance, would it?' He held out his hand and, dangling by its strap from his fingers, Rachel saw her handbag.

'My bag! However did you find it? Did you catch the chap with it?' She stared in amazement, hardly able to believe what she was seeing.

'No such luck, unfortunately. But Emma —WPC Hanson — and I, had a hunch that if he was just a kid and after money for drugs, he wouldn't be interested in anything else and he'd throw your bag away. He wouldn't want to be seen carrying anything like that, so we had a scout round on the waste ground near the end of the passage way, the area where you said he was heading. We found this in the bushes and by the look of it, it's still got plenty in it. Perhaps you'd like to check through it?'

Rachel's legs felt shaky all over again, and she sat down heavily in the chair, opening her handbag with trembling fingers.

'My purse has gone,' she said, 'but my chequebook and credit cards are still here. And everything else, as far as I can remember.'

'There wouldn't have been anything else of use to him. He wouldn't have risked the credit cards, if he was as young as you think; cash was all he wanted. No doubt your purse will be thrown over a hedge somewhere along his route, too, once he'd emptied it.'

'I — I don't know what to say,' Rachel whispered, overcome.

'I just need you to confirm that it is your property, Miss Hayward. Naturally, we'll be pursuing our enquiries with regard to the thief, but I doubt that your money will be recovered.'

'That doesn't matter!' Rachel exclaimed, clasping her bag to her. 'Money's just money. It's all the personal things I thought I'd never see again! Oh, thank you so much!'

'Glad to be of service, Miss Hayward. I hope your hand gets better soon. When we catch the chap, and we will in the end, he'll have a charge of assault and injury to answer to, as well as theft.' The policeman nodded to Michael. 'I'll take up no more of your time then, sir. Glad I caught up with Miss Hayward before she left.' He was gone before either of them could answer.

'My car keys!' Rachel exclaimed in delight, holding them up. Michael looked disappointed. 'So you won't be needing a lift home? But what about your hand? You shouldn't use it if you can avoid doing so. If the cut opens, it'll start bleeding again.'

'It's my right hand. I only need that to hold the steering wheel. I'm sure I can manage, and I ought not to leave the car here overnight.'

'If you're sure, then,' Michael said dully. 'But at least let me walk with you to where you've left it. I seem to remember you said you weren't too sure where the car park was. Best not to be wandering around on your own again.' He locked the shop door, and, taking her arm, walked her across the open space in front of the shops. 'There's a road along here that leads back to the town centre. You'll be able to get your bearings and work out which car park it's in.'

Rachel recognised the street as soon as they reached it. 'It's across here,' she said. 'There, I can actually see it. Thank you so much for all you've done. I don't know how I would have coped without your help.'

'Glad I was around. And glad that it was to my shop that you came for help.' Michael helped her into the driving seat. 'Now, you're sure you're all right to drive? You've had a few shocks, apart from the injury to your hand.'

Rachel laughed. 'I'm quite all right now. It's taught me a salutary lesson, never walk down lonely alleys with my bag swinging from my shoulder. I must have been the perfect target.'

'It could have been far worse. Take care now.' He closed the door on her and stepped back to watch her drive off. He was still standing, looking after her, when she turned the corner out of the car park and disappeared towards the main road.

On the way home Rachel considered what and how much she should tell the Prescotts. Aunt Freda would be horrified, and probably become nervous of letting her out by herself in future, which was ridiculous. She would have to tell them something, to explain her bandaged hand and the torn and bloodied trousers.

When she drove into the farmyard at High Topp she had to admit that her palm was beginning to throb slightly, due to the pressure from the steering wheel. She garaged the Metro in the barn and went into the farm kitchen, hoping to be able to slip upstairs and find herself some painkillers from the bathroom cupboard, before anyone noticed. Jennifer was laying the table and looked up quickly as Rachel came in through the back door.

'Had a nice day in town?' she asked. It was an innocent enough remark, but her tone implied that Rachel was lucky to have the opportunity to spend a day out. Then her sharp eyes noticed the bandage on Rachel's hand and she said, with what seemed like unnecessary loudness: 'What have you done to your hand? Have you had an accident?'

Freda, in the scullery adjoining, overheard the last words and came hurrying into the kitchen.

'Accident? What's happened, dear? Not in the car!'

Here we go, Rachel thought resignedly. She didn't want to have to lie, but the whole truth would certainly worry her aunt.

'I tripped when I was going over some rough ground,' she said. 'And I caught my hand on a piece of broken glass. It's all right now. It's been bandaged up very well.'

'Broken glass! Are you sure there isn't any still left in it? It was probably dirty glass — a cut could be dangerous.' Freda was fussing, as Rachel feared she might.

'It's quite all right now, Aunt Freda,' she said, edging her way out of the room.

'Have you had it properly looked at? Did you go to the hospital casualty department?' Freda persisted.

'It's been seen to and dressed by a paramedic, no less.' That, at least, was true. 'And he said to leave it untouched for the next day or two, so the cut knits together.' She was at the door now and through it quickly before Freda or Jennifer caught a glimpse of the damage to her trousers.

Up in her bedroom, Rachel changed, washed her grazed knees and noted that, with the dirt and dust gone, the damage was negligible. She rubbed some antiseptic lotion on to both knees, and an elbow where she found another graze, and hid her torn trousers in the bottom of her suitcase. When she came down to supper she was determined to put the whole incident out of her mind.

Later that evening there was a telephone call from a couple wanting bed and breakfast for the following week. 'That's all right with you, is it, if I look after them?' Rachel asked Jennifer, in an effort not to offend the Cornish girl.

Jennifer shrugged. 'It's all the same to me. I've enough to do as it is, without the B and

B's. If you want to fuss over 'em and give 'em the kind of breakfasts they'd have in London, that's up to you.'

'I don't give them the kind of food they'd have in London,' Rachel said patiently. 'I try to give them good, country breakfasts but with little extras, like good coffee or a choice of teas, so that they'll remember us as being rather more special than the average bed and breakfast stop.'

Jennifer sniffed. 'Can't see why you bother. They all come for the location, they're not bothered about the accommodation or the food.'

'There's a great deal of competition for tourists. I want people to choose us because we've been recommended as being special.'

'There are always plenty of tourists. We could fill the place with them every week even if we had uncomfortable beds and fed 'em bread and cheese,' Jennifer sneered.

'But we haven't filled our rooms every week, have we?' Rachel argued gently. 'You'll see. Next season our reputation will be made and we could double the rates and still have people clamouring for a vacancy.'

'Next season! You intend staying here that long, do you?' Jennifer sounded dismayed.

'I hope Rachel will stay with us as long as

she wants,' Freda remarked, with uncharacteristic tartness, overhearing Jennifer's last comment. Jennifer, who always treated the Prescotts with deference, fell silent, and scuttled off on some household job in another part of the farmhouse.

They were at coffee the next morning when the telephone rang.

'It'll be for me. Arthur said he'd ring me about those heifers,' said George, ambling to his feet and going into the hall to answer it. He came back a few moments later. 'It's for you,' he said to Rachel.

'For me?' She stared at him in astonishment. 'But no one knows I'm here. I mean — I didn't tell any of my friends in London where I would be staying.'

'Asked for you, clear as anything. Miss Rachel Hayward, he said. You'd better see to him, hadn't you?'

Rachel went into the hall and picked up the receiver.

'Rachel? It's Michael Conway. I rang to ask how you were? Your hand isn't giving any trouble, is it?'

'No, it's fine. Doesn't hurt at all now, thanks to you. You strapped it up beautifully. I don't want to touch it.'

'Look at it in a couple of days. It should be healed enough by then to wear just a light bandage or a sticking plaster, but if it hasn't begun to knit together, or it looks swollen in any way, do go and get it checked at your local hospital — '

'Thank you, Doctor,' Rachel giggled.

'How are you in yourself? Did you sleep all right? Sometimes there's a delayed reaction to shock.'

'I'm perfectly all right now, really. I had a good night's sleep. No nightmares of any sort. My only reaction is as it was then, anger, mainly at myself for being so stupid as to let him do that to me.'

'You couldn't have prevented anyone coming up behind you like that. Don't blame yourself. You did the right thing; if you'd struggled to keep hold of your bag he might have hit or kicked you and done far worse damage.'

'That's what I've been telling myself,' Rachel said. 'Tell me, how did you get this telephone number? I don't remember — '

'Heard you give it to the policeman when he took down your details. You don't mind my ringing you?'

'Of course not. But — I've just thought. I didn't say anything to my aunt and uncle — Aunt Freda's rather nervous, she'd have been worried for me — but if the police ring here she'll be even more worried.'

'They won't ring unless they find the chap or your purse, either of which I fear is unlikely. But look, Rachel, I didn't ring you merely to enquire about your health. I remembered what you were telling me about leaving your job, and I wondered — would you be interested in working here, with me, in my shop?'

'What?'

'It's not the kind of work you've been used to, I grant you but it would be more interesting than chambermaiding or waitressing. It's a genuine offer; I do need someone to take care of the place when I go to sales and to collect items of stock, and you seemed interested in antiques.'

'But I know nothing about them!' Rachel gasped. 'I might easily sell something far too cheaply! I wouldn't have a clue about values!'

'I'd see that most things had a price tag. And everything's listed in a ledger. I'd be around at first, until you got the hang of things. Please say you'll give it a try, Rachel.'

'Well, I — I don't know.'

'You said you were looking for a job. And I really do need someone. I've not found anyone who'd be suitable in weeks of advertising, and this is supposed to be an area of high unemployment. We'd get on well together, I think. We have things in common; not Cornish but here escaping from the rat race, leaving good London jobs for a totally different life.'

'I've involved myself with looking after bed and breakfast visitors,' Rachel said regretfully. Already the idea of working in the shop was beginning to sound attractive, but she couldn't abandon the paying guests back to Jennifer again. She could imagine the girl's comments if she did.

'No problem!' Came Michael's voice down the line. 'B and B is only part-time, in the mornings, isn't it? You'll be rid of your visitors by half past nine or ten, won't you? I wouldn't need you before then, anyway. We never have many customers before eleven, when they wander into town for a coffee and a look round the shops.'

'All right, then. If you really think I'd be any use —'

'I do! I thought of it while you were in the shop yesterday but it wasn't the time to ask. When can you start?'

'When do you want me to start?'

'The sooner the better. Whenever you can.'

They discussed salary and hours for a further few moments, then Rachel rang off and went back into the kitchen in a daze.

'Dear, you've let your coffee get cold!' Freda chided.

'I've been offered a job. In an antiques shop in Truro,' Rachel said.

'Hmm! So much for the bed and breakfast plans,' Jennifer sneered. 'I thought you'd lose interest soon enough, when something better came along.'

'No, it needn't make any difference. I can still cook and serve the breakfasts and make the beds. I won't be needed until half past ten or eleven in the morning.'

Jennifer scowled. 'Well, let's see. I give you a week and you'll be giving up one or the other.'

'You won't try to take on too much and exhaust yourself, will you, dear?' Freda said anxiously.

'No, Aunt. I'm sure I shall be able to manage both. And I think the antique shop will be exactly the kind of work I'll enjoy.'

'How did you come to know about the job?' George asked curiously. 'Who is this chap who rang you? How did he know you wanted a job anyway?'

'I met him in Truro yesterday. He owns an antiques business and we hit it off right away. He's also a Londoner; gave up a stressful job in the capital to come down here and start selling antiques. I'm sure I shall like working in the shop.' She didn't add that she was rather nervous about the idea; she knew nothing about antiques and dreaded the thought of being left to cope with customers.

'Hmm! From London?' George said in his gravelly Cornish voice. 'I'll bet he hasn't been here in winter yet.'

4

Rachel walked into Conway Antiques at twenty to eleven a few mornings later. At first, she thought the shop was unattended, but as the doorbell jangled she heard sounds from the office in the back, and Michael appeared.

'Good morning. Can I help — Good Lord, it's you!' He stared in amazement at Rachel. 'You look a bit different from the last time I saw you,' he said.

Rachel had made an effort to look the part of a knowledgeable antiques seller. She had put her fair hair up in a neat chignon, the way she'd always worn it at her London job; exchanged jeans for a smart skirt and blouse and added court shoes with more heel than she wore for loafing about on the farm.

She smiled. 'I hope you didn't think I'd come to work still looking like the dishevelled waif you rescued last week? Yours is a smart shop. I didn't want to let you down.'

'But this is Truro, not Regent Street!' he protested. 'You look stunning, but with you here I'll have to put up my prices to match! This is only a very small shop, after all.' He looked at her. 'How's your hand, now? I see you have the bandage off.'

Rachel held out her right hand, the palm now covered only by a sticking plaster. Michael took it and lifted a corner carefully.

'Yes, mending nicely. You clearly heal easily. Well, keep it covered if you're around handling grimy objects. Come to think of it, I suppose most of the stuff here is grimy to an extent. And mind you don't trip in those shoes and damage yourself again.'

'I probably won't last in these heels. I brought a pair of brogues with me. Now, what do you want me to do?'

'You've missed the first customer of the day. Chap came in to browse about half past nine, shortly after I'd opened, but it seemed he was merely killing time, waiting for his wife. Before the lunchtime rush occurs, perhaps I should fill you in with what's here. Tell you a bit about the items I have, so you can act knowledgeably if anyone asks about anything.'

'And then I think you ought to let me loose with a duster, if you have one,' Rachel suggested, looking round. 'All these things would look better if they were given a bit of a polish, don't you think?'

'I've never had the time,' Michael confessed. 'I can see having an assistant is going to make a great deal of difference to the place.'

He gave Rachel a conducted tour of the shop, explaining what each piece was, how old and valuable it was and how much he hoped to sell it for. 'I can drop ten percent but no further,' he said. 'And I usually start with the same amount above the asking price. People almost always haggle; it's part of the fun. I'll let you deal with the next person who comes through the door, but I'll be in the back if you need me.'

'You haven't told me how much you want for that bench,' Rachel said, indicating the long, high — backed, seat at the back of the right hand window. She remembered sitting on the end of it when she'd first come into Michael's shop. Now, it had a Chinese carpet draped over one end, and several pieces of porcelain displayed on the seat.

'Oh, that! That's worthless! An old pew from some derelict church. It was a mistake ever to have bought it, but it was in with a job lot of reasonable stuff. I'll never manage to sell it; it's far too big for most houses but it does a job as a display stand. It's too big for here, really. If I get much more furniture I'll have to put it out in the yard, or have someone chop it up for firewood.'

'Firewood! But it has a nice polish!'

Rachel exclaimed, shocked.

'Generations of churchgoers fidgeting while they listened to dull sermons caused that polish,' he laughed. 'Well, perhaps not firewood; some keen handyman might like it to cut down and make something else from it. They can have it for free if anyone wants it.'

Rachel's first customer came in at noon. She had been warned that most people just wanted to look round and didn't intend to buy, so she kept in the background, not approaching until she thought the customer, a middle-aged man, was becoming interested in one particular object. As he picked up a small vase, she sidled forward.

'That's beautiful, isn't it? It's a Victorian posy bowl. Ladies used to have them on their dressing tables, with lilies of the valley or other strongly perfumed flowers in it.'

'Is that so?' The man had an American accent, a tourist, of course. Rachel added boldly 'I don't suppose ladies in the States would have anything so small. Even in this country we tend to have larger flower displays these days.'

'We have flower vases of all sizes in the States.' He was still holding it, turning it in his hands. 'But I guess you'd go a long way to find anything as pretty as this. Kinda dainty and delicate, isn't it?'

'The workmanship is superb. It's a lost art, now.' Rachel babbled. The piece was about 1860, Michael had told her, but not particularly rare or valuable.

'I'm looking for a present for my wife,' the American continued. 'Some little memento of our holiday in Britain. I guess she might like something like this. On her dressing table, you say? That's what we call a dresser, I guess. What you put plates on and keep in a kitchen.'

He's been round lots of antique shops, Rachel thought. Aloud, she said 'You wouldn't find anything more English than that. See, it has roses and forget-me-nots painted round the sides. Very English flowers.'

'I'll take it. How much?'

Rachel was startled by the promptness of the man's decision, but recovered quickly enough to suggest 'Eighty pounds?'

'Sure. How much it that in dollars?'

When she had worked the amount out with the aid of the calculator by the till and told him, he didn't bat an eyelid, but produced a wallet from his back pocket, bulging with twenty pound notes. She wrapped the vase in tissue paper, found a suitable sized box under the counter and packed it carefully. As the man was leaving, she said on impulse 'Sir — I hope you don't mind my mentioning it, but please don't keep your wallet in your back pocket like that. It's a temptation to thieves and I know there are some operating in the town. My own purse was snatched recently. Please put it in your inner jacket pocket.'

He removed his wallet, replacing it in his breast pocket. 'Well, thank you kindly for your concern, Ma'am. You have some beautiful things here. I guess I'll bring Maisie to take a look before we leave. Goodbye now.'

He had barely closed the shop door behind him when Michael was at her side. 'You were wonderful!' he said. 'Eighty pounds! I don't know if I'd have dared ask for that myself. I'd marked it down as £50, but I'd have accepted £40.'

'Americans are easy; things always seem cheap to them,' Rachel said. 'Beginner's luck, but I must say it was fun. It gave me a buzz to make a sale but I don't imagine it'll be that easy very often.'

The rest of the day Rachel spent dusting the stock and attending to the half dozen or so people who came in, most of whom had no intention of buying. She made one more sale, a small, carved wooden figure, for twenty pounds.

'How ever do you make a living?' she asked Michael, as she prepared to leave at four o'clock. 'I can't see how you can afford this place, let alone pay me, on sales like today.'

'Main sales are through contacts with dealers, and customers who ask me to find specific items for them,' he explained. 'I was on the telephone doing business most of the day, and you've no idea how much easier it is when I don't have to keep an eye on the shop at the same time. Believe me, girl, I've needed an assistant for a long time.'

When Rachel arrived back at the farm, Freda was all agog to hear how she had survived her first day. 'You look like a high-powered executive, dear, dressed like that, and with your hair so smart,' she said shyly.

'That's London style; not what we're used to in Cornwall,' Jennifer added.

'Yes, I think I did go a bit over the top,' Rachel admitted mildly.

Jennifer looked startled, not expecting agreement. 'Do you know you're out of cornflakes, and low on that fancy tea you buy?' she offered.

'Thanks for telling me! I'll go down to Mrs Blamey's shop now, before she closes.' Rachel thrust her feet thankfully into her comfortable, flat shoes and picked up her handbag.

'Take the car,' Freda said.

'No, I'd like the walk.' She was out of the

door before Freda could remonstrate.

The truth was, Rachel loved the first view of the village where the road rounded the bend at the top of the hill and the whole panorama of little village street, oval shaped harbour and bobbing sailing boats was spread out before her. It had been her first sight of the village, a lifetime ago it now seemed, but she had fallen in love with the place at that moment.

'Good evening, m'dear! You're late; I was about to close the shop,' Ida Blamey greeted her.

'Sorry. I couldn't come any earlier. I have a job now, in Truro,' Rachel explained.

'A job! Well now, it seems you're planning to stay awhile. This isn't just a holiday visit.' It was hard to know whether Mrs Blamey approved or not.

'It never was just a holiday visit,' Rachel muttered, but she didn't want to get into a discussion with the Cornish woman, so she added quickly 'I need some groceries for tomorrow, please. For the B and B people.'

'I won't have any of that fancy coffee you seem so keen on.' Ida took the list from Rachel's fingers, leaving her open-mouthed in astonishment. Was there nothing that went unknown in small villages? How on earth had Ida Blamey come to hear that she'd walked into Pengarron and bought some special brand of coffee by chance?

'I don't want anything special,' she said, rather sharply, 'just your usual brands of cornflakes and tea. And a packet of butter and a loaf as well, please.'

Mrs Blamey collected the groceries together on the counter top, and did a few calculations on the corner of a paper bag. This must be the last corner shop in England without a calculator of any kind, Rachel thought, watching her.

Ida must have read her thoughts. 'I don't have any truck with these mechanical contrivances,' she said. 'I was taught to add up and I've always done it this way. You can check me if you like, but I've never been wrong yet.'

'I wouldn't dream of querying it, Mrs Blamey,' Rachel said demurely. 'I was just marvelling how quickly you did it.'

'You won't find many youngsters these days who can add up without help,' Ida said, with a touch of pride. 'That's one reason I wouldn't want any assistance in the shop. They're not trained like in the old days.'

Rachel looked curiously round the shop while Ida packed everything into the shopping basket. Apart from the food counter, everything looked almost exactly as it had done when she had first come into the shop, on her first visit to the village.

'Do you find you have enough customers to make a living, nowadays?' she asked. 'There never seem to be many holidaymakers here, and these days most people drive to the supermarkets to stock up.' Guiltily, she remembered that was what Aunt Freda did; only the odd, forgotten item was bought from the local shop.

'I survive,' Ida said tartly. 'Been here a good many years, I have, and I dare say I'll be here a while longer. Good evening to you.'

Thus dismissed, Rachel picked up her shopping basket and left. Behind her, she heard the bolts being pushed into place as Ida closed for the day. *Is she grumpy with everyone or is it just she dislikes newcomers?* Rachel wondered. *If she's often like that, it's no wonder she has few customers. How on earth does she keep in business?*

Rachel walked over to the sea wall to see if Sea Pie was back home. It was, but fastened to a buoy in the middle of the harbour, not in Stephen's usual place at the foot of the steps. There didn't seem to be anyone on board, though Stephen could have been out of sight in the cabin.

After watching the boats for a few moments, Rachel began the long trek back up the hill to High Topp farm. By the time she was half way, she was beginning to regret not having come by car after all, for the hill was steep and the shopping basket heavy. At the bend in the road, she paused again to look back at the sleepy little village. Hardly anyone ever seemed to be about, though the owners of the sailing boats must surely come and go regularly, and the inhabitants of the fishermen's cottages behind the shops must leave their homes occasionally.

When she finally reached the top of the hill and the road curved away from the cliff, she decided to walk back across the fields to the farm. It was a beautiful evening and she was loth to get back too soon, with only an evening of TV and George and Freda dozing beside her, to look forward to.

The path from the field followed the top of the cliff at first. Out to sea were three or four small sailing boats, the setting sun catching their sails at a slanting angle, making them look on fire. Rachel stopped to watch for a moment and noticed she was nearly opposite the great rock that rose up from the edge of the bay, Penhaligon's Rock. It looked peaceful and inviting, and she could imagine bird watchers or some naturist campers sitting on the flat, grassy top, inaccessible to anyone, able to sunbathe without fear of disturbance.

If what Stephen said was true, though, the only way to reach the top would be by being lowered from a helicopter.

She glanced down at the base of the rock, where the waves pounded against it. It rose sheer from the water, and jagged pieces of rock stuck up all round at this side. Certainly, it didn't look as if anything, neither a boat or a swimmer, could possibly land on the rock.

'Don't even think of it,' said a voice behind her. Rachel turned, startled, and found Stephen standing a few paces away.

'You were thinking what a nice place to acquire an all-over tan, weren't you?' he continued. 'I know you've been wanting to get yourself atop that place ever since you first saw it.'

'No, actually. I was looking at the waves beating against the rocks and thinking how very scary it would be to be in a boat down there,' Rachel retorted.

'Smash a rowing boat like matchwood. And as for a swimmer — there have been stories of people who swam out to it and tried to climb up it, being torn to ribbons. Those rocks are razor sharp. Though I suppose it's a bit too far out for your average holidaymaker to attempt to reach it.'

Rachel shivered. 'It does look very dangerous. But you have to admit, it would be a lovely place if one wanted a bit of complete privacy. It must be big enough to pitch a tent and have a camp fire.'

'Leave the top to the seagulls,' Stephen said dismissively. 'Are you on your way back to High Topp farm? I'll walk with you.' He held up a bucket. 'I've some fresh crab for Mrs Prescott. I promised her some, ages ago.'

Rachel turned away from the sea and fell into step beside him. 'I saw the Sea Pie in harbour,' she said. 'Have you been out today?'

'Tourist season,' Stephen replied. 'I don't go every day, only when I'm hired to take groups of them out fishing, mostly for shark. As a matter of fact, I'm going out next week — care to come with me?'

'What — shark fishing? I don't think that's exactly me, thank you!' Rachel laughed.

'That wasn't what I had in mind for you. I've a couple of men wanting to go out fishing, and the wife of one of them is coming too. She isn't interested in the fishing and I wondered, to save her being bored, if you would come as well, to keep her company? I'd be grateful if you would; the last thing the men will want is her demanding that we go back early because she's fed up.'

'Oh! Put like that, it's a bit different. But what about Jennifer? Why don't you ask her?' Rachel suggested. After Jennifer's behaviour recently, she was hesitant to have much to do with Stephen.

'Jennifer? I hardly think so. These people are on holiday, city types. The sort of people you would know and understand. Jennifer wouldn't have anything in common with them, whereas you would know the kind of things they'd talk about; the things that would interest them.'

There could be some truth in that, Rachel acknowledged, though it sounded rather snobbish. But Jennifer didn't seem to like anyone who wasn't Cornish.

'I'd like to come, but unfortunately I'm working. I have a job in Truro now,' she told him.

'It's a Sunday. Surely you don't work all through the week?'

Rachel made up her mind. Sundays at the farm were inevitably tedious and uneventful. And why should she take any notice about Jennifer's warnings against Stephen when the girl had another boyfriend of her own?

'Thank you, Stephen. I'd love to come,' she said.

'Early start. Be at the harbour by five thirty. They're bringing a picnic so there's no need for you to bring anything. They're well to do people, staying at the best hotel in Penzance so the food is sure to be plentiful and delicious.'

They had reached the gate into the farmyard. Stephen held it open for her. 'I'll put these crabs into the outside barn for Mrs Prescott. Let her know they're there, will you?'

He turned away and disappeared between two sheds at the side of the yard. He seemed to know his way around High Topp farm almost as well as those who lived there. Fleetingly, Rachel wondered if he was trying to avoid the risk of Jennifer seeing him with her, but it seemed a ridiculous idea. Stephen didn't seem to care much what Jennifer thought.

'Where's the book recording the B and B enquiries?' she asked, coming into the kitchen with her shopping. To her relief, Jennifer was not there; only Freda, preparing to serve the evening meal.

'Have you had another enquiry, dear? I must say, bookings have perked up since you took them over. I hope it won't be too much for you, with the job in Truro as well.'

'Don't worry; that's really only part time. Michael says I can choose my hours, up to a point, and he'll work round them. So far, he hasn't left me by myself in the shop, but he'll need to visit sales and auctions soon. I'm still a bit scared in case I make an awful boob and sell off something valuable too cheaply, but I rather suspect he hasn't much that's terribly valuable in the shop.'

'An assistant in a second hand junk shop!' Freda exclaimed. 'Are you sure it's really what you want, dear? You had such an important, interesting job in London.'

'That's over,' Rachel said firmly. 'I didn't expect to find anything similar here in Cornwall and I doubt I would have wanted it if I had. This job is fun; and I like Michael. He gave up an important, interesting job in London, too.'

She opened the book they used to register their bed and breakfast guests and glanced down the page where future bookings were listed.

'Oh, good. We haven't anyone staying over Saturday night. I've been invited to go fishing on Sunday, with Stephen and some holiday people. It's an early start.'

'That's nice, dear. I'm glad you're getting out a bit and meeting people. I've been worried that it must seem dull for you with just us for company.'

'You don't think Jennifer will be upset? It is with a group of his clients, Stephen thought I'd be company for the wife of one of them, since they're from London.'

'Jennifer? Why should she be upset?' Freda looked genuinely puzzled.

'Jennifer doesn't seem to like my being friendly with Stephen. She seems rather possessive of him, that's all.'

'I don't see why she should be. Stephen's a nice boy, always been kind to us. And he's had a very tragic life, too. If it hadn't been for Ida, I don't know how he would have coped. And she with troubles enough of her own, too.'

'Why? What happened to them?' Rachel was intrigued.

'Didn't you know? Stephen's father and Walter Blamey were great friends. They were drowned at sea together; must be four or five years ago, now. No one knew quite what happened to them; the wreckage of a boat was washed up along the coast but neither of the men's bodies were ever found. Caused quite a to-do at the time, with the Air-Sea Rescue and coastguards out, but they must have been swept far out to sea. No one knew exactly where they were, or what kind of accident befell them, but the report on the wreckage said it looked as if the boat caught fire, then exploded. It's terrible to have someone lost at sea, but I think it must be far worse if one doesn't know what happened, and the bodies are never recovered.'

'Poor Mrs Blamey! I never realised! So she must depend on the shop for her entire livelihood.'

'It's a wonder she manages,' said George, coming in for his supper and hearing Freda's last words. 'She's in the wrong place for a shop like that, though I doubt she'd ever consider moving. Had that shop and living space above it, long before Walter died. Now she looks after Stephen, in a manner of speaking, and Stephen looks after her. There's a bond between them, like, with the two men being killed together.'

'Does Stephen not have a mother, either?' Rachel asked, wanting to know more.

'Mother! Some mother!' Freda said scornfully. 'She disappeared many years ago. She was always something of a wild one.'

'Had a reputation in the village,' George put in helpfully.

'Poor Stephen!' The story put the two in a new light for Rachel. She felt she might be beginning to understand these Cornish people, for whom being lost at sea was an all too common tragedy. How did Stephen feel when he was sailing alone in Sea Pie, she wondered, knowing that somewhere beneath him his father and his father's great friend had drowned?

Sunday morning dawned with clear skies

and a slight land mist heralding a warm day. Rachel was up early, dressed in jeans and a shirt, with a bag containing shorts and swimming costume in case there was an opportunity to swim or sunbathe. She was at the harbour wall by twenty past five, but Stephen was already on board Sea Pie, sorting fishing equipment on deck.

'We pick them up round the coast,' he said. 'Come aboard. My, it's certainly going to cheer up my day to have you on board with me.'

There were three paying passengers who came aboard at the jetty a few miles down the coast, a Mr and Mrs Jarvis and a Mr Keegan. Mr Jarvis and Mr Keegan, who introduced themselves as Ted and Maurice, were work colleagues, both keen fishermen, out to catch 'the big one' as they gleefully informed Stephen. Mrs Jarvis, Sandra, was clearly a less enthusiastic passenger. She looked dubiously at Sea Pie, and asked 'Will it hold us all?'

'I've had twice as many on a trip, several times,' Stephen assured her, helping her aboard. The men passed over a large, wicker hamper plus a crate of assorted bottles.

'Our lunch,' grinned Ted Jarvis. 'Liquid or solid or both; whatever you fancy. The hotel's done us proud with that, a picnic fit for a king.'

Sandra looked a little pale and gulped. Rachel thought she ought to earn her place on the trip and smiled encouragingly at her. 'It's not so bad once the boat is out at sea. It's being tied up to the jetty and buffeted by the waves that makes it rock so much.'

'I've never been sailing before,' Sandra whispered confidingly as she took a seat beside Rachel. 'I didn't really want to come, I'd have much rather gone shopping or stayed by the pool in the hotel, but Ted was so keen on my watching him catch a shark. Men are so macho, aren't they?'

Stephen sailed the Sea Pie westwards, out beyond sight of land. It was a smooth sea but a brisk wind drove them along at a good speed. As soon as the sun rose sufficiently to give some warmth, Rachel changed into her shorts and sat, sunning herself in the prow. Sandra, who already wore a skimpy outfit, came and joined her.

'They're getting out the rods now. There's stuff all over the place,' she complained. 'If they do catch anything, I'm quite sure I don't want to be there to see. And if it is a shark, where on earth do they think they're going to put it? I certainly don't want to have to step over it every time I move.'

They sat, sunning themselves, talking in a desultory way. Rachel learnt that Sandra had been Ted's secretary and married to him only a couple of years. Maurice, it seemed, had shared Ted's passion for fishing for years, and looked set to accompany them on any holiday near the sea. 'It was a wonder he didn't want to come on honeymoon with us,' Sandra added morosely. 'Ted was going to bring his rods then, but I put my foot down about that.'

Rachel mentioned that she had lived in London until recently, but did not go into details. She was beginning to feel increasingly that that chapter in her life was over now. Instead, she told Sandra about Michael's shop in Truro, suggesting that she might like to explore the town one day and call in to have a look round. 'That's what most people seem to do, just come in and look round,' she said. 'I can't think he makes all that much of a living, but I suppose he must do a reasonable trade or he wouldn't be able to afford an assistant.'

A shout from the stern of the Sea Pie had them standing up and looking back over the cabin roof. 'Caught something!' Ted called in delight, holding up a fish. It was about two feet long, wriggling and squirming still.

'What is it? I thought sharks were much bigger,' Sandra asked Rachel.

'I've no idea. I don't think it's a shark, but

it seems to have made him happy.'

'Oh, dear! Does that mean we're here all day now? I had hoped, if they didn't have any success, they'd give up by mid day.' Sandra sat down again, her pretty face wearing a disgruntled expression.

'Why don't I persuade Stephen to land on one of the little islands for lunch? We can stretch the picnic out for as long as possible,' Rachel suggested.

'Land? On an island? It would be wonderful if the boat stayed still for a bit. But where is this island? I don't see any land anywhere.'

'There are lots of small islands dotted about, a bit nearer the coast,' Rachel said. 'Just sandbanks, some of them, but Stephen says it would be simple enough to row the dinghy over to one of the larger ones.' She put her head round the cabin door and found Stephen inside, making coffee on his diminutive stove. She explained her idea, adding, 'I think Sandra's feeling seasick. She didn't really want to come but a spell on land will cheer her up.'

'Stupid woman!' Stephen muttered unsympathetically. 'How can she possibly feel seasick when we're at anchor? Well, if I can get these two to stop for an hour or so, I can put you all ashore on a nice little secluded beach? Will that suit her ladyship?'

He sailed on, heading back towards the coast, and at noon anchored again and rowed them across to a small island within sight of land, so small it had not been marked on the commercial charts.

Sandra immediately cheered up and set about unpacking the picnic hamper. She seemed so keen on spreading out the hotel's lavish feast, that Rachel left her to it, wandering a little way away from the group. She felt she'd had enough of Sandra for the time being.

Ted and Maurice were sitting nearby, smoking. Rachel lay back on her beach towel, closed her eyes and let the warmth of the sun seep into her very bones. It was wonderful to have a day out like this; much as she enjoyed the shop or looking after the bed and breakfast people, she sometimes felt the summer was slipping away without her having time to notice it, far less enjoy it.

She must have drifted off to sleep, the men's conversation turning into an indistinguishable rumble of sound, but suddenly their words came to her clearly, a familiar name bringing her fully awake.

'FANECO, the subsidiary of J.P. Henson Ltd. It happened there,' Maurice was saying.

'FANECO?' queried Ted.

'Food and Nutrition Experimental Company,' Maurice explained patiently.

Rachel was fully awake now, though still lying with her eyes closed. Maurice had mentioned her old company and it seemed she was about to hear some gossip about it.

'Yes. Bad case of industrial espionage. They were on the verge of a breakthrough on something big when their confidential data was leaked to a rival company in a similar field. Great hoo ha and to-do about it. They never actually got to the bottom of it, who was responsible, but it caused a stink throughout the industry.'

'Wasn't there some row about who was to take over when Dennis Watson went? I think I read somewhere that he gave an interview shortly before his death, virtually announcing some woman as his successor, then she upped and vanished, soon after. There was some fuss about it, a few months back.'

'Sounds a bit fishy to me,' Ted said, with an easy laugh. 'Just as well there isn't the scope for that kind of scam in our company, eh?'

They went on discussing the business world, their own company and people they knew in other companies, but Rachel was no longer listening. It would seem there might well have been more to Roger Yateley's behaviour than stealing her research. But had her resignation and disappearance from London meant that people were now wondering about her own loyalties?

'I've done with all that. They can think whatever they want; I'm not going back,' Rachel told herself, rolling over on to her front and resting her head on her arms. Even so, she had an uneasy feeling at the back of her mind. There seemed to be some kind of unfinished business at FANECO, and would she really be able to stay here in Cornwall when winter came and all the tourists had gone, particularly if Michael closed his shop, as so many local people did.

'Lunch is ready!' Sandra called, and the two men rose eagerly to join her round the cloth, spread out on the sand. Rachel got up a little more slowly, still thinking about what she'd heard. She would have liked to ask Maurice, who seemed to know more about the story, for some further details, but she was unwilling to admit that she had been involved with the company they'd been discussing. No one knew she was here now and she wanted to keep it that way. No, not quite no one. When she'd first come to St Morwenna's Bay she'd bought some postcards at Mrs Blamey's shop, and, after sending one to her mother in Canada, had sent the other to her friend Claire, though she hadn't given an address or any details about her plans. For all Claire knew, she could have been taking a few days' holiday and now be settled somewhere miles away.

After lunch, Sandra persuaded Stephen to let her and Rachel stay on the island to sunbathe while the men rowed back to Sea Pie to resume fishing. Rachel helped repack the remains of the picnic, then Sandra changed into a bikini and lay down on a rug beside the water.

'This is more like it. The ground stays still, not like that awful rocking boat,' she said. 'Rachel, be a dear and put some sun tan lotion on my back, will you?'

They lay side by side on the sand, enjoying the sunshine and the sense of total idleness. Sandra raised her head to look out towards the Sea Pie, anchored some two hundred yards away.

'Idiots!' she muttered. 'Can't imagine what they want to catch a shark for. Can't eat the blessed thing, and I'm sure as hell not going to stand for having it put in a glass case on the mantelpiece.'

Rachel laughed. 'It's a macho thing. Man against Nature. They'll probably throw it back after they've photographed and weighed it.'

'Pitting one's wits against a fish isn't exactly challenging, is it? Now, Stephen I can understand. He fishes for a living, to supply food. He has a reason for catching the wretched things.'

'Mmm.' Rachel was dozing off again. Sandra was silent for a while, realising her audience was no longer paying attention, then she remarked, 'Your Stephen is quite a dish, isn't he? That lovely red beard and matching curly hair! And his eyes are exactly the colour of the sea, when the sun's on it. I could go for that lean, muscular type. You are lucky to have found a chap as good looking and sexy as he is.'

'He's not 'my' Stephen,' Rachel replied, somewhat annoyed. 'He's just a friend, that's all.'

'Oh, but I thought — ' Sandra sat up, her china blue eyes fixed on Rachel with a puzzled expression. Then she said awkwardly, 'But Stephen said — he told us that you and he — that you'd come to Cornwall to be with him. He definitely gave us the impression the pair of you were as good as engaged. I thought you shared his cottage.'

Rachel stared back, astonishment mixed with indignation rendering her speechless for a few seconds. At last she said coldly 'I can't imagine why Stephen said that. I don't even know him particularly well. I didn't know him at all when I came to Cornwall; I met him here and see him from time to time in the village. What on earth does he think he's playing at, saying anything like that?'

'Wishful thinking, perhaps,' Sandra suggested, with a laugh. 'I bet you're a bit different from the local girls and he's smitten. Wanted to pretend he'd found himself someone a bit more sophisticated than the local talent.'

'But he had no right — ' Rachel said angrily.

'Surely you don't mind that much? He's just a fisherman, I grant you, but he's frightfully dishy. I could go for him myself.'

'He shouldn't have said anything like that. It's embarrassing.'

Sandra lay back down on her rug. 'And there was me, thinking you'd landed yourself a gorgeous hunk and would be spending all your days sunning yourself on his boat. Don't give him the brush-off too quickly. He's clearly very keen to claim you as his regular girlfriend, though I agree his tactics were a bit gauche. I imagine there aren't too many eligible males in a place as small as this, so perhaps you should think about him a bit more positively. He'd certainly liven up your days while you're staying here, even if you don't want him long term.' She rolled over and closed her eyes, taking a deep breath as she revelled in the sunshine.

Rachel sat up, frowning. What was Stephen playing at? He couldn't possibly have thought —

She wondered if he was deliberately trying to upset Jennifer. Perhaps she'd been possessive once, and he wanted to make it plain to her that he wasn't interested, although the times she'd seen the Cornish girl with Alan, and from what Uncle George had said, it looked as if Jennifer no longer cared for Stephen. But, again, why had she warned Rachel off? Just the warning alone had made Rachel want to defy Jennifer and be as friendly towards Stephen as she wished, but it hadn't occurred to her that there would ever be more than the most casual of friendships. Sandra's words made her think. Did she, after all, like Stephen more than she'd realised? True, he was very good looking and a pleasant companion, but was there more to it? And, more seriously, had she been unconsciously sending out signals which Stephen might have misinterpreted?

I could surely only send out that kind of signal if I actually was attracted to him, she thought. And I'm not. He's nice looking, it's true, but he's not my type at all. There's something about him — something secretive. If I really was interested in him in the way Sandra suggested, I think there's something about him which would make me uneasy.

Stephen arrived back in the dinghy to collect them in the late afternoon. Neither of the men had caught the shark they'd set out for, but Maurice was delighted by an interesting collection of small fish he'd managed to hook, none of which, as Sandra pointed out, looked in the least edible.

'That's not the point,' Maurice argued. 'It's the skill in playing and landing that counts. Poor Ted didn't get a single bite this afternoon. He'll have to make do with that giant dogfish he caught earlier.'

Stephen made tea in Sea Pie's galley and brought them mugs out to the cockpit.

'Think we should call it a day now,' Ted said. 'We've been out about twelve hours, and I'm bushed. It'll be time for dinner before we get back to the hotel.'

'Why don't you and Rachel have dinner there with us this evening?' Sandra asked Stephen. Rachel looked at her in surprise, and was rewarded with a discreet wink.

'Thanks, but I'm hardly dressed for a place like that,' Stephen said.

'But you can stop off and change and come

along later, say about eight, can't you? They do an excellent dinner. Well, you've seen the standard of their picnic lunch.'

'I know they do excellent dinners. I supply the fish course often enough,' Stephen said drily. 'Thanks for the offer, but I'm not one for posh occasions. Besides, I have to be up early tomorrow. But Rachel might enjoy it.'

'Thanks, but I, too, am a working girl who has to be up early tomorrow,' Rachel said quickly. 'It's been a long day already.'

Stephen dropped his three passengers off at the jetty where they'd come on board earlier. 'Can't say I'm sorry to be rid of them,' he remarked, as the Sea Pie moved away from the shore, 'it's always tiring having to keep an eye on amateurs playing at fishing. They're quite likely to do something stupid and put themselves and everyone else in danger.'

'Stephen, I want to talk to you.' Rachel moved to sit alongside the tiller. Stephen kept a hand on it while turning enquiring eyes on her.

'Yes?'

'Why did you tell those people that I was your girlfriend?'

He shrugged. 'Seemed easier. Why, does it matter?'

'Of course it matters! I'm not your girlfriend! We hardly know each other! Did you realise, Sandra even thought we lived together!' Rachel said angrily.

'It could be remedied. I think I'd quite enjoy it if you were my girlfriend.' He gave her an appraising look. 'Why not?'

'Why not?' Rachel was furious. 'Because I have no intention of becoming your girlfriend, that's why. I thought we were friends, just friends. Now, I'm not sure that we're even that.'

'I don't see what you're making such a fuss about,' Stephen said calmly. 'I'm free and available. So are you, I assume. Presumably you don't find my company too objectionable, or you wouldn't have come out on this trip in the first place.'

'Perhaps Jennifer was right to warn me off,' Rachel muttered. She hadn't meant to say it aloud, but Stephen heard her.

'Jennifer warned you off me, did she? How interesting.' He threw back his head in a hearty laugh. 'You don't want to take any notice of Jennifer. She's always been a bit protective of me.'

'Protective of you? What is that supposed to mean?'

'It's none of her business what I do or who I see.'

127

'But it is my business if it includes me,' Rachel snapped. 'And I don't like people making assumptions or taking anything for granted with me. You had no right to tell those people I was your girlfriend. They must have had completely the wrong impression. Fortunately, Sandra told me what you'd said and I was able to explain the situation. Please, don't ever say things like that to anyone else.'

Stephen shrugged again. 'As you wish. I really don't see what all the fuss is about. One day you'll succumb to my charms, Rachel. You'll see.'

Rachel was speechless with indignation and decided that maintaining a stony silence was the only dignified way of dealing with the man. But while the Sea Pie sailed back into harbour in the still beauty of the summer evening, she thought about what Stephen had said. Did she fancy him? She could see his attraction, and yet — there was indeed something about him that made her uneasy. He was not entirely a comfortable person to be with.

When the Sea Pie finally moored at the foot of the harbour steps, she sprang ashore quickly, before he could reach out a hand to help her. 'Goodnight, Stephen,' she called from the top, without even turning round. She set off up the hill towards High Topp farm as fast as she could, and for the first time, did not pause at the bend in the road to look back over the retaining wall at the little boats bobbing in the evening light.

5

Rachel rushed into the farm kitchen with a trayful of used breakfast crockery, nearly colliding with Jennifer, who was about to leave the room.

'Whoops! Sorry, didn't see you there.' She banged the tray down on the table and began sorting the plates and cups, glancing hurriedly at the kitchen clock as she did so.

'You're going to be late into work,' Jennifer stated the obvious. 'But I suppose he doesn't mind what time you arrive, as you're part time.'

'Not normally, no,' Rachel muttered, filling the sink with hot water, 'but Michael's off to a house sale this morning and he particularly wants me to be in early. Those wretched PG's took forever eating their breakfasts this morning. They would be slow, particularly today.'

'I'll wash the crocs up for you. And make their beds. You get off now,' Jennifer offered.

Rachel turned to stare in astonishment.

'What? But you've got your own work to do.' There always seemed plenty of domestic work around the farm to be done, apart from the paying guests. Jennifer looked after all the family laundry and helped prepare meals, as well as cleaning.

'It won't take long.' Jennifer pushed Rachel aside briskly, reaching for the first plate. Glancing up at Rachel, she added awkwardly 'I never thought you'd stick it out this long, doing the PG's breakfasts and your job in Truro. You're certainly not afraid of hard work. I'm impressed.'

'Thanks.' It was the first time Jennifer had made a remark as friendly or complimentary as that, and Rachel was taken aback.

'Thought you'd be a bit lah di dah and expect to be waited on, when you first came,' Jennifer continued, seizing plates and cups and demolishing the washing up at a great rate. 'Thought you'd look down on people like us, after your high-powered London job. But you don't seem to mind being a skivvy for the paying guests and an ordinary shop assistant.'

Rachel forbare from commenting on the 'ordinary shop assistant' remark. Jennifer meant well and couldn't be expected to know that selling antiques was not exactly in the same category. Over the weeks that she had been working for Michael, she had learnt a great deal about the antique business. Several times now he had left her alone in the shop

131

while he went to local auctions, or to house clearances, and she had made sales by herself. So far, she had not made any disastrous mistakes, but then Michael kept records of the value of all his stock, which she referred to whenever a customer enquired a price. Today, however, he would be away for the whole day, as the sale he was attending was in Somerset, and he was anxious to set out as soon as she arrived to take over.

'Go on. I can do it all for you. And I will, too. I won't let you down.' Jennifer gave her another nudge. 'If you're going to stand there staring at me, you might as well be doing it yourself.'

'Yes. I'll go. Thanks a lot, Jennifer. I'll help you out in return,' Rachel said, snatching up her handbag and the car keys and hurrying out to the barn.

On the way to the shop, an unworthy thought crossed her mind. Was Jennifer being nicer to her now because she'd heard about her argument with Stephen? Since the day of the fishing trip, more than four weeks ago now, Rachel had hardly seen anything of him. She had seen his van driving past on a few occasions, and passed him going into his cottage when she'd been shopping at Mrs Blamey's stores, but they had not spoken to each other. In a village where gossip abounded and everyone seemed to know everyone else's business, it was quite likely that Jennifer had come to hear the story.

Why should it bother me why the girl's decided to be friendly at last, after so long? Rachel thought, dismissing the idea. It's just more pleasant that she is being friendly.

She parked in her usual place in the patch of rough ground near the shop and hurried over towards it. Through the window she could see Michael inside, and noticed that his van was parked beside the kerb outside.

'Sorry I'm late.' She pushed open the door with a rush.

Michael smiled at her. 'You're not late. I was checking a few price tickets and leaving you a note of what some things were. I'm not ready to go yet.' He paused and looked at her again. 'You've done your hair in that french pleat style again. What's this in honour of? Expecting an important customer in my absence?'

'Not that I know of. It's just that I thought, as I was going to be in charge today, I'd better look the part.'

'You do. That style suits you,' Michael observed. 'Though I must say I wouldn't like to see it every day. You look very efficient, but also intimidating.'

'Intimidating?' Rachel's eyebrows rose in surprise.

'The customers won't dare try to beat you down, looking like that. You look as if you've been in the business for years, and know it inside out.'

Rachel giggled. 'I must remember that when I'm feeling particularly ignorant about something here. Look, you'd better go, if you want to be there before all the best stuff is snapped up.'

'Yes, I had. Don't be nervous, Rachel. You'll manage splendidly. I've every confidence in you.'

She watched him climb into his van and drive off. It was still too early to expect any customers yet, so she filled in the time dusting and moving round some of the items. There were people who regularly glanced in the windows as they passed, most days; it would look as if they sold more if the display was changed frequently, and might encourage them to come in for a closer look, eventually.

By eleven o'clock she had sold a small china figurine and had had six browsers, none of whom appeared to be interested in buying anything. When the last one had gone, Rachel decided she'd make herself a cup of coffee. She went into the little back office and switched on Michael's kettle. She was spooning coffee into the mug when she heard the shop doorbell tinkle, followed by the sound of pewter tankards bumping together. Michael kept a row of them suspended by hooks from a beam across the centre of the shop. Anyone particularly tall might brush against them, walking underneath, but not many people were tall enough.

Rachel walked out into the shop. The customer was standing underneath the tankards, surveying the stock, and his bright red hair just brushed them enough to set them rattling together each time he turned his head.

He wasn't aware of her presence at first. She stood in the doorway, surprised to see him. In his navy jersey and seaman's boots, Stephen didn't look the sort of person who would be interested in antiques.

He became aware that he was being watched, and turned towards her. 'Good morning. I was wondering if Rachel Hayward was here?'

It was dark at the back of the shop, but all the same she was surprised he hadn't recognised her. 'Hallo, Stephen. What brings you here?' she asked.

He stared at her for a few seconds before exclaiming 'Good Lord, it is you! I didn't recognise you with your hair all done up like that. You look quite different.'

'One has to be formal for the serious business of selling antiques,' Rachel said primly, ignoring the fact that she usually came to work in jeans with her hair loose. Michael said most of his stock was dusty and there was no point in wearing good clothes.

'Is this a social visit or are you genuinely interested in buying something?' she asked.

Stephen looked disconcerted. 'I was delivering some lobsters to a restaurant in the town and I thought I'd drop by and see where you worked. You don't mind, do you? I'm afraid antiques are somewhat out of my range.'

'Of course I don't mind. More than half the people who came into the shop this morning, had no intention of buying anything. They just wanted to have a look round. I'm about to make myself a cup of coffee. Would you care to join me?'

'If you're sure your boss won't mind.'

'I am the boss for today. Michael's gone to a sale in Somerset. He won't be back until after closing time, so there's only me, minding the shop.'

She went back into the office and brought out two mugs of coffee, resting them on the counter. Stephen was looking round the shop with interest, asking a few questions about some of the goods.

'I don't think there's anything terribly valuable,' Rachel confided. 'Frankly, I think it's a thin line between antiques and a junk shop here, with some of the stuff. Michael seems to make a reasonable living, enough to employ me. I don't know what he does in the winter when the tourists have gone; they seem to be our main customers.'

'I imagine he does what we all do; heave a sigh of relief at having the place to ourselves, and go off and do something else,' Stephen said with a grin. He picked up his coffee mug and took a long drink. 'Actually, I didn't only come to look round your workplace. I wanted to ask you something.'

'Oh, yes?'

'I'm taking another party out on Sunday. They won't be after sharks or anything like that, just a sail and a picnic, and the men might put a line out, if they feel like it. Very relaxed. Would you like to come?'

'No, I don't think so.' Rachel spoke coolly.

'Look, I'm sorry about last time. It was no more than a misunderstanding —'

'Well, I hope you now understand the situation fully. But all the same, I don't think I'll come.'

'Please do. You were a great help last time, keeping the wife entertained so she didn't get

137

in the way and distract the men fishing. This time it's different; two young couples and four children. A family day out.'

'Then they won't want me,' Rachel said decidedly. 'Or had you the role of nursemaid lined up for me, this time?'

Stephen's face showed his disappointment. 'I was thinking more that you'd be company for me,' he said.

Rachel felt guilty for her sharpness. She looked at him, standing there so tall his hair was brushing against the pewter pots. Some girls would be flattered to have the attentions of a good-looking fisherman; Sandra had drooled over him, certainly. Was it that she was still annoyed with him that made her refuse? It was petty to be still harking back to that incident. Was it because she was now becoming friendlier with Jennifer and didn't want to damage that tenuous relationship? But why should she encourage Jennifer's dog-in-the-manger attitude? She was dating Alan, and seemed close to him; why should she care who Stephen wanted?

Rachel opened her mouth to accept, and found herself saying instead 'I'm sorry, Stephen. I'm doing something else on Sunday, so I couldn't come anyway. Thanks for inviting me.'

Stephen looked surprised. 'Doing something else? What?'

Annoyed, Rachel snapped 'I do have a social life apart from this shop and the farm, you know. And it's none of your business what I'm doing then.'

'It's not a very early start, like last time. I'll drop by the farm at around ten to see if you've changed your mind,' he said easily, draining his coffee mug and turning to leave. 'Bye, Rachel.'

She snatched up the mugs and flounced into the back room to wash them. The cheek of the man, to assume so much when she'd made it clear — She was glad she had refused, though what had made her say she was doing something else, she had no idea, except that there was still that odd feeling that she had about Stephen, that uneasiness, the feeling that there was something about him he didn't want to disclose.

The problem now was; she had to make some arrangement for Sunday, to back up the excuse. A trip out somewhere with Jennifer crossed her mind first, but Stephen would probably come to hear that it had been suggested after his own invitation. There were few other people that she knew well enough, and no one else likely to be available on a Sunday.

At twelve thirty Rachel locked up the shop and went along to the pub on the corner for a sandwich lunch, returning shortly after one. She had a few more customers and sold a pewter Victorian inkstand and a rather pretty, ornamental plate. She also had several more browsers, but one of them enquired about Clarice Cliff pottery, and she made a note for Michael to look out for any at future sales.

After the last browser there was a lull and she went into the back office to make herself some tea, feeling that, though she hadn't made many sales, she had just about justified being there, when she heard the shop doorbell and a man's voice call out: 'Mike! Hey, are you there, Mike?'

She went out into the shop and saw a shortish, rather thick-set man in his fifties, standing in the small space in front of the counter. He was looking at the stock with interest, but straightened up and looked startled when Rachel appeared from the office.

'Oh! Hallo. I was expecting Mike — Mr Conway. Is he about, do you know?'

'I'm sorry. He's away today, at a sale in Somerset. Can I help?' Rachel asked.

'Wasn't actually going to buy anything. Just thought I might look him up. He comes into my pub sometimes; we're old friends. Bill

140

Williams' the name.'

'How do you do, Mr Williams? I'm sorry you've missed him. Mike's usually here, but today there was a particularly interesting house sale he didn't want to miss. Can I give him any message?'

'Not really. I don't usually come this way, but I was in town on business and I thought I'd drop in and have a look at his shop. He often talks about it when he comes in for a pint. I keep a little pub on the edge of the Moor, not exactly Jamaica Inn, just a quiet, tucked away little place, mainly local people. The tourists don't often find us.'

'That must be a mixed blessing,' Rachel remarked.

'Yes, I suppose so. Can't say I'm sorry. I get by on local trade, everyone knows everyone in the bar of an evening. I like it that way, and it means business is steady throughout the year. No sudden drop in profits come autumn. I say, he's got some nice things here! Way he talked, I thought it might be some sort of junk shop, but he clearly goes for good quality. The patina on that little table is superb! A hundred years of housemaid's elbow grease, no doubt!'

Or, rather, two months of my dusting and polishing, Rachel thought wryly. The table top had looked dull and with a bloom of neglect on its surface when she'd first started at the shop, she remembered.

Bill Williams wandered round the shop, looking closely at everything. When he came to the window display he bent over it, peering at what Rachel took to be one of the smaller items. She stepped forward, about to suggest he picked up whatever it was that had taken his fancy, when he rested his hand on the long bench, and asked 'would this be for sale, by any chance? Or it is just here to display your stock?'

'That bench?' Rachel said in surprise.

'Yes. It would be the ideal thing for a little inglenook in my pub. I've been looking for something like this for ages. Would he sell it to me, do you think? As a special favour?'

'I — I'm sure he would,' Rachel said dazedly. What was it Michael had said, that first day when she'd staggered into his shop and he'd sat her down on it? 'I'll never manage to sell that. It was a mistake, ever to have bought it.'

'It's an old church pew. Michael's had it in the shop some time, I believe. It's too long to fit into the average sized house, I suppose.' She was glad now, that she'd given it an extra polish, out of affection.

'But not too big for my pub,' Bill said. 'How much does he want for it?'

'I really don't know. He's told me the price ranges for most things here, but he didn't say anything about that bench. There's no ticket on it, either.'

'Happen he won't want to sell it, then. It's a beautiful seat, with that deep shine on it, but I can see it's useful for displaying things.' Bill sighed, stroking the arm of the bench wistfully.

'I'm sure he'd sell it to you!' Rachel said quickly. 'Only I'm not sure how much for.' What had Mike said, that he might hope to get a fiver if someone wanted to chop it up?

'D'you think he'd take two hundred?' Bill asked hopefully.

'Two hundred!'

'Two hundred is all I can raise at present. Tell you what. He knows me. If I've done him down, next time he comes into the pub I'll give him a cheque for however much more he's asking. It really is exactly what I want. I do want to have it.'

'I don't suppose Mike would want more than two hundred,' Rachel said, feeling guilty about accepting even that much.

'I can borrow a brewery lorry to transport it. If I was to come back in say, twenty minutes, with a couple of lads, can we load it up and take it back now?'

'I suppose so.'

Bill pulled out his chequebook and wrote a cheque for two hundred pounds there and then. 'Tell him to come and see it in the bar soon,' he said. 'Be back in twenty minutes.'

Rachel barely had time to take off the china ornaments and small knick-knacks which had been lying on the seat, and remove the ancient Chinese rug draped across the back. She was giving it a final dust and polish when Bill returned, accompanied by two burly young men, who proceeded to lift the bench and manoeuvre it carefully out of the door and into the brewery lorry, parked outside.

'What's he going to say when he sees it isn't here?' Bill grinned at her. He was in high spirits, clearly delighted with his purchase, showing his companions the carved ends with pride.

'He'll be speechless,' Rachel assured Bill confidently.

'Tell him he can't have it back!' Bill called, as they drove off.

Rachel watched the lorry disappear round the corner. What was Michael going to think about the sale of the bench? He'd be astonished and delighted, she was sure. But two hundred pounds? And he'd told her he would have been happy to be rid of it for five!

She turned back into the shop. There was a large, empty space now, revealing a dusty floor, and a row of small objects lined up on the counter and on the floor beside it, needing to be re-displayed. Rachel spent the next hour, conveniently free of customers, reorganising the window display and putting the displaced items on a low table in the front of the window.

At ten to six, she was considering whether to lock up, leave a note for Michael and go home, when she saw his van drive up outside.

He breezed into the shop, looking pleased with himself. 'Hallo! You still here? You should have packed up and gone at half past five. No need to wait for me, I could have been ages. I was lucky with the traffic, though. In fact, I've been lucky all day. Come and see what I've bought. Since you're still here, you can help me unload.' He glanced round the shop, deciding where he could put his new acquisitions, and became aware that there seemed more space than usual.

'What's happened? You haven't had burglars, have you?'

Rachel giggled. 'No. But I made a big sale. Guess what.'

He stared for a moment, then exclaimed, 'The bench — you've never shifted that? Did someone really want it after all?'

'Yes, and paid a very good price. Two hundred pounds, and sounded as if he felt he

145

ought to pay more. The cheque is in the till. I was wondering what to do with it if you didn't come back tonight.'

She told him the whole story then, and Michael sat down on an embroidered Jacobean chair, quite lost for words until she had finished.

'You clever, clever girl!' He said at last. 'I've known Bill Williams ever since I came down here, and his pub. I know just where he is thinking of putting it. It will be ideal, yet I never thought to suggest it to him myself.'

'If you've quite recovered from the shock, there's the new stuff to unload. Come on, you need the two of us.' Rachel propped open the shop door and went out to the van.

It took them a further half hour to empty the van, with Rachel looking at the items with interest. Mostly they consisted on small pieces of furniture, but also some vases and good china ornaments and a couple of cartons of silverware. Even to her inexperienced eye, it all looked good quality, easily resaleable pieces.

Michael piled everything in the back of the shop, declaring that the sorting, cataloguing, pricing and displaying could all be done later, during the week. He fastened the steel mesh shutters that covered the windows and announced, 'I want to take you out to

146

celebrate your clever sale, and to thank you. I know a nice place, out in the country, where the food is superb. Come and have dinner with me tonight, Rachel.'

'What! Like this? I'm filthy. I've been cleaning your shop most of the afternoon,' she protested.

'Go home and tidy yourself up. I need to change, myself. I'll pick you up at the farm at eight o'clock. How about that?'

'Yes. You're on.' The thought of not spending another evening either watching TV or sitting in the Anchorage with Uncle George, raised her spirits considerably. All the way home, Rachel planned what she would wear, with the enthusiasm of a teenager on a first date.

Michael arrived promptly at eight. Instead of the van, which Rachel had half expected, he was driving a smart, two seater red sports car, the hood down since the evening was still warm.

'This is nice,' she greeted him. 'I thought you only had the van.'

'Did you imagine I was going to take you to dinner in a *van*? he asked, in mock outrage.

'I could have offered to drive us. But this is very nice.' She stroked the bonnet appreciatively. 'Come in and meet Aunt Freda and

147

Uncle George. They've been intrigued about you ever since you offered me the job.'

Aunt Freda welcomed him into the farm kitchen. She had been very keen to meet him and Rachel could see she had taken to him at once. While she finished making herself ready, George chatted to him and said afterwards that he'd never before come across a Londoner who could talk so sensibly about farming matters.

Michael drove her away from the coast, down winding country lanes, seeming to know the whole area very well. Eventually, he pulled into the car park of a small manor house, apparently in the middle of nowhere. There were lights in all the windows and an air of bustle and activity about the place.

'Pendragon Manor is always busy,' he said. 'It's very popular throughout the year, but I'm sure they'll manage to find us a good table. I think you'll like the atmosphere here, and, as I told you, their food is excellent.'

It was. They were shown to a corner table by the manager, who seemed to know Michael well. The waiter service was attentive, but not intrusive. Rachel was intrigued.

'You must come here quite often,' she remarked. 'They seem to treat you like a very valued customer.'

Michael shrugged. 'Well, you know, it's

148

always helpful to have even an ex-paramedic dining on the premises. Who knows when a customer will have a fishbone stuck in her throat, and choking to death would be so bad for the restaurant's reputation.'

Rachel's eyes widened. 'Do you mean you really saved someone who was choking to death, here?'

'The poor woman was going blue in the face. She couldn't breathe. Of course, they sent for an ambulance but it was lucky I was here and knew what to do. Speed was essential; the ambulance probably wouldn't have been able to arrive in time. As a result, the manager now sees to it that I have the best table in the house, any time I care to ask. And I always seem to be welcome, even if the place is completely full.'

'I've often wondered why you gave up your job as paramedic, to sell antiques. All that training gone to waste. Surely you could have found somewhere else, less stressful, to work, yet stay in the service?'

'That type of job is always going to be stressful. You never know what you might be called on to do. And as to wasting my training, that's never wasted. I used it on you, didn't I?'

Rachel glanced at the palm of her hand, where only the tiniest white scar showed now.

'I'm beginning to think I should thank that mugger,' she said. 'He gave me a job I enjoy, and opened up a whole new world of interest.'

'I'm glad you enjoy the job. Dealing with beautiful objects from the past takes hold of you, sooner or later. I collected things for years, ever since I had enough pocket money, and they became the basis of my stock when I first came to Cornwall. I wouldn't go back to being on the ambulances now, not for any consideration. That was my other life; this life is what I want.'

'But what do you do in the winter, when the tourists are all gone? They provide the majority of your sales.'

'Ah! You'll have to wait and see! And that should keep you working with me to find out.'

So this wasn't to be merely a summer season job. Rachel felt relieved; she had been dreading being told that she would no longer be wanted if the shop closed over the winter months.

'There's lobster on the menu. Fancy it? There's no bones to choke on,' Michael grinned at her.

The thought of lobster brought Stephen to mind. She didn't want to mention that he'd been in the shop, but she remembered his invitation and at once the perfect excuse for refusing it was there before her.

'Michael, do you fancy going out somewhere for the day on Sunday?' she asked. 'I've spent nearly every weekend since I came around the farm and, frankly, there's not a great deal of interest in the place, unless one's passionate about cows, or farm machinery.'

Michael laughed. 'Poor you! Of course I'd be delighted to spend next Sunday, or any Sunday, with you. Where had you in mind to go?'

'Oh, anywhere. I hardly know the county except for the area around the farm. I'd love to explore somewhere further afield.'

'And I'd love to be your guide! We can go across the Moor, stop off and have a drink with Bill Williams and assure him he doesn't owe me any more money for the bench. I feel guilty taking even that much for it.'

'He was delighted. He thought he had a bargain.'

'I suppose in a way, he has. It would cost more than that if he had had a seat like that especially made for his pub. I won't let him know how pleased I am to have it off my hands; I'll just say I'm glad it's gone to a good home.'

They made plans for their day out,

151

laughing and talking easily together. Rachel felt she had not enjoyed herself so much since coming to Cornwall. In the car going back to the farm afterwards, Michael said, 'I know I said I'd never go back to live in London again, but I have to confess, coming to Cornwall wasn't the complete success I hoped for, or that I pretend it is.'

'You mean, you still miss London?' Rachel asked in surprise.

'No, not that. I love Cornwall, but it's a close community. I've found it difficult to make many real friends here. Acquaintances, yes. I know loads of people after five years here and they're friendly enough, but I have this feeling all the time — I'm not Cornish. I wasn't born and bred here so I never can be. There'll always be a difference. Am I imagining things? Getting paranoid about people?'

Rachel thought of Jennifer. 'No,' she said thoughtfully. 'They are wary of strangers, especially people from somewhere like London. They seem to think it's a place as different as the other side of the world.'

'It is, in a way. You know that. The whole pace of life, their attitude to things, is not the same. Londoners must seem like aliens.'

'But we're not that different. We're happy to live at their pace, join in with them and become one of them, if they'd let us,' said Rachel.

'It's not so bad for you, having an aunt and uncle living here. I know I've felt not quite accepted, and perhaps I won't be, ever. Rachel, when you came into my shop that day and told me you were a Londoner, I felt as if I was welcoming a long-lost friend. I made up my mind right then that I'd offer you a job in the shop. I thought I'd have to persuade you to give up some other, far more interesting, occupation, so when you said you were actually looking for work, I couldn't believe what Fate had dropped into my lap.'

'And I was envying how well you seemed to have settled into the way of life here! I thought — perhaps they'll accept me like that in five years' time, if I'm not doing something they don't feel would be better done by someone Cornish.'

'You've let your friend Jennifer get to you too much,' Michael told her. 'There are people like that here as there are everywhere. Did you never meet anyone in London who believed that anyone not born and bred in the city, must be a hick from the sticks?'

'It's not only Jennifer. Mrs Blamey, too, seems to think if I'm not on holiday then I've no business being here.'

'I'm sure you can live with her attitude;

though whether she can, when she must rely on keeping friendly with her customers to make a living, is another matter. Just don't think of opening a rival general stores in St Morwenna's Bay!'

Rachel laughed. 'I wouldn't give much for my chances if I did! Even without animosity from her, I'd never make a living in a village like that. You can see the place is dying; there are empty shops all along by the harbour. There's only her general stores and the boat chandlers left, apart from the pub. It's not a place that tourists seem to want to visit, which is strange because the harbour looks so pretty in the sunshine.'

'This village of yours intrigues me. I'd never heard of it until you spoke of it. Shall we drive back that way? Do you think the harbour would look as pretty by moonlight?'

'Yes, I do. It's not all that much out of the way. I'd like you to see the village; I've spoken of it often enough and it's about time you knew what I've been describing.'

It was shortly after midnight when Michael drove along the sleeping village street and parked his car half way along the harbour wall.

'Lots of small boats at anchor,' he observed. 'They must need food supplies regularly. I suppose that must be what keeps her in business.'

'I've never seen much activity from them,' Rachel said. 'The place is always deserted when I come here.'

'Where does Stephen live? You said he had a cottage facing the harbour,' Michael asked.

'He does. There it is, along by the general stores. There's a little passageway between the two, leading to the back. There's another lane, running along the back of all the shops, I think. I noticed it from the car park of the Anchorage.'

'He's there now. Either just going home or coming out for some night fishing,' Michael said.

'Who is? What do you mean?'

'See, there's someone standing outside the cottage. Want to go across and say hallo to him?'

'That's not Stephen,' Rachel said, seeing the shadowy figure outside the cottage. 'Stephen's much taller than that. Slimmer, too. That man looks much older. I don't know who he is; I've never seen him before.'

'What's he doing, skulking around at this time of night, then? Look, he's gone to the door of the general stores.'

They watched as the man tried the shop door, then walked to the passageway between the buildings and disappeared down it.

'There's a post office at the shop,' Rachel said suddenly. 'Mrs Blamey must keep quite a bit of money, stamps and things, there. You don't think — ?'

'I do!' Michael reacted sharply. 'If you don't know who he is, he's probably up to no good. Come on, let's go after him!'

He opened the car door, then signalled to Rachel to close hers as quietly as possible. 'Leave it slightly open rather than shut it and alert him,' he whispered.

They crossed the street and paused by the entrance to the passageway. Michael looked down it very cautiously.

'Looks like he's gone round to the back of the shop. I'm going to follow him. Keep behind me and try not to make a noise.'

The passageway was narrow and dark, but had a concrete surface reasonably free of loose stones. Rachel slipped off her high heels and followed Michael on stockinged feet. Two thirds of the way down the passage they were startled by a light from the back of the shop suddenly coming on.

'Security light,' Michael muttered. 'Watch out, he'll probably run off, back this way.'

But the man stayed where he was, under

the full glare of the light. There came to them a rattling sound, of bolts being drawn and a door chain removed, then the back door of the shop opened and more light flooded out. They heard the man's voice, deep and gruff, saying 'Put that light out, woman. You don't want to alert the whole village,' and the security light was dowsed, though there was still some light coming from within the open door.

As they waited, wondering whether to go to her aid, they heard Mrs Blamey's voice, clear and calm: 'Come you in, m'dear. I've been expecting you this last half hour. There's a good fish supper waiting.'

The door shut and the light was dowsed. Michael turned to Rachel. 'A welcome burglar! Lucky I didn't tackle him, I wouldn't have been a popular hero!'

'Well! I wouldn't have thought Mrs Blamey was a lady to encourage gentleman callers at midnight.' Rachel began to giggle.

'Come back to the car quickly, before anyone sees us and thinks we're peeping toms!' Michael took her arm and led her back to the harbour wall. 'Did you say she was a widow?' he asked, as they regained their seats in the car.

'Lost her husband at sea, so Uncle George told me. He and Stephen's father were drowned together. She keeps an eye on him, since he apparently hasn't any other relations, and he helps her in return.'

'I suppose even a respectable, elderly widow shopkeeper is entitled to have a boyfriend, if she wants,' Michael remarked. 'Odd, though.'

'What's odd?'

'The way he was hanging round the shop and the cottage. The way he walked — as if he didn't want to be seen. And a bit late, turning up for supper at midnight. Wonder who he is?'

'I'd ask Uncle George, but somehow I don't think Mrs Blamey would like anyone to know she had a visitor so late. Perhaps we'd better not mention this to anyone.'

'Fair enough! I'd better get you home. I'd always had the impression the folk here keep to early nights. That doesn't seem to be the case with Mrs Blamey, though.'

Michael drove on, up the hill. Automatically, Rachel glanced back as the car turned the corner, away from the coast. There was a light glimmering from an upstairs room in Mrs Blamey's shop, but the rest of the village was in total darkness. She decided against saying anything about it to Michael, but she was puzzled. He didn't know Ida Blamey, but she did, and she was certain that the rather formidable shopkeeper was not at all the kind of person to entertain a gentleman late at night, not in the sense Michael clearly suspected.

6

Sunday morning dawned overcast, and looked as if there would be rain before long. Rachel wondered if this meant Stephen would not be taking his passengers out in Sea Pie. She rather hoped so; she didn't want the embarrassment of having him come to the farm and invite her out again.

At a quarter to ten, Michael arrived at the gate in his sports car. She ran to open it for him to turn easily.

'You're going to get mud spattered all over your lovely car, driving into the yard,' she said regretfully.

'Don't worry about mud. Doubtless we'll find plenty more before the day's out.'

Rachel was about to slip into the passenger seat when she saw Stephen's van coming up the lane towards them. She hesitated, and Stephen parked his van just inside the farmyard and came across to her.

'That's your fisherman friend, isn't it?' Michael asked quietly. 'Looks like he wants to have a word with you.'

Stephen looked annoyed when he saw Michael. He ignored him and said to Rachel,

'I thought you were coming out with me in Sea Pie today? The family are expecting you.'

'No, Stephen,' Rachel said patiently. 'I explained to you that I had something else arranged for today. I made it quite clear when you asked me that I couldn't come. There was no point in your coming to ask me again.'

Stephen stared at her as if he hadn't taken in what she was saying. Rachel turned to Michael and said, 'Drive on, Michael, or we'll be late.'

The sports car rolled forward, leaving Stephen still standing beside where it had been. There was a shout from the farm, 'Stephen!' and he looked up sharply. Rachel looked up as well and saw Jennifer waving to him from the kitchen door. She came quickly across the farmyard towards him and it seemed as if Stephen turned towards her with a show of reluctance. As they drove through the gate on to the lane, Rachel glanced back and saw Jennifer, on tip-toe, reach up to kiss him on the cheek. He didn't respond and a brief wave of sympathy for the Cornish girl, swept over her.

'Poor Jennifer! She's besotted with Stephen, but he doesn't seem to care anything for her,' she remarked.

'I can sympathise,' Michael said, with a touch of grimness. 'I thought I was being

161

invited out because you wanted my company for the day. I didn't realise I was being used as an excuse for not going out with Stephen. Or was I invited just to make him jealous?'

'What!' Rachel stared at him in astonishment. 'Whatever makes you think that? I wasn't going out with Stephen whatever happened.'

'You said you told him, when he asked you, that you had made other arrangements. But that must have been before you suggested we went out for the day. So aren't I being used as an excuse?'

'No! I wanted to come out with you! It wasn't at all like that!' But, Rachel thought guiltily, she had thought of Michael as the perfect let out.

'Why did you say I wanted to make Stephen jealous?' she asked, genuinely puzzled. 'Why should I want to do that? I don't want to encourage him, for heaven's sake; quite the reverse.'

'He's a good-looking chap,' Michael said flatly.

'So he may be but so what? I don't even think I like Stephen very much. There's something about him that makes me uneasy. I just wish he'd see sense and realise that Jennifer is clearly in love with him. She's the one trying to make him jealous, by going out with Alan, but it doesn't seem to have worked. She'd be exactly the right sort of girl for him; they're two of a kind, both staunchly Cornish, both — both a little secretive, I think. Come to think of it, they both make me feel a bit uneasy.'

They drove on in silence for a while, then Michael said awkwardly, 'I'm sorry I was so petty over Stephen. Stupid of me. I suppose I was looking forward to today so much I didn't want anything to spoil it, so the first thing I do is put my foot in it and damn nearly did spoil things.'

'It's all right. Just so you know I'm not harbouring any romantic notions about him, in spite of what Jennifer seems to think. And some other people as well.' She thought of Sandra and her frank comments.

'None of my business,' Michael muttered.

'I really don't want anything to do with Stephen, but it's impossible to avoid bumping into him in a village the size of St Morwenna's Bay, and he seems to be a friend of Uncle George and Aunt Freda's.'

'Let's forget Stephen,' Michael urged.

She agreed, but added, 'All the same, he's probably the one person we could ask about that mysterious visitor to Mrs Blamey's shop. I'm sure he'd know who it was.'

'But would he tell you?'

She had to agree that it was more than likely he would not.

They drove towards Bodmin Moor, reaching the edge of the Moor near lunch time. 'Let's see what our bench looks like in its new setting,' Michael suggested. 'Bill Williams' pub is not far from here.'

A few moments later he pulled into the car park of a small, stone building at the side of the main road. The pub, the Black Horse, was old and quaint. Though not as famous as Jamaica Inn, Rachel could imagine it had seen its share of smugglers and free traders meeting there in the past, to plan their secret activities.

There were a few local people in the bar, farmers they looked, sitting over their pint glasses discussing sheep sales. They seemed to know Michael, nodding to him courteously as he entered, but not interrupting their conversation.

Bill Williams greeted them warmly, insisting that whatever they wanted to drink would be on the house.

'Seen the new acquisition?' He nodded towards the end of the room, near the fireplace. 'Looks good there, doesn't it?'

The old church pew had regained a new lease of life. Bill Williams' wife had made a tapestry covered cushion to fit the whole length of the seat, and a tasselled hanging of the same material to go over the back. It fitted perfectly into the space beside the fireplace, with barely inches to spare.

'You don't have another one, by any chance, do you?' Bill asked wistfully. 'Look nice if there was a pair, one either side, like.'

'Unfortunately no, but I could always look out for one for you,' Michael replied. 'Remind me, Rachel,' he said to her, 'to look out for another bench and snap it up quickly.'

To Bill, he said, 'Rachel's my assistant and right-hand woman. Best sales assistant I've ever had.'

'And the only one, from what I hear,' Bill grinned at them both. 'Well, are you staying here for lunch, or what? We've a selection of roasts, or there's home-made pasty or pie.'

'We'll lunch here,' Michael said at once. 'Then we'll plan how we're going to spend the rest of our day out.'

When they eventually left the Black Horse, the weather had changed. The overcast skies had dispersed and the day had become hot.

'I think a deserted beach and a swim would be nice,' Michael suggested, as they walked back across the car park. 'It's a long time since I've been to the coast with time to laze. Which shall it be, north coast or south? We're midway between the two at present.'

'You'd be hard put to find a deserted beach anywhere on a hot summer Sunday,' Rachel said, laughing. 'You must have been working very hard not to notice that this place is crammed with visitors and they all head for the beaches. And at weekends you have half the locals joining them.'

'It's too humid for the walk over the moor I had in mind,' Michael complained. 'There must be somewhere still undiscovered, near the sea.'

'Well, the beach below High Topp farm never gets very busy, mainly because there's a steep cliff path down and no other way of reaching it,' Rachel said thoughtfully. 'As to swimming, I never thought to bring a swimsuit with me, but if we dropped in at the farm I could collect one and then we could reach the beach over the fields to the cliff path.'

With the hood down, the sports car produced a delicious, cooling breeze as they sped along the main road. There was a good deal of traffic, but all of it moving smoothly so nothing held them up. By mid afternoon Michael was turning into the farmyard at High Topp and Rachel leapt out to collect her swimsuit and a towel.

'Back so soon, dear?' Freda asked in surprise. 'I wasn't expecting you before

166

supper time, at least.'

'We're going to find a beach and have a swim,' Rachel explained. 'Michael fancies one to ourselves but I suppose that's a hopeless wish at the weekend, especially now the weather has improved so much.'

'You may just be in luck there,' George said, getting up from his chair. 'I'll check with the tide charts, but I think it should be on the turn about now. By the time you've climbed down the cliff path here, there should be about six feet of sand exposed, with the tide going out. Anyone looking over the edge from the top would think tide was still right in to the cliff. You'll have the place to yourselves for an hour or so, I reckon, until folk can see a bit of beach and come down the path to investigate.'

'That's wonderful!' Rachel exclaimed. 'I'll get my swimming things and we'll be off.'

As she turned towards the stairs, Freda cautioned 'Now you be careful, dear. Tide's going out. The current can be strong there. Bring Michael back with you to tea, won't you? I'll have pasties ready, home-made and fresh. I doubt he'll have had many genuine Cornish pasties.'

'I'll try to persuade him.' Well, why not, she thought. Aunt Freda didn't get to meet all that many people, and Uncle George had enjoyed talking to Michael when they'd met previously.

'I'll have to see what he wants to do. He is my boss, after all,' she called over her shoulder as she ran out of the kitchen door. No harm in reminding them of that fact, thereby hopefully scotching any romantic ideas Aunt Freda might be harbouring.

They left the car in a corner of the farmyard and walked across the fields to the cliff edge. The path down to the beach was steep but had been left in good repair, with steps and railings at the more tortuous parts. When they arrived at the bottom, Michael looked around in surprise.

'Couple of feet of damp sand! No wonder we have the place to ourselves! Sure we won't be cut off by the tide?'

'Uncle George says it's going out. He checked with the almanac of tide tables so I'm sure he's right. People won't start coming down here unless they can see beach from the top of the cliff.'

For the first half hour they kept on the base of the cliff, near the end of the path, ready to move back if a particularly large wave came close, but later they were able to spread out towels and a rug which Michael had brought from the car.

'How far does the tide go out?' he asked,

lying lazily on his towel, eyeing the water.

'I'm not sure. Quite a long way, I think.'

'As far as that big rock at the entrance to the bay? Could we swim out to it, or even wade out, in a while? It looks the ideal place to go to avoid the day trippers.'

'That's Penhaligon's Rock,' Rachel said. 'I've been warned more than once to stay clear of it. It's very dangerous, apparently.'

'Dangerous? Why? Looks all right to me.'

'I've been told there are strong currents surrounding it, and the rocks all round the base are jagged and sharp as razors.'

'If it's that dangerous, why isn't there a notice to that effect, displayed prominently on the beach? It's the kind of place anyone swimming out from here might try to reach. Are you sure it's really that inaccessible?'

'It's what Stephen told me. I wanted him to land on it when he was taking me out in his boat, and he was quite horrified at the idea.'

'Perhaps it would be difficult for a sailing boat. It looks perfectly safe to me. When the tide's gone out far enough, I'm having a go at seeing if I can reach it.'

'Are you a strong swimmer?' Rachel asked.

'Reasonably. I'm not going to do anything foolhardy, but the rock intrigues me. What did you say it was called?'

'Penhaligon's Rock. Apparently he was a

smuggler, or a wrecker, probably both, some two hundred and fifty years ago, when the Cornish mostly lived by smuggling and wrecking. He used to lure ships on to the rocks by lights on the top, so that the steersmen thought they were coming in to land. Something like that.'

'Then he must have been able to reach the top easily enough. Come on, I'm going to try. Coming with me?' Michael stood up, exchanged his shorts for swimming trunks and strode down towards the sea. Rachel quickly discarded her own shorts and sun top, put on a one piece swimsuit and hurried after him.

'I'm not sure we should be doing this,' she panted, catching up with him. 'Aunt Freda warned me to be careful when the tide's going out.'

'Your Aunt Freda sounds like a perpetual worrier,' Michael laughed. 'Has she also warned you to be careful of strange men from London who might lure you into danger?'

The water was now waist deep around him and he suddenly dived forwards and began to swim towards the rock. Rachel followed. She had the tide to help her, but after a quarter of an hour she realised that the rock was still some way ahead, further beyond the mouth of the bay than she had at first thought.

'Michael! I'm going back!' she called, turning. She was battling with the tide now, and beginning to feel tired. Try as she might, the beach seemed never to come any nearer. She began to feel uneasy, and then frightened.

'Michael!' She looked over her shoulder but the sea behind her was empty. Surely he hadn't reached Penhaligon's Rock already? But if he hadn't, wouldn't he have turned back too, by now?

Her arms were aching and the beach was still so far ahead. Perhaps she wasn't going to make it back, after all? They'd been stupid to swim out when the tide was going out. Everyone knew that was a dangerous thing to do. Stephen had been right to warn her to stay clear of Penhaligon's Rock.

Rachel felt herself sinking. Her shoulders ached and her arms felt like two lead weights.

'Michael!' she screamed. 'Michael, help me!'

There was a rushing sound of water and suddenly she was grasped from behind. A strong arm came round her, supporting her, and a voice gasped out 'keep going — you'll make it! Just keep going!'

Gradually, the grey wall of cliff came closer. Rachel struggled to keep her arms and legs moving but it was only the strong arm

171

supporting her, dragging her through the water, against a tide that threatened to push her back every time she thought she had gained some distance, that kept her going.

When she thought her arms would part from her shoulders, and her breath was coming in great, sobbing gulps, her foot touched against the pebbly beach, and she staggered into a standing position, finding herself shoulder high in the sea.

'Mike — oh, Mike!' She clung to him, still frightened.

'Come on. We can walk it from here.' He, too, was standing now, and together they waded towards the beach, the retreating tide buffeting them every few seconds.

Rachel staggered across to where her beach towel was still spread out beneath the cliff, and flung herself down on to it. She felt as if she ached in every limb and had had all the breath knocked out of her by the waves.

'Are you all right?' Michael leant over her. 'Rest a bit, and get your breath back.'

'Oh, Mike! I never realised how strong the current was! I'd never have made it back without you,' she gasped.

'You wouldn't have tried to swim out if it hadn't been for me. How could I have been so stupid?'

Rachel sat up. 'It wasn't your fault. You

weren't to know. I thought I was a reasonable swimmer but I should have realised it was further than I've swum in the sea before. It's quite different doing a few lengths in a swimming pool.'

'I turned back as soon as I realised you weren't behind me. I thought I might have drowned you.' Michael sat beside her, his face still white with shock.

'You'd have managed it by yourself. I was silly to think I could keep up. That's all.' She put a comforting arm round his shoulder. Michael turned to her.

'Rachel, I've never been so scared before. I thought I had lost you in the sea. It made me realise — ' He gulped, then raised a hand to lift wet tendrils of hair from where they lay, plastered on her cheeks. 'You've become terribly important to me. Do you know that? I don't just mean the way we work together. I mean — ' He leant forward, cupping her face in his hands, stroking back her wet hair with infinitely gentle fingers.

His kiss was long and sweet. Rachel lifted her arms, twining them round his neck. After a while he moved his lips but still held her close. She felt a strong sense of safety, held in his arms. She rested her head against his shoulder, nuzzling into his neck, wishing the sensation would go on for ever.

At last he released her. 'Just thank God you're safe,' he muttered.

'It was the tide. We shouldn't have swum when it was going out. And I'm out of practice; I haven't swum in the sea here at all.'

Michael looked out across the bay towards the rock. 'Your fisherman friend was right to warn you. We should have paid more attention.'

Rachel shook her head. 'No, I'm sure it was that we chose the wrong time. I've always had the feeling that Stephen was deliberately warning me away from the rock for some reason of his own, not because of any danger. As you said, if it was that dangerous there'd be a notice up, on the beach, warning people not to attempt to approach it. The way Stephen spoke of it, it made me all the more keen to try to climb on to the top of it. It looks such an ideal place for secluded sunbathing. I must say, though, that I've never seen anyone on it, or any boats trying to get near it.'

Michael glanced up at the cliff path behind them. 'We're going to be invaded by a couple of family groups in a moment. Perhaps it would be as well to dress and leave now.'

Rachel nodded. 'Yes. I don't think I want to stay here any longer. Aunt Freda has invited

174

you back to tea, by the way.' She made a face. 'She has rather old-fashioned ideas, I'm afraid. I think, in her day girls were supposed to bring their men friends home to be inspected. Say if you'd rather not. Be warned there will be genuine Cornish pasties on the menu.'

'What could be nicer?' Michael smiled. 'I'd be delighted to have tea with your aunt and uncle. But I think it would be wiser if we don't make any mention of this swimming episode. Let them think we sunbathed, and merely splashed around in the shallows.'

Rachel nodded. 'It would be the last thing I'd want, for Aunt Freda to get to hear how I might have drowned. You might end up a hero for saving me, but she'd never let me near the water, ever again.'

As soon as the cliff path had disgorged its new visitors on to the beach, two sets of parents with a clutch of children each, complete with buckets, spades, beach ball and several holdalls of towels and picnic food, Rachel and Michael made their way slowly back up to the cliff top. As they crossed the fields to High Topp farm, Michael took her hand and kept hold of it until they came to the farm gate.

'I wasn't carried away by the drama of the moment,' he whispered, as they entered the

175

farmyard. 'I meant what I said. I'd been plucking up courage to say something for some time. It was just that — '

'Shhh!' Rachel murmured. 'Uncle George will be in the milking shed. Don't let him hear you or he'll be dragging the whole story out of us.'

Jennifer was, surprisingly, at the farmhouse and joined them for tea. For once, she seemed quite friendly and asked some sensible questions about Michael's antique business.

Aunt Freda was clearly charmed. She had been impressed with the idea of Rachel working in a shop full of beautiful and valuable objects, and had taken to Michael on the earlier, brief occasion when they'd met. She plied him with pasty, fruit pie drenched in Cornish cream, and innumerable cups of tea, until he laughingly exclaimed that he wouldn't need to eat again for the rest of the week.

'Oh, I know you men who live on your own,' Freda chided. 'Live out of tins and never get to cook yourself a decent meal. Isn't that the truth of it?'

'Not exactly. I do cook for myself occasionally. But I eat out quite a bit.'

'Restaurant food!' Freda snorted. 'Chips with everything, I dare say! Far too much

176

stodge and fat for a healthy diet.'

Michael caught Rachel's eye and winked, looking pointedly at the bowl of Cornish cream. Rachel, in the act of sipping tea, nearly choked and had to turn it into a cough.

Afterwards, as they strolled across George's fields, Michael said, 'Does your aunt really feed everyone as much as that? So why aren't you twice your size by now?'

Rachel laughed. 'We don't get that kind of feast every weekend. It was all done for your benefit. Aunt Freda means well, but she can overdo things a bit. I feel very indebted to her for letting me stay here so long, but I'd like to move out and find somewhere of my own, especially if I'm going to be staying on in Cornwall.'

'I hope you will. The job's permanent, even though I'll probably shut the shop at the end of October. I might open it on Saturdays only in the winter, but I can assure you there's plenty to do, without it. The last four years I've been travelling round the country, going to auctions and country house sales. A lot of the time I'm looking for specific items for customers, then I have to deliver them, all over the country, anywhere. I've customers abroad, too, but so far delivery has meant no more than taking the goods to the airport. I'll need an assistant just as much and it's an interesting life, so please say you'll stick with me once summer's over.'

'I'd like that,' Rachel said softly. Since the episode on the beach, her feelings towards Michael had changed subtly. She had always enjoyed his company, but now there was a new closeness. They shared so much; the job, their interest in the seeking out and selling of antiques, and the common background of being ex Londoners, to be treated warily by the Cornish, as different.

She felt strangely safe with Michael. Instinctively, she had always felt she could trust him, rely on him as she had relied on him that first day when she had run, shaken and bleeding, into his shop. If ever they find that thief and bring him to trial, she thought, I shall hope he is let off. He did me a bigger favour than ever those few pounds could have done for him.

It was a few mornings later, when Rachel was about to leave for the shop, when she saw the elderly postman trundling up the lane on his bicycle. She ran to open the gate for him, then left it propped open for her car. As she turned towards the barn where the Metro was kept, he called after her:

'Don't you want your letter, then? I've come all this way with just the one for High

Topp today — you are Miss Rachel Hayward, aren't you?'

'A letter — for me? It must be from the Tourist Board.' She reached out a hand to take it, then changed her mind. 'I have to be off now. Leave it with Mrs Prescott and I'll read it when I get home.'

'Tain't Tourist Board. Hand written, and a London postmark. A real letter, not them pesky junk mailings.' He held it out, clearly disappointed by her lack of enthusiasm.

'But no one knows I'm here,' Rachel said in astonishment. 'There's no one in London knows this address.'

'Someone do,' the postman grinned. 'First letter you've had here, I reckon. Quite an occasion. Don't you want to read it straight away?'

She did. Rachel took it from him and glanced at the handwriting. She thought she recognised it, but surely, Claire, her friend in London, couldn't possibly know this address?

She sat in the car but didn't drive out of the barn. Instead, she ripped open the envelope and unfolded the handwritten sheet of paper inside. She didn't need to glance at the name at the end to know that it was indeed from Claire. She remembered, then, that first time she'd bought postcards in Mrs Blamey's shop, she'd sent one to Claire, along with another to her mother in Canada, but she certainly had never put any address on the card. Intrigued, she began to read.

'Dear Rachel,'

'I'm hoping this letter will reach you. I've had to play detective to try to find out where you are. You simply disappeared off the face of the earth after that fiasco at work. You didn't even leave a forwarding address at your flat. No doubt the mail is piling up there, until they get round to returning it all to sender.

'When you sent me that postcard from Cornwall I thought you might have included an address, but at the time I supposed you would be there for only a few days' break. It was only when the great scandal broke, and I needed to get in touch with you urgently, that I remem-bered you'd once said you had an aunt living there. I had to do a really clever bit of detective work, involving raiding the records at Personnel — all very illegal! — and came up with your mother's address and telephone number in Canada, as you'd given her as your next of kin. I rang her — on the Company, of course, and asked her if she knew where you were living now. She didn't, but said she thought your Cornish aunt might know, as you'd been to visit her recently, so she gave me this address. Here's hoping that she can send this on to you as it's VITALLY IMPORTANT!

Roger Yateley has been found out! Revelations about his murky past have been surfacing, thick and fast. Apparently, he's been up to his eyes in criminal activities for years, but up till now no one ever suspected a thing. The discovery came when Dennis Watson's daughter was going through his papers as executor, and came across some of his work notes which she thought ought to be passed to FANECO. She'd no idea what they were, and might have given them all to Roger, which would have suited him very nicely, but instead she sent them to the MD and I had the job of looking through it all to see what should be done with it. My dear, it really dropped Roger in it! Proved beyond doubt that the department had been working on the Kenya Third World Project long before Sanson's produced their results. Someone had to have passed our data on to them, and it couldn't have been anyone but Roger. And Dennis had notes about your work, too. I know you hadn't said much, but he'd recorded all you told him and it was enough to prove you'd been working on it long before Roger stole your research and claimed it as his!

The MD ordered an enquiry. I think he wasn't too keen on Roger anyway, too cocky and brash by far, but once the investigation started, it seemed there was no end to the criminal activities that came to light. He's been up to these tricks for years, selling confidential data; stealing other people's ideas and passing them off as his own. A lot of people in places where he'd worked previously said it explained a lot, but they'd never been able to prove anything, until now.

Roger has been given the boot, and will never work in the industry again, not even as a cleaner, if the MD has his way. So, the message is, come back, all is forgiven, and the Head of Department job is up for grabs. If you make an appearance now, the word is, the job's as good as yours. You'd have had it anyway but for Roger, and the MD feels he owes you, after all you've been through. So, come back, Rachel, old girl, and take up the reins that were rightfully yours. Your job awaits! You'll be hearing from the MD with a formal offer as soon as he knows where to write you.

Everyone here is longing to see you

again. Do get in touch and come and see us quickly. I hear there's a HUGE increase in salary going with the post!

Love and kisses from us all.

Claire.

Rachel sat, staring at the letter. At last, the work she'd done, sweated over for years, was proved to be rightfully hers. She could go back, take up the work again, in the job she'd always wanted, a trusted and valued member of the company.

Why then, she wondered, did she feel no enthusiasm for the news? It was good to be vindicated at last, to know that her name was finally cleared, but the idea of going back to work in London now felt depressing. She was happy, here in Cornwall, and though she was earning a fraction of her London salary, and not using the skills she had studied so long and hard to gain, she wanted to stay here, stay working with Michael in the shop.

She tossed the letter into her handbag and started the car. She knew she ought to think about her old job seriously. It was silly to turn it down out of hand. At the very least, she had been working on projects which would benefit hungry people in famine hit countries. Had she any right to turn her back on something like that?

Rachel was still in a thoughtful mood when she arrived at the shop. Michael was in the back room, making the coffee they always had together as soon as she appeared.

'What's up? You look rather pensive. Has your fisherman friend been propositioning you again?' He handed her a steaming mug.

'I wish you wouldn't keep calling him my fisherman friend,' Rachel said irritably. 'You make him sound like a throat lozenge. His name's Stephen. And no, I haven't seen him for days.'

'Sorry,' Michael said meekly. He held out a packet of biscuits. 'Here, have one. Special issue for sweetening customers and cheering up forlorn looking assistants. There is something wrong, isn't there? You're not usually as subdued as this. Has your aunt asked you to leave?'

'Heavens, no! As far as aunt Freda's concerned, I could stay with them at the farm permanently. I don't think Jennifer would like that, but Jennifer doesn't have any say in it.'

'Then what's the matter? Come on, you know you can tell a member of the medical profession. Discretion is our watchword. We get to be privy to all kinds of secrets.'

Rachel managed a feeble laugh. 'Sorry, Michael. I have a lot of things on my mind but I shouldn't be taking it out on you. I had

184

this letter from a friend I used to work with, the MD's secretary.' She pulled the letter out of her handbag and held it out to him. 'Read it. It was a bit of a shock, actually. I don't know what to think.'

Michael read the letter silently. His face had a bleak, lost expression as he handed it back to her.

'I suppose you'd better go back, then. Yours was a good job. No sense in wasting all your qualifications working as a shop assistant when you have the chance to go back and have the job you always wanted.'

'I think I've stopped wanting that job now,' Rachel said.

'Don't be silly! There's a great career being offered you. You can't turn it down.'

'You did!' Rachel turned on him angrily. 'You gave up a career that was helping people and saving lives. If you could, why not me? There are others who can work on the famine project just as well as I could.'

'I gave up being a paramedic because the job was getting to me. Stress was making me incompetent so I got out before I made some disastrous error. I had to leave. With you it's different. You've got your whole future to think of. This job in antiques isn't much. There aren't any real prospects —'

'Would you go back to London if the

opportunity offered?' Rachel demanded.

'No. I'd never work there again. Or live there now. But for you it's different — '

'No, it isn't!' Rachel interrupted. 'You told me once that Cornwall had worked a spell on you. Well, it has for me, too. I don't want to leave here. I want to stay here permanently.'

'You're wasting your qualifications. Lord, I felt guilty enough employing you when I knew you could have done much better — '

'Not in Cornwall! And if you sack me, I'll find another job here, which will probably be as a chambermaid or a waitress, and that's if I'm lucky. I didn't know what I was missing until I came to live here. Now, I'm not going back.'

'You know what the locals all say? Wait until you've lived through a winter here.'

'I hardly think it can be colder, wetter or snowier than London.'

'It isn't. But it's dead and empty. The locals seem to go to ground — I'll swear a lot of the Cornish simply hibernate. And the incomers, and those who depend on the tourist trade have a thin time. A lot of them go away.'

'You manage. You said you'd been here five years,' Rachel pointed out. 'Mike, what's wrong with you? Anyone would think you wanted me to leave.'

Michael looked directly at her. 'I don't,' he

said. 'God knows, that's the last thing I want. But I don't have any right to hamper you if you have the chance of resuming an important career.'

'I'm not going back to my old job. I decided that as soon as I walked in the door here. Here is where I belong. The shop itself feels like home.'

'I'm very happy to hear you say that. But you should at least wait for the MD's letter, and go and see him, before making a final decision.'

'What's the point? That's what I think of his offer!' Rachel ripped the letter into pieces and tossed them into the waste paper bin. 'It's good to have my name cleared, I'll own that. But the thought of going back to work there is the most depressing idea.'

'If you're really sure, then I'm more pleased than I can say!' Michael took her by the shoulders and planted a gentle kiss on her lips. 'I always hoped you would want to stay, but I thought you'd soon get bored here.'

'Bored! How could I possibly be bored? And certainly not now we seem to have the first customer of the day.' She slipped out of his embrace as the doorbell tinkled and an elderly gentleman came diffidently into the shop.

Some hours later, while they were taking

their lunch break in the back office, Michael said 'I've been meaning to say — you were doubtful about staying with the Prescotts and I wondered — there's a flat above this shop, not much of a place, admittedly, but it's yours if you'd like it.'

'A flat? Of my own?' Rachel paused in the act of selecting a sandwich and looked up at Michael eagerly.

'I've been using it as a store, but it could be cleared easily enough, there's not a great deal there. And we could pick up some suitable furniture at house sales. It would take a little while to clear, and give it a lick of paint, but it seems pointless to have it hardly used if you could make use of it.'

A place of her own! Fond as she was of Aunt Freda and Uncle George, life at High Topp farm could be stifling. And, with the end of the tourist season looming, there would be no more bed and breakfast visitors to look after before work.

'Mike, that would be wonderful!' she exclaimed, and startled him by giving him an exuberant hug.

7

September was mild that year, and there were still people coming to spend a long weekend in the county. Although she and Michael had made a start on clearing the flat, it was not yet habitable, and since there were still enquiries from people wanting accommodation at the farm, Rachel felt she should stay on with the Prescotts and help out for the present. Jennifer seemed surprisingly pleasant now, probably, Rachel thought ruefully, because Michael was a frequent visitor to the farm, and she had seen little of Stephen.

Michael planned to curtail the shop's opening hours at the end of the month, and told her that they would both be attending sales on their closed days, possibly as far afield as Somerset and Dorset.

'Might even take a couple of days off and travel north,' he said. 'There are some interesting sounding house sales in Yorkshire. That's always a good area and we don't want to miss out. Prepare to be travelling the whole country for the next six months.'

The letter from FANECO's MD duly

arrived, a generous apology in the circumstances, explaining the present situation and inviting Rachel to an interview 'to discuss future prospects.' Michael made her wait until she had given the letter some thought, but her answer had never been in doubt. She wrote back, thanking the MD for his offer, but explaining that she was happily employed in another job now and did not wish to return to FANECO. To Claire, she replied with more detail, but was deliberately vague about the antique shop. Claire wouldn't have understood how Rachel could reject the olive branch being offered, but then Claire had never experienced the magic of Cornwall. And never met Michael.

The telephone was ringing in the back office. Michael went to answer it while Rachel dealt with the customer who had come in at that moment. He was enquiring about long-case barometers and clearly expected that she would know nothing about them. The man was almost certainly a dealer, who would try to haggle the price down, thinking that she would not know the true value of any piece, and then sell it on at a vastly inflated price. His patronising manner annoyed Rachel and she decided to teach him a lesson.

'Barometers pre 1650?' She asked. 'I doubt it. They weren't invented until 1643.' She smiled helpfully at him. 'You could try doing what the children here do, and hang a piece of seaweed up beside the door. I'm told it's extremely accurate as a weather forecaster.'

The man gave her a furious look, muttered something and left. Michael came from the back, laughing. 'One of those dealers from London, thinking we don't know our job, eh? You showed him! Good for you! I wish I could say things like that and keep a straight face.'

'They'd never believe you meant it about the seaweed,' Rachel said. 'What was the phone call? You look rather pleased with yourself.'

'Something that sounds as if it might be interesting. An old lady who lives not far from Pengarron village wants us to take a look at her houseful of furniture. It seems she's intending to sell up and move to a sheltered flat and won't have room for most of what she has now. She suggested next Sunday; how do you feel about coming with me to take a look?'

'I'm not doing anything in particular next Sunday. In fact, as you know, I rarely do anything when I'm around the farm on a Sunday, except spend most of the time recovering from Aunt Freda's enormous lunches.'

'I thought we might go and see her mid-morning, then take a drive out somewhere. Spend the day on the moors. Last of the fine weather and we'll have the lanes to ourselves.'

Michael arrived in the sports car at half past ten the following Sunday morning. Freda was keen that Rachel should invite him back for lunch, but she had her tactful excuse ready.

'I'm sure he'd have loved to, Aunt Freda, but we're off to see a possible client this morning. She has a whole houseful of furniture and things she wants to sell, so I can't say how long we'll be. It might easily take the rest of the day to value everything and I wouldn't want to mess up your lunch arrangements.'

Freda looked disappointed. 'I could always keep two platefuls hot for you,' she offered hopefully.

Rachel shook her head. 'It would be much simpler and quicker to grab a sandwich at the nearest pub, unless the lady herself offers us something. By the time we've finished, it could well be tea time.'

They drove down the deep, Cornish lanes with their high banks topped with ancient hedges. 'I love these secret little ways,' Michael said, slowing the car to negotiate a

192

bend. 'So many visitors moan about meeting farm carts and having to back up to a passing place, as if they had more right to use the road than a working vehicle. If I were Cornish born and bred, I wouldn't like being invaded by pushy strangers every summer. I can understand how Jennifer feels about us incomers.'

'Jennifer seems to have accepted me as a fixture in the county now,' Rachel replied. 'But she's still a very strange girl; she behaves so oddly. She goes out to the Anchorage or somewhere in Truro most evenings with Alan, who seems to be her regular boyfriend, yet if Stephen drops by with some crab or fish for Aunt Freda, she acts as if she's pleased to see him but doesn't want him there. I feel sorry for Alan; he's clearly devoted to her but she seems to care only for Stephen, while he treats her as if he hasn't noticed how she feels at all.'

'Why should he notice a rather plain, dumpy girl like Jennifer when he can spend his summers having sophisticated city women, here on holiday, clamouring to be taken out in his boat?' Michael said. He drove into the outskirts of Pengarron village and took a turning to the right, off the main road. 'It should be about half a mile along here. Look out for a cottage set back from the road, with no immediate neighbours.'

'I think Stephen's too much of a loner to be seriously interested in women,' Rachel said thoughtfully. 'He seems to enjoy sailing by himself in Sea Pie more than anything. I'm always seeing his boat passing the coast, out beyond the bay. It would be a lonely life, married to a fisherman.' And an anxious one, too, she thought, remembering Mrs Blamey and the double tragedy that had robbed her of her husband and Stephen's father.

'Here we are! Pyder Cottage! I say, what an attractive house!' Michael pulled up outside a large, slate roofed cottage, its stark white walls softened by a covering of creeper and rambling roses still in bloom. The garden in front was ablaze with autumn flowers, and, unlike most homes, where the flowerbeds were now beginning to look straggly after the summer, these were neat and tidy, with sharp-edged grass paths and a gravelled area for parking to one side.

Rachel opened the gate and Michael drove into the space provided.

'The lady's name is Mrs Dudley. She's elderly, I imagine, though she had a young-sounding voice over the telephone. If the interior of the house is as attractive as the outside, I think we should be in for an enjoyable visit.'

Rachel rang the bell and within moments there came the sound of quick, light footsteps on quarry tiles, and the door was briskly opened to them.

Mrs Dudley was probably in her early seventies, but there was no sign of the slowing up that comes with age. Small, slimly built and trimly dressed, she beamed at them and held the door wide.

'Mr Conway and Miss Hayward, isn't it? Thank you so much for coming! How would you like to begin? Would you care to have some coffee first, or would you prefer to get down to work straight away?'

'Coffee would be very nice,' Michael answered for them both.

Mrs Dudley led the way into a sun-filled sitting room, with french windows leading out on to a narrow terrace, beyond which was an immaculate garden, bright with colour.

'You must have discovered the best gardener in Cornwall,' Michael exclaimed, stepping to the windows to look out on the scene.

Mrs Dudley laughed. 'I don't employ a gardener. It's been my hobby, keeping the place in order.' She sighed. 'I'm going to miss all this when I leave. Perhaps I should say if I leave, because I haven't sold the place yet.'

'Not sold! I'd have thought you'd have a

queue of potential buyers for a lovely house like this!' Rachel said.

Mrs Dudley gave an embarrassed little laugh. 'I could have sold it, but the couple who viewed it were talking all the time about how they'd alter it, build an extension on the side, and another bedroom in the roof. You'll think me terribly silly, but I couldn't bear the thought of my home being changed so much. What they wanted to do sounded like vandalism, so I refused their offer. I think now, the estate agent has decided I don't really want to sell and that I'm a silly old woman who can't make up her mind.'

She bent over a small table on which rested a tray of cups and saucers, and began to pour coffee from a large, earthenware pot. 'Please sit down, both of you. I'll take you round the house afterwards and show you the pieces I'm selling. You know, it's a great pleasure to be showing people round who don't want to buy my home.'

When Mrs Dudley left the room to take the coffee cups out to the kitchen, Michael said, 'Who on earth would want to change anything here? It's perfect! It's the prettiest house I've come across in the county. I wish she'd been selling when I first came to live in Cornwall, but I imagine it would have been way out of my price range then.'

'Now,' said Mrs Dudley, coming back into the room, 'I'm wanting to sell most of the larger pieces of furniture. It's only a one bedroom flat I'm moving into, so most of it will have to go.' She sighed and stretched out a hand to caress the top of a walnut ladies' desk. 'This was my mother's. so I simply cannot part with it, even if it means I have to do without a bookcase. Most of the furniture here belonged to my parents, good, solid stuff though probably out of fashion for today's families.'

'You have some lovely pieces here,' Michael said admiringly. 'There's always a market for genuine, well-crafted furniture.'

'My father always went for the best,' Mrs Dudley said gently. She smiled wistfully. 'So much here he had made to his own designs. So many memories are tied up in this house. I've lived here for nearly fifty years, you see. I came here as a bride; this was our first and only marital home and we filled it with my parents' furniture. They'd both died only a year or so earlier, you see. And there was no one else to inherit.' She shook her head sadly. 'No one else by then.'

'Are you really sure you want to sell at all?' Rachel asked impulsively. 'It must be a terrible wrench for you, parting with things that are so much a part of your life.'

'My dear, I don't want to at all. But I have to. I can't look after this house and garden any more, my doctor says I really should be somewhere where there's a warden on call. I've had one heart scare, you see. And I know he's right. If I didn't move, I'd have to watch my lovely garden turn into a wilderness and the house grow uncared for. I can't manage to look after a place this size any more.' She shook her head and smiled at Rachel. 'I mustn't be a sentimental old fool. I'm just so glad to be selling my things to someone who appreciates fine furniture.'

She led them round the house, showing them each piece she wanted to sell. Michael made notes while Rachel privately tried to decide how much each was worth. She did her best to remain professional and unemotional about the sale, though her heart ached for Mrs Dudley.

At the top of the stairs, having shown them three bedrooms, Mrs Dudley said 'I think that's everything. There's my bedroom furniture, but you wouldn't want that. It's quite modern, run of the mill stuff.'

'But surely, you wouldn't be selling your bedroom furniture anyway,' Rachel said. 'You're going to need that, at least.'

'No, my dear. The bed and wardrobe are too big for the new flat. I'm getting rid of what's in there and buying myself a smaller, single bed.' She smiled shyly. 'I thought I might treat myself to one of those beds that tip up, so I can read in bed in comfort. When I've sold all the rest, I'll be able to afford some really luxurious things, like an armchair with a built-in footrest. I've always wanted one. They remind me of a dentist's chair. So comfortable if one wants a doze!'

'May we look at your bedroom furniture?' Michael asked. 'I don't only deal in top of the range antiques. I could give you a price for modern pieces too,'

Mrs Dudley pushed open a door to her right. 'I don't have the same sentimental feelings about this room. I bought most of its contents after my husband died, ten years ago.'

'It's good quality,' Michael said, looking round. 'Rachel, you're going to need some furniture for the flat when you move in over the shop. How about having this?'

'It's lovely,' she said. 'I wasn't expecting anything as good as this.'

'You might as well take the lot; curtains, carpet, everything. They won't fit my new place,' Mrs Dudley said.

'Oh, that would be — ' Rachel looked round the pretty room, then a picture hanging on the wall opposite the bed, caught her attention. 'Look, Michael!' she exclaimed. 'Do look at this! Do you recognise it?'

Mrs Dudley interrupted quickly 'Not the picture. I'm happy to sell everything else in this room, but not that picture. You wouldn't want it, anyway, it's of no value to anyone. Just an amateur watercolour.'

'It's of Penhaligon's Rock, isn't it?' Rachel asked, moving across the room to take a closer look. 'I live on top of the cliffs, opposite the bay, at High Topp farm. I know that rock very well.'

'My sister Charlotte painted it,' Mrs Dudley said. 'Poor dear girl! She died young, and I still miss her. We lived near the bay, you know, when we were girls. What fun we had! We used to row out to the rock and have picnics on the top, with a camp fire, sometimes. Pretend we were wreckers, signalling to storm-tossed ships like they did in the old days.'

'What!' Rachel gasped. 'You mean you actually landed on the rock? But it's sheer up from the sea, and there are rocks all round it. Surely it was a terribly dangerous thing to do?'

Mrs Dudley gave a little, silvery laugh. 'Oh, no, dear. Not if you know where to go. It looks unapproachable, I grant you, but there's a little gap in the rocks, on the right-hand side, looking from the sea. You can get a small boat in between them and there's a tiny jetty, like a toy harbour, and a flight of steps leading up to the top. Old John Penhaligon himself is supposed to have built it, or some of his men, more likely. It was a secret way on to the rock, known only to Captain John Penhaligon and his crew in those days.'

'But I was told — ' Rachel stopped abruptly, then said 'everyone I've spoken to in St Morwenna's Bay seems to think it's impossible to land on the rock, that there are dangerous tides round it, as well as the rockface being unclimbable.'

Mrs Dudley stood in front of the picture, giving it a long, considered look, as if she was noticing it for the first time. 'I expect it does look impossible to reach, and there are tricky currents, particularly when the tide's going out. It's strange how ideas can get passed on down the years. John Penhaligon used the rock for other things besides wrecking. He was supposed to have hidden smuggled goods there, too, kegs of brandy and crates of tobacco, mostly from France. He wasn't above smuggling the occasional Frenchman ashore, too, for a fat fee. Since we were at war with France for a lot of the time, that would have been a treasonable offence, I suppose. Particularly as the Frenchmen would have likely been spies.'

'I've often wondered about the man who gave his name to the rock,' Rachel said. 'No one seems to have known much about him, apart from his being a smuggler.'

'Like most historical characters, there are plenty of legends and folk tales attributed to him, which probably aren't true,' Mrs Dudley said, 'but I like to think I know as much about him as it's possible to know, from this distance.' She hesitated, then continued 'I don't exactly publicise the fact, but he was an ancestor of mine. My name was Penhaligon before I married, and we lived quite near the bay, in a house that was reputed to be built from stones left from the ruins of John's own house. Charlotte and I were fascinated by him as girls, and researched everything we could about him. Apparently, in his day he discouraged the locals from going near by tales of boats being dashed against the needle-sharp rocks, and, of course, when he lured passing boats on to the rock, flashing lights from the top to make the helmsman think he was near harbour, it confirmed the story.

'Easy to do, I imagine, in rough seas. I hadn't realised the tale was still believed, two hundred and fifty years later.'

'And he was your ancestor? I've been intrigued by him ever since I came to live in St Morwenna's Bay,' Rachel said.

'We had often wondered, my sister and I, how he could have reached the top of the rock, and one summer we rowed right round it. And we found the way in! I don't think anyone would have found it, unless they were as determined as we were that there had to be somewhere to land. The story is that he kept the landing place and the steps a well-guarded secret, only he and his crew knew, and the secret died with them, when they were hanged for piracy. But one of the crew betrayed them, and was saved from the gallows by giving King's Evidence. I'm sure our parents wouldn't have been pleased that we were out on the rock — it had such a reputation for being dangerous, you see, but we thought that if Captain John could land, then so could we. And so we did. After that, we often went out to it. We were good oarswomen and strong swimmers so we were probably quite safe. It was that good summer of 1940 that Charlotte painted that picture, I believe. She was only fifteen but she had quite a talent, even then. Had she lived, she might have made a name for herself as an artist.'

Mrs Dudley looked fondly at the painting. 'That's going with me to the new flat. It's the only thing I have left now that was Charlotte's.' She turned away. 'All the rest of the furniture I'm selling. There are fitted wardrobes at the new place so I won't need any of it.'

She moved towards the door. 'You can work out a fair price at your leisure. I can't sell it to you until I've moved, so there's no immediate hurry. But I'll accept any reasonable offer. I need to be rid of it all.'

Rachel hardly paid attention to the rest of the visit She took notes, as Michael directed, but her mind wasn't on the job. Stephen had been so insistent that no one could reach Penhaligon's Rock, that she had developed a fascination for it. Now, she wanted to explore it more than ever.

They spent a further hour with Mrs Dudley, examining and pricing her furniture. It was only as they were about to leave, standing in the hallway with the front door open, that she said to Rachel: 'Oh, I nearly forgot! You might like to see this, since you seem so interested in our Captain Penhaligon. There's an oil painting of him I found in a junk shop in Penzance, years ago. I don't think it can have any value. I was going to throw it out, but you might like to have it.'

She opened a cupboard and from the back, pulled out a dusty picture, darkened with age and dirt. It showed four men sitting round a capstan on a quayside. In the background, a three-masted sailing ship floated on the sea.

'It's supposed to be him and his crew,' she said, brushing a hand across the frame. 'I can't see the name of any artist, but it's not very well done, as you can see. At the time I saw it, I was just a teenager and collected anything to do with my notorious ancestor, but it's so poorly done I never wanted to hang it anywhere. Here, my dear, have it. You've been so helpful and considerate about my furniture, and you're the only person I've come across who's been interested in the man. Take it.'

'But I couldn't — ' Rachel began.

'I was going to throw it away. It's a terrible daub. It couldn't possibly be worth more than the canvas it's painted on.'

'It's very kind of you. I can see it's not quite an old master, but, you know, sometimes it's the age, or the subject that makes a picture valuable.'

'It's certainly not valuable, I assure you. I didn't give more than a couple of shillings for it at the time. I couldn't have afforded more. Here, let me put it in a plastic bag for you, it's so dusty it'll make your hands and clothes filthy.'

Mrs Dudley scurried into her kitchen and came back with two supermarket carrier bags, which she pulled on to either edge of the picture. 'I'm delighted to give it to you. After I'm gone, he'll just be legend. He'll have no more descendants, no one to think of him as a real person.'

They drove away from the cottage almost reluctantly.

'That furniture looks so right there; it's a shame she has to sell,' Rachel said, looking back.

'But that's how we make our living,' Michael replied. 'Now, any ideas for where you'd like to have lunch?'

'Not really. The weather looks as if it's clouding over for rain. If you were planning an invigorating walk over the moors — '

'I wasn't,' Michael interrupted. 'I have a much better idea. You've never been to my home, have you? I'll cook you lunch and we can sit and work out what we can offer Mrs Dudley for her heirlooms.'

'You — cook?' Rachel looked at him in surprise.

'Of course I can cook! How do you suppose I've looked after myself all these years? Did you think I was living with a landlady, or ate out all the time? I've cooked for myself ever since I left home, at the age of eighteen.'

Michael's home was a small, unremarkable semi-detached house in the eastern outskirts of Truro. 'You can see why I hanker after Mrs Dudley's house,' he said, as they drew up outside and he led the way up the short front path. 'Absolutely no character, this place. I needed somewhere in a hurry when I first arrived in Cornwall and this was available and conveniently near the shop. I've been too lazy to think about moving ever since.'

While Michael busied himself in the kitchen preparing lunch, Rachel found a cloth and wiped the dust from the painting of Penhaligon and his crew. She sat in the wicker chair beside his kitchen stove, drinking wine and studying the picture.

'He looks just like a pirate,' she said. 'It's a wonder the artist didn't give him an eye patch and a hook for a hand.'

'It won't be anything like him,' Michael said. 'That painting isn't contemporary. Might be valuable if it was, but it's no more than an amateur effort, done in the twenties. It probably got thrown in with a job lot of other bits and pieces at some auction. That's how we end up with rubbish in with what we really want, or, if we're very lucky, find a treasure we weren't looking for.'

'There's no artist's name,' Rachel said, peering at the bottom of the picture.

Michael, busy peeling vegetables at the sink, glanced over his shoulder and suggested, 'try taking it out of its frame. That is, if the artist hasn't been too embarrassed to sign it. It really isn't very good.'

Rachel dropped to her knees on the rug and carefully prised the back of the picture away from the frame. The surrounding couple of inches beneath the frame, were much lighter in colour with clean paintwork. At the bottom, right hand edge she saw the signature. 'A H Henderson, 1906,' she said aloud.

'Never heard of him.' Michael was whisking something in a bowl and didn't sound interested. 'There are some reference books in the front room if you want to look him up.'

Rachel went into the sitting room and found a bookcase full of reference works on antiques. She found one dealing with paintings, but there was no record of anyone called Henderson, listed.

'Told you it was some amateur. The picture's terrible, anyway,' Michael said when she told him of her lack of success. She began to put the canvas back into its frame. Behind the picture was a scrap of thin, brown paper, probably used as protection when the picture had been originally framed. She smoothed it out, then saw there was some writing and a rough diagram on it. The outlines of the four men were sketched in their relative positions on the painting, and underneath was written, in an old-fashioned, sloping hand 'Captain Penhaligon and his crew. First mate Tobias Penrose, Able Seaman Elias Blamey, who were hanged with Penhaligon at the Penzance Assizes in 1785, and Daniel Tresillian the cabin boy who betrayed them and escaped death, being given ten years penal servitude.'

She turned the picture over in her hands again, looking at the four men grouped round the capstan. Three were bearded, grizzled, and looked in their fifties, the fourth, a young lad of perhaps eighteen, was clean shaven with a mop of red curls.

Strange how names still lingered in this part of Cornwall. These men could all have descendants among the local folk, who might now, after more than two hundred years, be proud of having a notorious ancestor hanged for smuggling.

'Lunch will be ready in five minutes!' Michael announced. 'You don't mind eating at the kitchen table, do you?'

The meal was excellent; far nicer than the

solid roasts that Aunt Freda cooked with monotonous regularity. Farm workers needed to keep their strength up with large, heavy meals, Rachel knew, but it was usually far too much for her, and a steak, cooked in a delicious wine and mushroom sauce, with tiny slivers of mixed vegetables, and a fresh fruit salad to follow, was, to her mind, an ideal meal.

Afterwards, they sat in the small and unkempt garden, drinking coffee. There was a small patch of lawn, mostly run to daisies and other weeds, surrounded by a dull assortment of shrubs which had no other virtue except to provide a certain amount of screening from neighbouring gardens.

'What would Mrs Dudley think of this, I wonder?' Michael laughed, gesturing at it. 'It's all I can do to keep the grass reasonably short. I'd do more, but the plants are so gloomy it's disheartening to work in it.'

'You never thought of living in the flat over the shop yourself?' Rachel asked.

'I did. I camped there for a few weeks, but I was surrounded by surplus stock from various sales and it wasn't a long-term option. I wanted somewhere away from work, though I suppose I didn't need a whole house, just for myself.'

Rachel glanced sideways at the clean lines

of Michael's profile; his dark hair, slightly rumpled now from his efforts in the kitchen, his hazel eyes, light brown with greeny flecks and his humorous mouth, lips curved in a reminiscent smile.

'You've not been married, have you?' she asked tentatively. The question seemed an intrusion, but she wanted to know.

'No. Never married. I came near to it, once.' Michael was gazing unseeingly towards the end of the garden, his thoughts elsewhere. 'I was engaged when I was twenty, and a student.'

'What happened?'

'She was killed in a car crash.' He spoke flatly, without emotion. After a moment, he said 'that's what made me want to join the Ambulance service, train as a paramedic. The ambulance crew who came to her aid were magnificent. They did absolutely everything they could. If it had been humanly possible to have saved her, they would have done it. She was still just alive when she reached hospital, but she was too badly injured to survive. I felt then that I wanted to do something like that myself, to give back something in return, for all they'd done. What I didn't realise, or perhaps was too fired with misplaced zeal at the time, was that I was psychologically unsuited for that kind of work. It takes a special kind of person to deal with horrific injuries day in, day out, and cope with the emotional stress. I couldn't, in the end.'

'How long did you work for the ambulance service?'

'Ten years. I suppose you could say it was a waste of the training to have given it all up. But if I'd stayed — I was always afraid, towards the end, that I wouldn't be able to cope any more. That, one day, I'd turn my back on someone who needed me, and run away. I had to leave before that happened.'

Rachel reached out a hand and clasped Michael's, pressing it comfortingly. She didn't know what to say, so said nothing.

'It was all in the past, many years in the past, now,' Michael said, his voice brisk and matter-of-fact again. 'Sixteen years since Carol died and I can't pretend I've lived like a monk ever since, in her memory. I've had my share of girlfriends and some I was very fond of, and grew close to, but there was never anyone I wanted to marry. I suppose you think at the age of thirty six I might be feeling that it was now or never if I wanted a wife?'

'Not at all!' Rachel said. 'I'm twenty nine and, frankly, I've never given marriage much thought at all. I suppose you could use that awful cliché that I was 'wedded to my work' but it was such interesting work I was quite content to give all my energies to it. I had a social life, but there was no time for serious commitment to anyone.'

'And yet you didn't want to go back to it, when you were offered your job back, and a promotion?' Michael asked curiously.

'Perhaps I might have done, if the letter had come sooner, but by then I'd realised there was more to life than work, and, as it happened for you, the magic of Cornwall had got to me. I couldn't go back.'

'I think the magic truly happened for me when you walked into the shop that day, bloody and bedraggled and needing help. Perhaps I'd been missing not being needed. Well, that at first. But later, I realised that, although I loved this place and didn't want to leave, I was terribly lonely and there wasn't anyone who understood what it was like to have lived and worked in a busy metropolis like London.

'Then you appeared. Can you wonder I'm almost grateful to that chap who mugged you?' Michael leant towards her, kissing her at first tenderly, then with a deeper passion. 'Rachel — you can't imagine the difference you've made to my life,' he murmured, and it was then that she realised exactly why she'd had absolutely no desire to return to her old job. The magic of Cornwall was also the magic of falling in love.

Much later, Michael said 'I suppose you'll want to make another attempt to reach the top of Penhaligon's Rock, now you know Mrs Dudley and her sister managed it?'

'Do you think the tides could have altered since she went there? Stephen was so insistent about the danger,' Rachel replied.

'We could try. If we found the tide was too strong, we'd have to give up, and accept that perhaps there has been a change, or that the Penhaligon sisters were exceptional oars-women. Perhaps they inherited the skill from their ancestor.'

'It's too late to think of trying today,' Rachel said. 'I'll have to look at Uncle George's tide charts and work out when would be the best time. And we'd need to hire a boat. Not from anyone Stephen or Mrs Blamey know; they'd ask too many questions. But the very fact that she and Stephen warned me off the place, makes me want to land on it, now I know it can be done.'

Rachel was glowing with happiness when she eventually returned to High Topp farm that evening. She and Michael had talked for hours, and now there was a closeness between them that was more than had ever been before. He'd talked of a partnership in the business, and though Rachel had protested that she still knew hardly anything about antiques and was fit to be no more than a sales assistant, he pointed out that she'd shown enthusiasm and an ability to pick up knowledge about the trade which had surprised and delighted him.

'After a winter of touring the auction rooms and house sales, you'll know more than you ever imagined,' he'd promised. 'It will be wonderful to travel the country with a companion for once, finding pieces for our customers, and things we can sell in the shop come next summer. It will be the greatest fun, I can assure you.'

'Had a nice day, dear?' Aunt Freda greeted her as Rachel came into the kitchen. 'Michael not with you? I was hoping he'd stop by for a cup of coffee with us.'

'No, Michael has some paperwork for the business to sort out.' It wasn't exactly true, but their love was so new and sparkling they didn't want to share the secret with anyone yet, and anyone seeing them together, even aunt Freda, would have guessed at once.

'You look pleased with yourself,' Jennifer remarked perceptively, looking up from the table.

'We had a house full of superb furniture, offered to us,' Rachel explained. 'And Mrs Dudley's home is beautiful. She's a delightful lady, too. Made us very welcome.'

'That's Pyder Cottage, off the Pengarron road, isn't it?' Freda asked. 'Such a pretty place I always thought, but what a strange name to call it! I wonder why.'

'Pyder is the name of this Cornish Hundred,' Jennifer said. 'An old name; it means place of oaks.'

'Really? As a matter of fact, there were several oak trees nearby,' Rachel said.

Jennifer looked at her scornfully. 'Well, there would be, wouldn't there? That's why it was called Pyder.'

'Did you buy a picture from her?' Freda asked, seeing the corner of the painting sticking out from the plastic bag.

'Mrs Dudley gave it to me because I was interested. It's a painting of John Penhaligon and his crew. Would you like to see it?' Rachel pulled off the wrappings and laid the picture on the kitchen table.

Jennifer glanced at it, then turned away. 'Ugh, it's horrible. Penhaligon and his men never looked anything like that. It's ridiculous.'

Rachel was inclined to agree, but was stung to retort 'How would you know? They were hanged over two hundred years ago.'

'They aren't Cornish faces,' Jennifer said dismissively. She turned towards the door.

'I'm for bed. Goodnight, Mrs Prescott.'

Freda smiled apologetically. 'It's a very interesting picture, dear. Quite old, I expect.'

'But not old enough. Jennifer's right. The artist painted this more than a hundred years after Penhaligon's time. He couldn't have known what they looked like.' She refused a cup of coffee or even cocoa and went upstairs to her room. Though there were unlikely to be many more paying guests now, until next Easter, Rachel still slept in the tiny single room. It had hardly seemed worth moving now, when she would be moving into the flat over the shop as soon as she and Michael had time to clear it out and make it habitable.

Rachel propped the picture against the mirror of the dressing table facing her bed. She had intended to read for a while before settling to sleep, but found herself unable to concentrate.

She stared at the picture. Jennifer was right, there was a Cornish look; she'd noticed it in the faces of some of the local people, a tendency to be short, dark and thin-faced, with a rather large, hooked nose. Penhaligon and his crew looked more like a serious portrait of Captain Pugwash. The cabin boy, though, was different. He looked to have his own personality, sitting a little apart from the other three, a young man with brilliant blue eyes and a towsled mop of red hair.

Rachel gazed sleepily at the picture. It wasn't well painted, so what was it that made her keep returning to look at it? What was it Mrs Dudley had said? Only John Penhaligon's crew knew about the steps and the secret died with them. But one other must have known, the cabin boy who saved his own life by giving King's Evidence. He'd passed the secret down to his own family. Looking at the boy now, she hardly needed to get up and check his name on the piece of paper stuck to the back, but she did so, anyway.

Red hair must run in the Tresillian family. Now that she looked at him again, Daniel Tresillian the cabin boy did indeed look rather like his descendant, Stephen Tresillian, owner of the Sea Pie.

Perhaps red hair was not the only thing Daniel Tresillian had passed on to his descendant, Stephen Tresillian?

8

Rachel didn't know why she hesitated over telling Michael about Penhaligon's cabin boy. She knew he didn't like Stephen much, but whether it was from a feeling of jealousy, or merely because they were such different people, she had no idea. Michael sometimes wore an odd expression when she mentioned Stephen, a bleak look, though now he had no reason to be jealous of anyone. Michael had never seemed the jealous type, yet mention of Stephen brought out a tension in him that Rachel thought was best avoided. If, indeed, the traitorous cabin boy really was an ancestor of Stephen's, it might explain why he was so protective of Penhaligon's Rock, though what there could be now that needed protection, she had no idea. All the same, the story she'd heard from Mrs Dudley and the idea that Stephen might have some particular interest in the rock, made Rachel more determined than ever to visit it.

'Uncle George, may I borrow your tide charts?' she asked on Monday morning, on her way out to work.

'By all means. Don't have much call to

consult them after the end of summer.' George handed her the book. 'Not thinking of going swimming, are you? Water gets very cold this time of year, even if the land seems warm.'

'No. It's only something Mike wanted to look up. I'll bring the book back when he's finished with it.'

Rachel entered the shop waving the tide tables in her hand.

'I guessed you'd want to take a trip to your favourite place as soon as possible,' Mike grinned at her. 'Come into the office for a moment, will you?'

Innocently, Rachel followed him into the back of the shop. Michael closed the door, which was something he rarely did, his desk being placed so that he could watch for customers while working at it.

'I've been wanting to do this ever since last night,' he said, taking her in his arms and kissing her. 'Not had second thoughts, or changed your mind over what we talked about, yesterday?'

'Of course not!' She hugged him. 'Yesterday was magic. It was hard to keep calm at breakfast this morning and not give Aunt Freda any ideas. She's surprisingly perceptive, I've realised.'

'We'll tell them soon. When we're used to

the idea ourselves. I think it will be shock enough for her when you tell her you'll be moving out and living over the shop.'

'I haven't mentioned it yet. I don't want to tell her too soon and have her trying to persuade me to change my mind, for weeks on end. I think she'd accept my leaving more easily if I was going back to London. She still talks sometimes about my 'important and interesting job' I had there, though she doesn't know why I left, or that I had the chance to go back. All she really knows about my work at FANECO was what my mother told her in letters, so it's all a bit vague and third hand. But she doesn't seem terribly interested in it anyway, she's just glad that I'm staying with them, not alone in a big city with no family nearby. She and Uncle George look on London as dangerous foreign parts. They've never been there in their lives.'

'We'll go back to visit, this winter,' Michael promised. 'I've noted several sales in and around the capital. Now, before we have any customers, let's go upstairs and look at the condition of the flat.'

Rachel hadn't been into the rooms above the shop before, and was a little startled at what she saw.

'It needs a lot doing to it,' she said, eyeing the thick dust on the floor and cobwebs

221

clinging to every corner.

'Painting and decorating,' Michael said. 'And I'll have to clear out the junk that's here. Most of it is oddments from job lots; unsaleable. I'll put it outside at the back.'

'Unsaleable like the church pew?' Rachel's eyes were twinkling. 'I don't believe you even know what you've got here. When did you last come up to have a look?'

'I looked up here before I offered you the flat!' Michael retorted indignantly. 'Admittedly, I only came to see how big it was and if there really were kitchen and bathroom facilities. I suppose most of this stuff dates from the time when I first took the shop over. I wasn't so experienced at buying at sales then and I had to take a fair amount of rubbish to get what I really wanted.'

'It's going to take weeks to sort out what you have here and decide if it's worth cleaning it sufficiently to put it in the shop,' Rachel said. 'And by that time you won't be opening except on market days and we'll be travelling round the country to sales. I can't see myself using the flat all that much. I might as well stay at the farm until next spring.'

'I suppose that makes sense,' Michael conceded. 'It might be worth cleaning the place up, whether you have it or not. We're going to need somewhere to keep all the smaller things we bring back from the winter sales.'

'I'm not sharing my home with a load of dusty Victoriana,' Rachel said decidedly. 'You said you didn't like it much when you slept up here, and that was only a matter of a few weeks.' She glanced out of the window, down to the street below. 'It looks like we may have our first customer of the day. There's a couple looking in the window and something seems to have caught their attention.'

The couple were interested in a small, marquetry card table and Michael went to deal with them. He came into the office looking pleased with himself.

'A good sale, that! The table's worth quite a bit, and the chap appreciated it. He's bringing his car round to collect it in a few minutes.'

'Now you have a space in the window, you can bring something down from upstairs to fill it,' Rachel said. 'A few more sales like that, and we might have enough room upstairs to start thinking of making it halfway habitable.'

'Hey, don't be mad at me! I was trying to be helpful because you said you didn't want to go on living at the farm. I wasn't expecting you to live in the flat with the place looking as it does at present.'

'Have some coffee before we have any more

customers,' Rachel said. 'I'm not mad at you, I just think the idea of living in the flat is impractical, having seen it.'

'Probably as impractical as rowing out to Penhaligon's Rock.' Michael picked up the tide tables. 'Is there a suitable time over the next weekend? Have you looked? If you're set on going, we ought not to leave it too late in the year.'

'Next Sunday is a possibility. The tide turns at midday so if we went soon after two, we'd have the tide with us, out to the rock. We'd have plenty of time to explore before we'd need to leave, in time to catch the tide with us on the way back.'

'Explore! It's hardly that big! And exposed to the wind, it'll be too cold to sit around; I'd think we'd have had enough of the place in half an hour at most. I don't understand about tides;' Michael handed her back the tide tables. 'I'll leave it up to you to plan when we go.'

'The point is, the tide will be low but still going out at two, so it's the easiest time to take a boat out, we'll have the tide with us. By six the tide will be coming in again, so we'll have the tide with us coming back. I know it's silly, but I have this childish feeling that I want to get on to the top of the rock because I've been told not to.'

Michael nodded. 'I know the feeling. What about hiring a boat? We can hardly ask Stephen.'

'I'm sure there are places here in the town would put me in contact with someone who hires out boats,' Rachel said. 'I could try the tourist office, if it's still open at this time of the year. Shall I go round to the High Street now and make some enquiries? I can sort out something to replace the marquetry table when I get back.'

'Might as well. I can see you are keen about this bleak lump of granite. You've had an eager gleam in your eye ever since you saw Mrs Dudley's sister's painting.'

Rachel picked up her shoulder bag and slung it over her shoulder. 'I won't be long,' she said, opening the shop door.

The quickest way into the main shopping streets was down the passageway between the two derelict shops, where she'd come all those weeks ago and been mugged by someone the police hadn't caught yet. But Rachel was wary now, and tucked her handbag firmly under her arm as she approached the narrow entrance. She didn't mind going down here again; after all, the chances of being robbed in exactly the same place twice, were extremely unlikely.

She was half way down the passage when

she heard running footsteps pounding behind her, and a hand fell on her shoulder. This time she was ready. She whirled round, aiming a punch at the man's body and at the same time, screaming as loudly as she could.

'Ow! Rachel!'

She looked in horror at the man now in front of her.

'Mike! Oh, my God! I'm so sorry!'

Mike was clutching his ribs, doubled up and gasping for air. When he finally recovered, he said, with some respect, 'I never knew you could pack a punch like that. I can see I shall have to watch myself in future.'

'I'm *so* sorry.' She was concerned for him, afraid she might have inflicted some real damage and still shaking from the shock of the encounter. 'Mike, I thought you were the mugger again. It was just here that he pushed me. I thought I'd got over it and then I heard running footsteps behind me and it was like it was happening all over again. When you put your hand on my shoulder it brought it all back back, all the anger that last time I'd let him get away with it and I was determined that this time — ' She stopped. 'I'm babbling,' she said. 'Did I do any damage? I'm so sorry.'

'I'm all right.' Mike put out a tentative hand and felt his ribs. 'I should have realised.

You've never mentioned it since and I thought — but I should have known that the memory of that kind of experience doesn't go away for a long time. It was stupid of me. I should have known better.'

'Why did you come after me?' The shaking had stopped, now that she knew it was Mike and not some potential thief. Rachel leaned against the wall, breathing deeply.

'After you'd gone, it occured to me that you could pick up some paint charts while you were at the shops. We might as well have the flat looking clean, whether or not you live in it. I never thought twice, just ran out after you. I'd forgotten for the moment that this was where — ' Michael broke off to look round the passageway. 'This isn't a very pleasant way to come. And you were screaming your head off and no one's come to investigate.'

'Like last time. But just as well now, or someone might think you really were attacking me. If I don't need to take you to Casualty to repair any cracked ribs, I'll go and sort out the boat hire. And collect some paint charts.'

'You winded me, that was all. I'd better get back to the shop. Oh, and why not buy some sandwiches or a pasty, and we can plan this great expedition over lunch in the office?'

It took Rachel some time to find someone willing to hire out a boat for the day, at this end of the holiday season. She was given a list of boatyards by a helpful assistant in a fishing tackle shop, but most of those who hired out boats had already laid up the smaller ones for the winter, and were not prepared to hire cut anything without coming themselves.

'I found someone in the end,' she said. 'His boatyard is a little way up the river. We can go directly to Penhaligon's Rock without going anywhere near the harbour, but we have to pick the boat up from him ourselves.'

'Up the river? You aren't telling me I'll have to row miles before we even reach the sea? I've only ever rowed a boat on the Serpentine before.' Michael was horrified.

'No, this has an outboard engine. It's as small as a rowing boat but he says it's easy to steer and handle. I couldn't ask him to bring it to Penhaligon's bay. For one thing, it would be difficult to bring it inshore, with the tide low, and I didn't want him to guess we were going out to the rock. I don't know how many people have this habit of warning folk off the rock, but he might have refused to let us take it if he knew where we were going.'

Over lunch, Rachel worked out with the aid of the tide tables, when they would need to start for Penhaligon's Rock, and when to think of leaving it. 'Though if the boat has an engine, I suppose the tides are irrelevant,' she said. 'I telephoned the boatyard from the tackle shop to find out if they were willing to hire. I said I'd confirm it before the weekend. If they ask us, where can we say we want to go? It's hardly the season for a pleasure trip.'

'People come down here for autumn breaks,' Michael said. 'We can say we fancy seeing the coastline from the sea; it's attractive enough and that's the only way you can see some of the bays. There are places where it's virtually impossible to climb down the cliffs, but there's a marvellous beach at the bottom. He'll be glad enough to take a hiring when business must be all but finished for the year.'

Rachel turned her attention to the paint charts, but with some lack of enthusiasm.

'Did you really mean that I should have Mrs Dudley's furniture in the flat?' she asked. 'It's very good quality, but I'm thinking it might be too big to fit in. And the stairs are narrow if we're to bring it all up. It might not look nearly so nice as it does in her room.'

'What are you suggesting?'

'That we forget about my having the flat to live in. At least until next year. I won't be there much if we are going to be away at house sales all winter.'

Michael gave her a long, thoughtful look. 'Did you like looking after the bed and breakfast people at the farm?'

'What?' To Rachel, the question seemed beside the point. 'Yes,' she said, after a moment's thought. 'I enjoyed doing that. It was fun, meeting people, and they were all so appreciative. But there won't be any more of them before next Easter. And I suspect that, in spite of what she said, Jennifer won't be sorry to do it again. I felt awful, taking tips which she should have had.'

'You earned them.'

'Perhaps, but I'd more or less taken her job away from her. She claimed she didn't care, but it must have meant less money for her. No wonder she looked on me as a cuckoo in the nest.'

Michael stood up. 'I have to go out for a while. I may be out for a couple of hours. You can mind the shop for the rest of the afternoon, can't you?'

Rachel looked at him in surprise. Michael hardly ever left the shop for any length of time unless it was to see about a sale, and then he invariably told her about it beforehand. She was about to ask him where he was going but decided it was none of her business.

'Of course,' she said with a shrug. 'I might

230

even have a plan for redecorating the shop when you come back.'

Michael didn't return until nearly closing time. When he walked into the shop Rachel thought he had an air of suppressed excitement about him.

'Had any customers?' He glanced round briefly, almost as if he expected empty spaces in the shop every time she was left by herself.

'Three or four. I sold a silver snuffbox and a man showed interest in one of the Dresden figurines. He said he would come back; didn't seem daunted by your asking price. Ah! Here he is now!'

Rachel looked up as the shop doorbell tinkled and a man entered.

'I'll leave you to deal with him,' Michael said. 'I'll be in the office if you need me. Shut the shop after he's gone.'

The man had evidently already made up his mind about the Dresden statuete. 'Rare now, ever since the war,' he commented. 'I've been looking for pieces like this for a long time. Not many antique shops have anything at all like this.'

'Would you like us to look out for some others? We shall be spending the winter touring house sales. I imagine by Easter we'll have seen most of what's on offer in the country.'

'I'd appreciate that. Here's my card. I'll make out your cheque while you pack the figurine for me.'

When Rachel brought in the cheque and the man's card after he'd left, Michael whistled. 'Clever girl! I didn't expect to get that much for it.'

'He didn't even haggle,' Rachel said. 'And he'll be interested in anything else that's genuine Dresden, that we come across at the sales.'

'I truly believe my business turnover has doubled since you came to work for me,' Michael said. 'I should thank that mugger, instead of wanting to brain him for what he did to you.'

'He doesn't matter,' Rachel dismissed the thought. 'I rarely think about him these days. It was only being in that passageway and hearing footsteps behind me, just like then, brought it all back for a moment.'

'Sit down. I've something to say.'

Rachel sat down, frowning. Michael seemed more serious than usual and she wondered what he could possibly be about to tell her. His manner made her feel nervous, especially when he began pacing about the tiny room, as if not knowing where to begin.

Finally, he said 'I've been thinking. It's not

fair to let you live in the flat upstairs. You'd be using that passageway every time you needed to reach the shops. It would be a constant reminder.'

'No, it wouldn't. I've told you, normally I rarely think of the incident at all these days. And as you saw just now, I'd be ready and able to defend myself — oh!'

Sudden enlightenment dawned. 'You didn't go to the hospital casualty department, did you? I didn't break a rib, or rupture something?'

He broke into a laugh at her expression of horror.

'No, I didn't. You did nothing worse than wind me. But I'm worried the chap might still be hanging around this area. The police seemed to think he was a junkie, and that means he could be unpredictable.'

'Mike, I've lived by myself before. I can manage.'

'And it's clear you hate the flat. I'm not surprised; it's full of rubbish and filthy. And it would be small and poky even if it was cleaned up and made habitable.'

'Not half as small as the attic room I have at present at the Prescotts.'

'So I got to thinking. And I've been to see my bank manager.'

'Whatever for? You don't want to spend

loads of money on that flat. Please, Mike, don't feel you have to do that.'

He raised a hand to silence her. 'No, not the flat. I wanted to discuss my finances with him before I put this idea to you. If he'd told me it wasn't possible, I couldn't have said anything, but it is possible, just about. So now you can tell me what you think.'

'What about, for heaven's sake?'

'Suppose I sell my house, which is in a good location, even though it doesn't have much character about it, and buy Mrs Dudley's cottage, which she'll sell to us because she knows we love it just as it is and won't want to change it. And you come and share it with me? And I thought — if you still wanted to — we could run a bed and breakfast business in the summer, as well? The cottage would be big enough, and it's well-furnished already. That way, we'll still have upstairs here for a store for the goods we buy this winter, and come Easter we'll have two businesses, providing the Tourist Board approve the B and B. Which they will do, because you've been doing it all summer and have appreciative guests to recommend you. I'd always dreamed of expanding the business, but I thought that would mean another shop. This is a much better idea, and it provides us with a beautiful home as well. What do you think?'

'Hold on a minute! You're going too fast for me!' Rachel raised her hands in protest. 'I'm bewildered. I thought you said you would have liked to buy Mrs Dudley's cottage when you first came to Cornwall, but it was far too expensive.'

'It wasn't even for sale then. That was five years ago, when I was starting out in the antiques business and I needed all my capital for that. Now, it's become a comfortable living and it's time to think of branching out. Another shop, or a new, different venture. A bed and breakfast business in Pyder Cottage would be perfect, and you fell in love with the place, just as I did.'

Rachel gave him a long, hard stare. 'Are you doing this for me? To give me somewhere to live, that isn't with my relations or in a poky flat?'

'I'm doing it for both of us. Perhaps I'm being selfish in wanting to spend more time with you, but I was hoping it was what you wanted, too. If it isn't, and I've taken too much for granted, tell me.'

She shook her head. 'No, it isn't that. I'd love to share living in Mrs Dudley's cottage with you. You must know that. But you wouldn't have considered buying it if it was just yourself. Isn't buying the cottage now going to mess up any long term plans you must have for the antiques business?'

'To put it bluntly, you messed up all my long term plans the day you staggered into this shop, shaken and bleeding and looking like — like the person I'd been waiting for, for years? Don't you realise, meeting you changed everything for me? I wanted to see you again, and offering you a job here was the perfect opportunity.'

'So you didn't really want an assistant? Offering me a job was just an excuse?'

Michael looked at her in exasperation. 'Of course I wanted an assistant! Didn't I tell you I'd been looking for someone for months, but the only people who applied were school leavers who'd have been more suitable for Woolworths? I admit, I was taking a chance, but it was a risk for both of us. It might not have been what you wanted, and we might not have hit it off together.'

'Instead of which, we seem to have become — ' Rachel hesitated, searching for the right word, which would not be mawkish, or assume too much.

'Lovers?' Michael's arm was round her, drawing her close to him. 'Was that the word you were too shy to say?' He kissed her on the lips. 'The shop door is locked so we won't be disturbed. And, because you won't say it, but undoubtedly you'll be thinking it, the cottage has four bedrooms. It would make better business sense to let out three of them rather than two, don't you think?'

Rachel entwined her arms round his neck, looking up at him with laughter in her eyes. 'If I agree, you'll have to be with me when I tell Aunt Freda that I'm moving out. You do realise, don't you, that as well as leaving the farm, by next Easter we could be rivals with her in the B and B business? The cottage is near enough to take people who might have stayed at the farm.'

'Always plenty of tourists for everyone, in this county,' Michael said lightly. 'Why don't we go and visit Mrs Dudley now, and make her an offer, since the bank seems to think I can afford it? I'll have to sell my own home first, but the way she was talking, I feel sure Mrs Dudley will give us the first refusal, especially if she knows that some of her furniture will stay in the house. I'll telephone her now; see if it's convenient.'

Mrs Dudley welcomed them like old friends. 'And now you've decided you'd like to buy my house, as well as my furniture?' she said, ushering them into her pretty sitting room. 'I'm delighted! I could see you liked my home but I never expected you would want to buy it.'

'Neither did we, then,' Michael said. 'But we've had some new ideas since, and we thought we would like to own somewhere where we could offer bed and breakfast to paying guests in the summer.'

'What a splendid idea! You know, I've been asked, more than once, if I'd take paying guests. The cottage is in such a good location, but I couldn't face the extra work and responsibility. If my husband had still been alive, perhaps I'd have considered it. But we were both too old, even then.'

'How are we going to keep your garden looking as good as it does now?' Rachel wondered, looking out of the french windows. There was still plenty of colour in the flowerbeds, bright with dahlias and chrysanthemums.

'You'll manage, dear. And if you find you don't have the time, there are plenty of people in the village who would be glad to put in a few hours' work to keep it tidy.'

Rachel privately doubted that would be enough, but there was the winter to come before she needed to worry about the garden. Michael was talking house prices, and Mrs Dudley sounded eager to sell to them.

'I haven't had so much as an enquiry since

I turned down the last people,' she said. 'The estate agent tells me it's the sort of place someone might want for a holiday cottage, and no one's interested in them until the spring. I was told I couldn't expect to sell before next Easter, but if I don't, I shall lose my flat. If you can make me a firm offer, I'd be willing to drop the price.'

By the time they left, the cottage was all but theirs, once the legal formalities had been completed and Michael had sold his present house, which he seemed to think would not present any difficulties. While he was out at the car, collecting his diary and notebook, Rachel said to Mrs Dudley, 'That picture of Captain Penhaligon and his crew that you gave me — do you think the crew could still have descendants living round here? I was wondering.'

'It's not a true likeness of any of them, you must realise,' Mrs Dudley said. 'That picture must have been painted long after they were all dead and gone, and I don't suppose there were any contemporary portraits to go by. The artist painted what he thought typical pirates might have looked like. Why, have you seen someone who looks like one of them?'

'No, it was the names. They're common enough in Cornwall, I know —'

'The names are accurate. As to whether the

crew had any descendants, no one knows, but they were old enough to have been married with families by the time they were caught and hanged. Not the cabin boy, of course, but then he escaped being hanged. I imagine they all came from this part of the county so there might still be descendants here. People move about much more these days, though, and all the crew had Cornish names that one might come across anywhere.'

Driving back through the deep, narrow lanes, Michael said, 'Do we go and celebrate, or do we stop at the farm to tell your aunt and uncle first?'

'I suppose we ought to tell them before they hear it from someone else,' Rachel replied. 'The strange thing about these villages is that, even with houses isolated from each other, news travels faster than it ever seemed to in London. I bet Mrs Blamey will know all about us buying Pyder Cottage by the time I next visit her shop.'

Aunt Freda and Uncle George took the news of Rachel's departure very well, even the fact that she would be sharing a home with Michael didn't produce the frown of disapproval that Rachel had feared.

'It had to come, lass. We knew you'd be looking for somewhere of your own, eventually,' George said. 'And you're near enough to drop by and see us, now and then. Freda was worried you'd go back to London. That's no place for a lass on her own and we'd have lost touch with you. Your mother'll be relieved to hear we'll still be near enough to keep an eye on you.'

'Really, George! Rachel is a grown woman! She doesn't need any eye kept on her,' Freda replied tartly. 'I shall miss you, though,' she added.

Jennifer was disposed to be friendly as well. 'I shall miss having someone near my own age around,' she said privately to Rachel. 'I was bored rigid whenever I had to stay in in the evenings. I was almost driven to move in with Alan before you came, I was that desperate.'

'Why didn't you? Alan seems a nice chap and he's devoted to you. You could do a great deal worse,' Rachel ventured. She'd never discussed Jennifer's personal life with her before, but the girl seemed to be inviting confidences tonight.

Jennifer made a face. 'Alan's all right, I suppose. But he's ordinary. Not what I'm really looking for. You're lucky; your feller is great. Don't worry, he's too posh for me, but he's right for you.'

Rachel laughed. 'Mike's hardly posh, though I think I know what you mean. But,

Jennifer, are you going to spend all your life looking for someone who matches up to Stephen?'

'Stephen?' Jennifer looked surprised. 'But no one's like Stephen. He's a one-off.'

'If he's the kind of man — ' Rachel began. Now might be her only opportunity to encourage Jennifer, if Stephen was the man she really cared for.

'Stephen's wild, and not to be trusted,' Jennifer snapped. 'He's impossible. And he's not the sort of man who'd ever want to be married. He doesn't ever want to be tied down.'

'But you're fond of him, all the same?' Rachel pressed.

'Of course I'm fond of Stephen. Why wouldn't I be? There'll never be anyone else like him. But God help the woman who has the misfortune to fall in love with him,' Jennifer said with a touch of bitterness. 'I'll probably end up marrying Alan, breeding a load of kids and having a waistline like a river barge.' She smiled at Rachel. 'I'm glad you came here, and I'm sorry I wasn't always as friendly as I could have been. I don't take to incomers much. Tourists are all right, they're our bread and butter, but Cornwall's for the Cornish, I always say.'

The following week Michael took time off

242

from the shop to show round potential buyers for his house. There seemed to be an encouraging amount of interest, but by Friday he felt they were taking up too much of his time, so he left his spare key with the estate agent, with instructions to let him know at once, as soon as there were any firm offers.

It was a telephone call when she was alone in the shop that reminded Rachel of the trip she had been planning until Michael's surprise plans had swept it out of her mind completely.

'Miss Hayward?' came the diffident voice with the West country burr to it. 'I was wonderin', do you still want to hire a boat? Only I'll be laying them up for the winter come the weekend.' The voice tailed off, waiting hopefully for her answer.

'The boat! I'd forgotten all about it! I'm terribly sorry, we've been involved with some business deals and I completely forgot that I said I'd call you back to confirm it. Yes, we'd still like to hire your boat. It has an engine, you said?'

'Small outboard. Just a small boat, you said. Not planning to go far?'

'No, oh, no. We wanted to see the coastline from the sea. Take photographs, that kind of thing.' Rachel began hunting round the desk for George's tide charts.

'When would you be wanting it for, then?'

'At the weekend. This Sunday. About one o'clock?'

'Next Sunday? Beginning to be a bit cold for a trip on the water. I don't reckon on using them open boats after the end of the month. T'ain't no call for 'em, so I lays 'em up till Easter.'

'We'll wrap up warmly.' What on earth was the man fussing about? Fishermen were out all year long. She couldn't find the notes she'd made on the tide charts, about high and low tides, but surely, if the boat had an engine, it wouldn't matter anyway?

'Would you want me to bring the boat somewhere? Harbour at St Morwenna's Bay would be convenient,' the voice continued in its unhurried tones.

'No, not there. We'll come to the boatyard and collect it.' Even if Stephen was not around, Mrs Blamey would see them and would be certain to ask awkward questions.

'Got a trailer on the back of your vehicle, have you?'

'What?' Rachel frowned into the receiver mouthpiece.

'To tek her to the water. My yard's not near the coast.'

'I didn't realise. I thought — no, we haven't

244

a trailer or anything. How can we get it to the sea?'

'My yard's up river. Mebbe half a mile from the sea. If you want to start from here, that's all right by me. She'll do fine if you keep to the centre of the flow. I was thinking to save you time.'

'Thank you, but we'd just as well collect it from your yard and go down the river. Where, exactly, do we find you?'

He gave her directions and Rachel moved across to Michael's ancient map of the county. The names might have changed but the position of the river mouth hadn't, and she saw it was not very far from Penhaligon's bay. Probably they'd be able to reach the rock in an hour or so.

'We'll be there to pick the boat up at one o'clock next Sunday,' she said, putting the receiver down.

Too cold for a picnic on the top of the rock, in October? She'd once dreamed of sunbathing up there, but then she remembered Mrs Dudley's tale of building a camp fire and roasting potatoes. That sounded more appropriate, though she couldn't imagine wanting to stay too long on the exposed summit. It wasn't all that big, and, apart from the certainty that there would be gulls' nests, nothing much to see. Now that she was so near to fulfilling her ambition, she realised it would be far more sensible to wait until summer came again and enjoy the feeling that they would be the only people to lie on the grassy summit in complete privacy. It was only the fact that Stephen had been so much against any idea of her trying to land on the rock, that made her want to defy him and reach the top. He must, she was certain, have learnt the secret of the way in between the rocks, from his cabin boy ancestor. Did he ever go there himself, she wondered? Or did he merely want to preserve Penhaligon's secret from everyone else?

Well, she and Michael would show him that he couldn't keep secrets from incomers, any more than she could keep them from locals.

9

On Saturday evening, Rachel was late leaving
the antique shop, a customer taking time over
the purchase of a set of dining chairs. As she
and Michael walked out to their respective
cars, he said 'You didn't need to have stayed,
but thanks, all the same. It made it worth
while that he bought them in the end.'

'I wanted to stay. I was keen to see if he
really would buy,' Rachel replied. 'But I could
have done with him not coming in quite so
near closing time.'

'Better than after we'd closed.' Michael
yawned. 'Tomorrow we don't have to think
about the shop or anything connected with it.
Tomorrow we set sail on a voyage to explore
your mystery island at last.'

'Not sail, but engine,' Rachel laughed. 'And
it's hardly a mystery. You can see the whole of
the top with binoculars from the cliffs.
Penhaligon's Rock can't hold any secrets
these days, I'm sure. I only want to go there
because Stephen was so adamant that no one
could.'

'You must have been a terribly difficult brat
when you were a child,' Michael said

affectionately, opening his car door. 'See you at this boatyard around one o'clock tomorrow, then?'

Driving home, Rachel wondered why she had had such a fascination with a mere lump of rock, out in the middle of the bay. Was it only because of Stephen's attitude that she wanted to visit it? But she'd been attracted to it the first time she'd seen it from the sea, sailing past in Stephen's boat that morning in early summer, when she'd newly arrived in Cornwall and walked to the village for the first time.

Would it be an anticlimax, once they stood on the top, with nothing but the gulls swooping round them? I know, I'll buy a bottle of wine to drink on the top, to toast the purchase of Pyder Cottage and the successful future of all our joint ventures, she thought. But where, along these country lanes, would she find somewhere she could buy wine?

Moments later, she was turning into the road that led to St Morwenna's Bay. The general stores was often open late on a Saturday night; in fact, Mrs Blamey seemed to keep erratic hours and Rachel suspected that she had so few customers these days that she might be prepared to open at almost any time to make a sale.

Rachel parked her car alongside the

harbour wall, opposite the shop, and was relieved to see there was still a light on downstairs. The shop door was unlocked, but the bell did not make its usual jangle as she stepped inside. Mrs Blamey wasn't in the shop, but presumably she was in the back, counting the day's takings, or checking on stock. Rachel selected a bottle of wine from the rather limited range Mrs Blamey kept, then looked around for anything else they might need.

It probably would be cold on top of the rock, exposed to the wind. Perhaps wine wasn't such a good idea, unless she brought a flask of hot soup along as well. She giggled at the thought of toasting their future in soup, but the idea seemed practical. She chose two tins and left them on the counter with the wine while she looked at the rest of the stock. Mrs Dudley had said she and her sister had built a campfire, though there couldn't have been much in the way of wood to fuel it. Perhaps it might be fun to try lighting a small one, in memory of her sister Charlotte, with whom Mrs Dudley had had so many happy times picnicking on the rock. Rachel added a box of matches and some firelighters.

After the small pile of shopping had gained a packet of biscuits and a packet of sausages she thought they might have fun cooking on the fire if they managed to light one, she began to wonder where Mrs Blamey was. She had deliberately made noise in putting her purchases on the counter and fully expected that by now the dour Cornishwoman would have appeared to see who was in her shop.

Rachel coughed loudly, then scuffed her feet. There was still no sign or sound of anyone on the premises. Finally, she went to the door at the back of the shop and knocked. When there was no response, she began to feel uneasy. It seemed very unlike Mrs Blamey to leave everything open and unattended, especially with a post office on the premises. She turned the handle of the door and pushed it open a little way. There was a dark passage beyond, but at the far end a staircase led to the upper floor, and there a light glimmered at the top.

'Mrs Blamey?'

When there was still no response, Rachel stepped into the passage and walked as far as the foot of the staircase.

'Mrs Blamey!' She shouted, anxiety making her voice unexpectedly loud.

There was a scurry of feet on the landing above, Mrs Blamey came to the head of the stairs and leaned over the banisters. Behind her, Rachel saw there was a man, wearing a thick dufflecoat and with a cap pulled well down over his face.

'Who's there? What is it?' What do you want?' Mrs Blamey sounded frightened, and Rachel hastened to reassure her.

'It's me, Rachel Hayward. I wanted to buy a few things but I couldn't make you hear when I knocked on the door. I'm sorry to disturb you but I really do need these things.'

Mrs Blamey glared at her. Rachel had the distinct impression that she moved deliberately to block any view of the man behind her, but she was not quick enough.

'The shop is shut. How did you get in?' she demanded.

'The door was not locked. And you still have your 'open' sign up. I'm sorry if I disturbed you but I assumed I could still buy groceries. If you've already cashed up, I might be able to offer you the exact money.'

The man behind Ida Blamey muttered something which Rachel could not catch, then Mrs Blamey, without glancing back at him, came down the stairs and hustled Rachel in front of her, back into the shop. 'I suppose I can deal with your shopping,' she grumbled. 'In future, ring the bell, don't come wandering into places you've no call to be in.'

Rachel was about to apologise again, then thought better of it. There was no bell inside the shop that she could see, and if Mrs Blamey had left the shop door unlocked by mistake, she should be grateful that it was a genuine customer who had come in, not someone who might have made off with the stock.

Mrs Blamey raised an eyebrow over the odd assortment of goods Rachel had left on the counter, but she did not make any comment beyond a scornful sniff. With great speed, she totted up the prices on the edge of a paper bag, and Rachel, searching in her bag, was glad she could indeed give her the exact amount. Ida Blamey followed her to the door and held it open for her.

'Goodnight, Mrs Blamey.'

There was no reply but as Rachel stepped across the road she heard the bolts of the shop door being pushed fiercely into place.

Well! Rachel thought, sitting back in her car with the bag of shopping on the seat beside her. It was uncharacteristic behaviour for the normally garrulous and inquisitive Ida Blamey. Rachel had expected to have been quizzed about her strange assortment of purchases, but then, Ida had been unexpectedly interrupted while entertaining her gentleman visitor and it had been clear that she hadn't wanted Rachel to see him.

Rachel was certain it was the same man

that she and Michael had seen going round to the back of the shop on a previous occasion. Though she had only seen a glimpse of him then and at neither time had seen his face, his clothes had been the same, a heavy dufflecoat and cap well pulled down. He'd looked the same build and height, too.

Well, why shouldn't Mrs Blamey entertain a gentleman friend if she had a mind to? Though with her neighbours inclined to gossip, Rachel could understand her reluctance to let anyone know about him. 'Good luck to her'! she said turning the car's ignition. I wouldn't say a word about this to anyone at the farm, but it's something I'll enjoy sharing with Michael.

She drove the car towards the steep hill at the end of the street, heading for High Topp farm. As she began the ascent, she glanced in her rear mirror and saw a dark, shadowy figure leave the general stores and walk briskly away towards the harbour wall. She'd have liked to know more about this mysterious caller, but she knew that was something she could never ask Ida Blamey.

Next day, after an early snack lunch to avoid Freda's huge Sunday roast, Rachel drove to the boatyard, arriving to find Michael already there.

'I've seen the boat we're hiring,' he told

her. 'Looks a nice little craft and seems easy to handle. The chap has already given me a run down on using the engine and the sea looked very calm as I passed the bay.'

Rachel took her place in the bows of the boat, clutching the carrier containing her makeshift picnic.

'What's that?' Michael eyed it curiously.

'You'll see. Wait until we're on the top.'

The boatman pushed them off from the jetty and they drifted into midstream. Here the river was as wide as a road, shallow except for a narrow channel midway between the banks.

'If you want to row, look out for them water weeds,' he called. 'Only use the engine when you're clear of them midstream, else you'll likely clog it.'

Michael fitted the oars into the rowlocks and took a few experimental strokes. 'This isn't bad at all,' he said. 'We've the current with us. We could float down to the sea without any effort, if we wanted to. Save ourselves for when we reach the mouth of the river.'

Rachel lay back, looking up at the trees that overhung the banks on either side, their leaves gold and brown now, and falling into the water like large, slow snowflakes.

'How far to the sea? I like this. I could drift all afternoon.'

'I thought you were the one desperate to scale the heights of Penhaligon's Rock,' Michael teased. 'And we can't drift for long. I've realised, if I don't row, we'll collide with the bank every few yards.'

It was not long before the scenery changed and the trees gave way to rocky banks; later they passed through the edge of a small town, the banks now built up concrete walls, with a path high above their heads, then, suddenly, they had left the river and were at sea, rocking more now the waves reached them.

'What's the tide doing?' Michael asked.

'I forgot to check! I didn't think it mattered much if we had an engine.'

Michael shipped the oars and scrambled to the stern to start the engine. After a couple of false starts, it gave an encouraging splutter, then a roar, before settling into a rhythmic chug-chug. The boat gathered speed, cutting through the water and soon leaving the land behind.

'I'll go out of the bay and round the headland,' Michael decided. 'If we're to locate this gap in the rocks, we need to approach from the outside of the bay.'

The boat rocked more than Stephen's larger Sea Pie, which was the only other small boat Rachel had experienced at sea before. Though the water was relatively calm, there was a steady breeze, and the waves slapped round the sides of the boat and occasionally splashed over the side, spraying them with salt water. Rachel was beginning to feel uneasy, and wished they had not planned to reach the rock from this direction. It meant they would not have had to risk being seen and questioned, but it would have been a great deal nearer had they begun their trip from the harbour in St Morwenna's Bay.

The boat chugged along, keeping the coast in sight but still some way out to sea. They could make out the houses on the top of the cliff, but it was too far to see if there were any Sunday afternoon walkers along the cliff path.

After half an hour since they'd left the river, when the land was beginning to look disconcertingly unfamiliar, they passed a headland jutting out into the sea, and Rachel cried out and pointed ahead: 'There it is! There's Penhaligon's Rock! It looks different, approaching it from this side, but there still seem to be rocks all round the base of it. I can see white spray where the waves crash against them.'

'Now comes the tricky bit.' Michael had been steering the boat with a light hand on the tiller, keeping a course straight ahead but not too concerned if the boat wavered a little from side to side. Now, he turned the boat's prow towards the great pile of rock rearing out of the sea and slowed the engine until they were moving gently forward, almost drifting with the tide.

'Where did Mrs Dudley say this landing place was?' he asked.

'She didn't say it was a landing place here, just a gap in the rocks. Towards the right as you face it from the sea, she said. Go round slowly, as near as you can, and see if we can see anything.'

With the engine barely ticking over, and using the oars to fend them off when they threatened to be swept too near the rocks, Michael made a complete circle of the rock. Nowhere did there appear to be a place where it would have been possible to steer a boat between the jagged rocks which stuck up out of the water all round.

'This looks a dangerous place,' he said, when they were facing out to sea again. 'Was she making it all up, do you think? She's old; she could have been romanticising, or perhaps she dreamt it, or read a story about old Penhaligon doing impossible things and believed she had, too.'

'She didn't seem like that,' Rachel

defended Mrs Dudley. 'She sounded like a perfectly rational, truthful person. Could there have been some geological changes since her day; a rock fall, or something? In a storm, perhaps, rocks could have been loosened and fallen from the top to block any entrance. It must be nearly sixty years since she and her sister came here.'

'I'll go round once more, and you look carefully,' Michael said. 'I can't look myself; I have to concentrate on keeping us from getting too close. If we don't see anything this time, I vote we call it a day and go back to the boatyard.'

Rachel let her eyes follow the rock up towards the summit. Something caught her attention a yard or so below the top. 'Mike, can you move back a little way?' she asked.

'Not easily. This isn't a car, you know,' he grumbled, but cut the engine completely and began to paddle the boat backwards, using the rocks to push against.

'There! Between those two rocks! Quick, before the boat drifts past again!' She was pointing to a space that seemed hardly big enough for a person to edge through, let alone a boat.

Michael stared where she pointed. 'Surely not. I'll crush us if I try to go in there.'

'It's the place! I know it is! Look up, you

can see a path near the top, immediately above. Follow it down with your eye and you'll see steps. It has to be the place.'

The boat was already nosing against the rock at one side. Michael leaned over to fend it off, when, to his astonishment it slipped forward, past the ring of rocks and entered a small, enclosed space of still water, barely big enough for a sailing boat and completely hidden by surrounding rocks. Ahead, against the bulk of the rock itself, a small platform had been cut, with steps leading upwards from it to the top of the rock. Beside the platform, a rusty iron ring was fastened in the rock face. It was clear that this was the harbour Mrs Dudley had meant, and that it had once been used frequently by her pirate ancestor.

'We've found it!' Rachel cried.

'You found it. Wait while I tie her up and you can have the honour of being the first to land.'

'It's perfect,' Rachel exclaimed. 'We're completely hidden from the sea and from land. I wonder, did Penhaligon and his men build this or was it a natural gap in the rock that he developed into this secret harbour? Either way, it's the perfect smugglers' harbour.'

Michael slipped the boat's painter through

the ring and made it fast. He held the boat steady against the side of the tiny landing stage and handed Rachel ashore.

She reached back to him, grasping his hand while still clutching her carrier bag. 'Welcome to Penhaligon's Rock,' she said. 'We've made it at last. And we might well be the first two visitors since Mrs Dudley and her sister were here.'

The steps were worn and rather dangerous in places, the flat stones that shaped them having loosened with the years, but it was still possible to reach the top of the rock with relative ease.

The top was a flat expanse, some fifty by thirty metres, sparsely covered with grass but thick with gull droppings.

'Did you really want to come for this?' Michael asked, surveying it. 'I wouldn't fancy sunbathing here however private it was. I hadn't expected that the birds would have taken it over quite so completely.'

'I'm here at last,' Rachel said. 'I can understand Stephen not wanting to encourage me to come here either swimming or by boat by myself, but if he knew about the harbour, why didn't he bring me in Sea Pie? I'm sure he knew about it. I believe he's a descendant of the cabin boy, Daniel Tresillian. The secret of the harbour would have been passed down and Daniel was the only one left who knew.'

'That's fanciful; there are hundreds of people called Tresillian in Cornwall,' Michael said. 'You've only got to look in the phone book. But if it means so much to you, I'm glad to have been the one who brought you here.' He spread out his waterproof anorak on the ground. 'Here, sit on this. You can enjoy the view for a while and then we might as well go back. There isn't anything of interest here.'

'There's something I want us to do first.' Rachel pulled the bottle and two plastic tumblers from her carrier bag. 'If you will open this for me, I'd like us to drink a toast to the old pirate Penhaligon. I feel as if we've put one over on him, finding the way to his secret place at last.'

'You don't like to be bested at anything, do you?' Michael opened the wine and poured two measures into the tumblers. 'That's what I think attracted me to you, right at the beginning. You were so full of fight after being mugged, and then, when you told me how you'd been cheated over your job — '

'I didn't fight back then. If I had, if I'd stayed on in London I'd have missed all this. And you.' She raised her tumbler. 'Here's to Captain Penhaligon! And to us.'

'To us!' Michael echoed. 'Gosh, it's breezy up here! How long do you want to stay?'

'I had planned a kind of picnic, if you could bear it. Mrs Dudley gave me the idea when she said she and Charlotte used to light campfires. I can't see what she could have used for firewood, but until we've solved that one, here's some hot soup to help you keep warm.'

'Your carrier bag is full of surprises!' Michael laughed. 'Had you planned all this from the beginning or was it a last minute idea?'

'I called in at Mrs Blamey's shop yesterday evening and bought the wine and some other things.' Rachel giggled. 'Guess what? She wasn't meant to be open but she had forgotten to lock the shop door and I interrupted her entertaining a man upstairs. She was furious with me because I went into the back part of the shop, which is private, to look for her, and saw them both.'

'Did you recognise who it was? My, there'll be some village scandal there.'

'I barely saw him, and not his face at all, but I'm sure it was the same man that we saw coming out of her shop late one night; same build, same kind of clothes.'

Michael raised his tumbler, draining it. 'To Ida Blamey! And to her secret admirer! He must be a brave man to be courting her, she's a bit of a battleaxe, isn't she?'

'To Ida Blamey!' Rachel solemnly raised her tumbler and drank a toast.

'What have you brought for the rest of this picnic, then?' Michael finished the last of the soup and looked at her hopefully.

Rachel looked at him ruefully and produced the sausages from the bag. 'I thought we could cook these over the fire,' she said. 'But it doesn't look as if a fire is going to be possible. There's simply nothing we could use. Mrs Dudley and her sister must have brought their own wood.'

'Let's walk once round the edge of the rock and then go back,' Michael suggested. 'If we're lucky, we might be in time for a late lunch in one of the pubs, if they haven't all closed their restaurants for the winter. Bill Williams at the Black Horse would find us something and, frankly, I'd prefer anything he could produce, to raw sausages, or even sausages cooked on a camp fire.'

'That's a most sensible idea.' Rachel stood up. 'It's cold up here, and there's nothing to see. But at least I've satisfied my curiosity about this place. Thank you for pandering to my obsession with Penhaligon. I promise I won't ask you to bring me here again.'

They set off, walking round the edge of the

flat summit, stepping carefully round the debris left by the gulls, while the birds screamed and wheeled overhead.

'The seagull population must have increased since Mrs Dudley and her sister sunbathed here,' Rachel remarked. 'I don't think I like the idea of it at all, now I've seen the top.'

'I don't think they like us invading their territory,' Michael said. 'They're beginning to remind me of that Hitchcock film and I shouldn't be at all surprised if they don't attack us, if we stay much longer.'

Rachel stopped by the seaward side, looking out to sea. There was a small boat, not all that far out, but about to pass out of sight, round the headland. She wondered if it could be the Sea Pie; there weren't many boats out at this time of year. What would Stephen say, if he knew she had come here, in spite of all his warnings? She had a sudden urge to wave, a childish gesture of defiance, but the boat was already slipping away behind the headland.

She followed Michael round towards the landward side, finding a gull's nest and a small ring of pebbles which she felt sure was where Mrs Dudley and Charlotte had made their campfire. There were no longer any twigs or sticks left, having been taken by the gulls long ago, to build their nests, or blown over the rock edge in the many gales since those days.

Rachel raised Michael's binoculars and studied the cliff top. 'I suppose anyone walking along the cliff path might see us from there,' she said. 'But I can't see anyone today. Nobody's dog walking, or walking off a heavy lunch. The whole stretch of the cliff path looks to be deserted.'

There was silence behind her.

'Michael?' she asked.

There was no answer. She turned round and the whole flat top of the rock was empty.

'Michael!' She called sharply, sudden fear clutching at her. It would be all too easy to slip over the edge anywhere here, and anyone doing so would strike jagged rocks before being swept out to sea.

'Michael!' she screamed again, and, crouching down, looked fearfully over the edge. Fifty feet below, waves crashed against the rocks. If Michael had fallen, he wouldn't have stood a chance.

'Michael!' There was despair in her voice, and then she heard, 'I'm over here. It's all right, Rachel. Did I scare you?'

She looked for a disembodied voice, and then saw him standing on the side which looked out obliquely towards the left headland. She could have sworn that he hadn't been there a moment before.

'Rachel, come over here,' he called. 'I've found something rather curious. There's another flight of steps cut in the rock.'

She crossed the summit to join him, her knees still feeling wobbly from the fright she'd had.

'Where were you? I turned round to speak to you and you'd gone. I was terrified you might have fallen over the edge.' She clung to him and he put a comforting arm round her. 'Sorry, I shouldn't have scared you like that, but I was only there for a moment. Look!' He pointed to where a set of steps led over the side of the rock.

'But why cut steps here? It's nowhere near the landing stage, and that rockface is sheer. You couldn't bring a boat in close here, even if you could reach the base of the rock.'

'They don't seem to go further than about fifteen feet down, and then there's a flat ledge. I only went down a little way, but you can see they've been well made and look well preserved.'

'Yet there seems no reason for them,' Rachel said, frowning as she looked down at them. 'Do you think Captain Penhaligon made an experimental flight before cutting the steps to the landing stage? These don't go anywhere.'

'He'd have had to cut those at the landing stage first, and from the bottom upwards, before he could reach the top of the rock,' Michael pointed out. 'But these are in even better condition than those. They must have been cut for some purpose. Perhaps he did his signalling from here.' He put one foot over the edge. 'I'm going to explore and see where they go. Perhaps there's another flight at the other end of the ledge.'

'I'm coming too.' Rachel had recovered from her fright at the thought of losing Michael, and these steps were definitely intriguing.

'Be careful. Keep close against the side of the rock.' Michael led the way along the ledge, which was about four feet wide and curved away to the left, round the wall of rock.

'There must be more steps, or something,' Rachel heard him saying, then his exclamation 'Good Lord! A cave! That's something I didn't expect!'

Rachel peered over Michael's shoulder. There was a rough coloumn of rock at the end of the ledge, and, behind it, a narrow fissure which had been widened and smoothed to an entrance just big enough for one person to edge through. The rock pillar sheltered it in such a way that it would have been impossible to see the opening until one was on the ledge itself, no more than two yards from it.

'A cave! How can there be a cave up here? I thought caves were made by the sea wearing away at the rock. The sea's never come up this far,' Rachel said.

Michael was running his hands round the edge of the entrance and just inside. 'This was probably once only a split in the rock, due to a fault, or a landslide, but it looks as if the whole thing has been enlarged inside by human hands. Look at the wall here; there are marks of a tool of some sort, a chisel or an axe.'

'Penhaligon's cave!' Rachel exclaimed. 'It would make sense, wouldn't it? Somewhere for him to shelter until it was time to set lights on the top and lure ships on to the rock on stormy nights; somewhere to hide all his stolen goods and contraband until it could be taken ashore later. Perhaps we'll find the odd doubloon lying forgotten in a corner somewhere.'

'You read too many boys' adventure stories,' Michael said drily. 'Don't imagine this place has lain undiscovered since Penhaligon's days. I bet some of the locals must know of it. I bet Mrs Dudley knew about it too, though she didn't mention it. She and her sister probably used it as a modest changing room before they sunbathed on the top. I wish I had a torch or something. It would be nice to know how far it goes back.'

'I've got matches! I was going to light a fire, remember?' Rachel hurried back, retracing her steps to the top of the rock, where the remains of their meagre picnic were still lying on Michael's waterproof.

She was back within minutes, but by then Michael was fully inside the cave, feeling his way round the walls and trying to gauge its extent.

Rachel struck a match and held it up. By its light they could see the cave was not large, but high enough for a man to stand upright, and went back some ten feet, the roof lowering at the back and filled with a pile of loose stones and rubble.

The match burnt low and Rachel dropped it before she burnt her fingers. Michael had stepped forward and his foot struck against something that gave off a sound unlike that of a rock. He bent down and felt around by his feet. 'I think there's something rather interesting here,' he said excitedly. 'Strike another match and let's have a look.'

It proved to be a lantern, with a sizeable piece of candle still in it. Rachel lit the wick and Michael held it up. 'It's an old style, but I wouldn't say it dated from Penhaligon's time. More like something they sold in that ship's chandlers shop near Mrs Blamey. Ten years old at most, I should think. It doesn't look very worn, and it's not even rusty. I'd say it had been used until fairly recently. Not even left here by Mrs Dudley.'

By the lantern's light they had a clearer view of the cave. Along one side were stacked a row of small sacks made of thick polythene, and beside them, some old wooden packing cases. Michael prodded one of the sacks with his foot. 'A smuggler's hoard, that's for sure,' he said. His face, in the lantern light, looked grim. 'But not from Penhaligon's time. I'm pretty sure those sacks contain drugs, heroin. That's the modern smuggler's trade and it goes on round here in spite of all the vigilance of the Customs officials. This coast is ideal for bringing in illicit cargoes in small boats and landing them secretly. Always has been. And this place! Penhaligon has handed some modern smuggler the perfect set up. It could have been going on for years with no one ever knowing about it.'

Someone knew. Rachel shivered. What if the smuggler came back while they were here? It would be easy enough to silence them by throwing them off the rock, and no one would know they hadn't fallen to their deaths by accident.

'Let's go,' she urged Michael.

'No, wait a moment. I'm curious about that pile of rocks at the back. Perhaps there's something more hidden underneath it. Or perhaps it blocks a passage — '

'You can't have a passage in this cave, we're on an island,' Rachel said impatiently. 'It can't go anywhere. If these sacks really do contain heroin, why don't we throw them into the sea now?'

'No, we mustn't do that. It's evidence. We need to be able to prove there's drug smuggling going on. Look, hold the lantern while I move some of these rocks.' He bent down and began to pull away some of the looser stones.

'Surely, they just piled up the left over stone when they enlarged the cave,' Rachel protested.

'They'd have thrown it over the cliff, not left it inside. This pile looks — well, odd, to me. There's something deliberate in the way the stones have been piled up.'

Michael moved two more stones and started a small avalanche that rolled down and across the floor of the cave. After they'd subsided, he bent down to examine the space they'd created. He moved aside a couple more rocks, then stopped, his body crouching very still beside the pile.

'Pass the lantern down to me, Rachel,' he said quietly.

Puzzled, she put it on the floor beside him.

'Oh, my God, it is!' She heard him whisper softly.

'What is it? What's the matter?' She dropped to her knees beside him and then she, too, saw what Michael had seen.

Jutting out from the pile of stones and rocks was the lower part of a human leg, encased in stout sea boots and faded blue denim.

10

'Is it — is it what I think it is?' Rachel whispered, staring at the leg protruding from beneath the pile of rocks.

'Yes, I'm afraid it is. You'd better not look.'

'Don't be silly! I'll help you move the rest of the rocks.' Rachel set the lantern to the top of one of the packing cases, where it could shed the maximum amount of light on the back of the cave. Together, she and Michael began lifting the remaining rocks away, piling them against the side wall. Soon, her hands were grazed and stinging, but she carried on, ignoring the pain, until they had uncovered the rest of the body.

The man lay on his back, his arms by his sides. He might almost have been asleep. He wore seaboots and denim overalls with a worn, navy sweater over the top. On his head he had a knitted cap. He was tall, as far as they could judge, and slightly built, though perhaps by now the body's flesh had disintegrated.

'A fisherman, by the look of him,' Michael said, holding the lantern up to study the body. 'And I should say he's been here some time. He's begun to decay, though there's still skin on his face and one hand. The salt air might have helped to preserve him, but my guess would be that he's been here maybe some years.'

'Did these rocks fall on him?'

'No, I don't think so. He'd have been crushed, otherwise, and he'd have curled his body to protect himself. He's lying flat, quite peacefully. I'm almost certain he must have been put here after he'd died. Covered with stones as a kind of tomb.'

'I want to see his face!' Rachel said suddenly, taking the lantern. She held it up so that the light shone down on the man's head. His cheeks were sunken, but that could well be the flesh already rotting away. There was still some skin, drawn tightly like parchment over the bones and there were tufts of sparse, red hair round his chin and showing under his cap.

'It couldn't be anyone you know,' Michael said gently. 'He must have lain here since long before you came to Cornwall.'

'He has red hair,' Rachel said wonderingly. 'I wonder, would he have had deep blue eyes as well? Could he possibly be Stephen's father, do you think? He was supposed to have been lost at sea with Ida Blamey's husband, six years ago, but their

274

bodies were never recovered.'

'Don't jump to conclusions. He could be anyone,' Michael warned. 'He could have been put here six years ago, I suppose, but the only certain fact is that he didn't end up dying of starvation, marooned on Penhaligon's Rock. Someone hid him here, or made an attempt at burial.'

'Do you think he was murdered?'

'I've never studied forensics and the body has been dead too long for any obvious marks of violence. But the evidence does seem to point that way. I think we'd better think of leaving this rock before our smuggler comes back to collect his drug haul and finds us. I wouldn't give much for our chances of ever getting back to the mainland again if he came now.'

'But what are we going to do about him?' Rachel nodded towards the body of the sailor. In the dim light from the lantern he looked almost as if he were sleeping. Only closer scrutiny showed how far decomposition had progressed.

'We'll leave him as he is. I don't fancy covering him up with the rocks again,' Michael said. 'We'll get back to the boatyard as quickly as possible and go to the police.'

Rachel stared a long time at the man's face, before blowing out the lantern and following

Michael out to the ledge.

'He looks so much like — You did say he could have been there about five or six years, didn't you?'

'Really, it's impossible to tell, just by looking at the condition of the body. But, yes, I'd say more likely four or five years than a matter of months. He'll probably crumble to a skeleton as soon as he's moved.'

'I have this feeling that he must be either Stephen's father or Ida Blamey's husband,' Rachel said, as they crossed the top of the rock towards the landing stage steps. 'He looks the right age, and he's a fisherman. Their bodies were never washed up, which Uncle George told me was very unusual, round these coasts.'

'A drowned man would hardly land up in a cave, fifty feet above sea level,' Michael pointed out.

'No, but what if they weren't drowned? What if they discovered the smuggling activities and were murdered because of it?'

'Are you suggesting there might be a second body under that rubble?' Michael asked. 'If so, it can stay there. I'm certainly not going back to look.'

They reached the landing stage and Rachel stepped into the boat. Michael reached out a hand to untie it, then paused. 'Rachel, you haven't been down here and touched this rope, have you?' he asked.

'Touched the rope? What do you mean? How could I have come down here? I was with you all the time.'

'I didn't tie it up like this.' Michael was staring at the rope, twisted in the rusty ring.

'But you did. I saw you.'

'I didn't fasten it like this. I pushed the rope through the ring several times and tied it. This,' he gestured to the ring 'looks like a proper boatman's knot. How the fishermen tie up their boats in harbour. I didn't do it like this.'

'You must have done. Maybe you copied the way they do it without realising. Or perhaps the boat has drifted round and twisted the knot on the ring, made it look different. How could it have retied itself? I never did it. I wouldn't know how to do a proper boatman's knot anyway.'

Michael shrugged and pulled the rope free from the ring. 'Suppose I must be imagining things. But I was so sure — '

'No one could have been here. We'd have seen them, or they'd have come to the cave. There's nowhere else on the rock anyone could be, without us seeing them.' Rachel protested. 'And if there was anyone, where was their boat? We'd have seen that, surely?'

'Of course we would. I'm imagining things.' Michael climbed into the boat and took an oar to steer them out through the narrow gap. He was frowning, though, and looked thoughtful.

Dusk was beginning to fall as they chugged round the headland, and lights from houses on the top of the cliff twinkling out over the sea.

'Mike,' Rachel said tentatively. 'If that body does have something to do with Mrs Blamey, she ought to be warned about it before we tell the police. She's not a young woman. It could be an awful shock for her if the first she hears about it is a policeman on her doorstep.'

And if it was Walter's body, wouldn't she feel even more shock, if the police arrived while her mysterious gentleman caller was with her?

Mike nodded absently, concentrating on steering the boat in the growing darkness. He heard what Rachel was saying, but was too busy steering the boat and hoping he'd find the mouth of the river before it became completely dark, to pay attention or enter into a discussion about the possible identity of the body they'd found.

'Mike, could you put me off in the harbour at St Morwenna's Bay?' Rachel asked after a pause. 'I think I ought to see Ida and warn

278

her before anyone else does. They might want her to identify the body. Or the police might come when she had customers in the shop. That would be terribly embarrassing for her.'

'But we don't know the body is anything to do with her,' Michael protested. 'And your car is at the boatyard.'

'I can collect it later, or tomorrow. Look, it was definitely a fisherman, and you thought he'd been dead about the right length of time. This is a small community. How many people here do you think have been lost at sea, drowned without trace? The bodies of drowned people are almost always washed up eventually, even if it's miles down the coast. But even if it turns out not to be Walter, it'll be a shock for her to hear a body has been found, and in such a place. If he was a local man, it's almost certain she'd have known him.'

'All right. I understand your concern. But I'm worried about getting this boat back up the river before it gets completely dark,' Michael said.

'You needn't come as well. I know she's a sharp-tongued woman and a bit grumpy, but I have a — a kind of affection for her. I really do think she should be told about the body before the police see her.'

Michael nodded and altered course. It

wouldn't be far out of their way, and there seemed no point now in hiding where they'd been. The whole village would be bound to be buzzing with the news before long.

He aimed for the lights which showed the gap between the ends of the enclosing harbour wall, manoeuvred the little boat easily into the harbour and, within seconds, was nosing against the steps below the street. Rachel leapt ashore, and, mindful of the time and darkness coming on, he drew away before she had even reached the top.

The shop was in darkness, but on a Sunday evening that was only to be expected. The upstairs room in the front was also unlit and for a moment Rachel feared Ida Blamey might be out. Then she saw a glimmer of light shining out from the rear of the shop, and guessed that might be a kitchen. Ida might be making herself some tea, and it would be easy to knock on the back door and ask to speak to her. Rachel only hoped her mysterious friend wouldn't be there too, though if he was, he might prove helpful in comforting her.

Rachel entered the passageway that led to the back of the shops. She had hardly gone three paces when a voice called to her 'Rachel? Where are you going?'

She was momentarily startled, but the

familiar voice reassured her.

'Stephen!' she said. 'I was going to see Mrs Blamey.'

'Shop's shut. She never opens on a Sunday.'

'I didn't want to buy anything, but I have to speak to her. I have to tell her something urgently.'

'She won't thank you for disturbing her on a Sunday evening. What is it you want to tell her?'

Rachel ignored the question. 'Has she got her friend with her?' she asked.

'Friend? What do you mean, her friend? Who do you think is with her?' Stephen's voice was sharp. Protective of Ida's reputation, Rachel thought, with a smile.

'Her man friend. The one who looks like a fisherman. I've seen him there a couple of times in the evening. I wouldn't mention it — '

'How do you know about that?' Stephen gripped her arm and looked angry.

'Heavens, there's nothing wrong about her having a man friend in to supper! I happened to see him when I went to the shop yesterday and couldn't find her to pay her.' Rachel was surprised at Stephen's fierceness. 'I didn't say anything about it to anyone at the farm. I don't gossip, but for heaven's sake, what's it matter?'

'You can't go disturbing Ida now, anyway,' Stephen said. He kept hold of her arm and began to steer her down the street, past the front of the shop.

'But I have something very important I must tell her!' Rachel tried to disentangle her arm but Stephen kept hold of it.

'What is it you have to tell her? You can tell me. Ida and I are — well, she's been a second mother to me. Tell me and I'll judge if it's that important. If it is, I'll tell her myself.'

It was true that Stephen was a great deal closer to Mrs Blamey than she could ever be. Perhaps the news would be better coming from him, especially since it might very well concern him even more. Rachel made up her mind.

'Stephen, we went out in a boat today, Michael and I.' She began. 'We went to Penhaligon's Rock.'

'What!' The pressure on her arm increased. 'What on earth possessed you to attempt such a thing? Haven't I told you that the currents round the rock are terribly dangerous? It's a wonder you weren't dashed against them and drowned. You know nothing about boats, do you? And I don't suppose Conway does, either. Don't ever try to do anything like that again. I've warned you of the dangers often enough.'

'That's not quite true, though, is it?' she said. 'The currents aren't as strong as all that, and there's a way to get on to the rock, if you know it. I'm sure you do, but you wouldn't tell me. I had to discover it for myself.'

'Are you telling me that you actually got yourself on to the rock?' Stephen was facing her, his face a mixture of anger and rage. She felt decidedly uneasy. Stephen's reaction seemed unnecessarily extreme.

'Yes, we did,' she said defiantly. 'We found the little harbour with the landing stage and the steps leading up to the top.'

'And I suppose you were disappointed then. There's nothing but a whole flock of gulls and the mess they leave. It's nothing but a bare rock.'

'But we found a cave.'

There was a stillness about Stephen that she found even more frightening than his anger.

'What has all this to do with Ida Blamey?' he asked.

'In the cave we found — ' It struck her that the body could as well be that of Stephen's father as Ida Blamey's husband. It might come as much of a shock to him as to her.

'Stephen,' she said, as gently as she could. 'We found a body.'

'A body?' His voice was quiet, deadly cold.

'There was a body in the cave, buried under some rocks. We — I thought it could have been Mrs Blamey's husband, or — ' she hesitated, then said in a whisper, 'your father. There was still some red hair under his cap, and a bit of red beard.'

Stephen gave a harsh laugh. 'Red hair! So you thought it must be my father! My father and Walter Blamey were drowned at sea, six years ago. And neither of them had red hair. This body you found has nothing to do with them or me. Perhaps old pirate Penhaligon left one of his enemies to starve to death there, and you found the skeleton.'

'No, it couldn't have been. The body wasn't anything like as old — ' She stopped. She didn't want to tell Stephen any more details. It occurred to her that he hadn't seemed at all surprised to hear about the body.

'You said you and Conway went out there? Where is he now?' Stephen demanded.

'Michael had to take the boat back to the boatyard, up river.' She was going to add 'before he goes to the police' but stopped herself. It was suddenly all too blindingly clear. Stephen hadn't wanted her to go out to the rock, not because of any dangerous tides or razor sharp rocks; he wanted her to keep well away because he knew she would find the cave if she landed on the rock, and find what was in the cave. Not perhaps the body, but the sacks piled up waiting for someone to collect them, sacks of heroin. And he knew about the sacks because either he had put them there, or would shortly be collecting them and bringing them secretly to shore.

'I'll have to go home to the farm now,' she said. It was imperative she left Stephen as soon as she could. No point in trying to see Ida Blamey now.

'I'll see you back there safely,' he said easily. 'I need to collect some eggs for the shop, ready for tomorrow when Ida opens.'

'It's all right, really. I know my way.' She was frightened now. Stephen must know what she knew.

'Don't be silly — it's dark up the hill once you leave the village street.' He took her arm, steering her away from the harbour lights. She didn't want to make too much fuss arguing; she must act naturally towards him, not let him realise she had guessed how much he was involved. At least, she thought thankfully, he hadn't offered to drive her to High Topp. If they walked back together it wouldn't be so bad, but she wished he hadn't taken her arm in quite such a firm grip.

He hustled her along, almost dragging her up the hill. 'Oh, please, do slow down!' she gasped, as the gradient began to steepen.

'I forgot you city types aren't used to walking.' He slowed fractionally but still kept a grip on her arm.

'I don't much care for being called a city type.' Rachel snapped, with the little amount of breath she had left. 'Even if I did live in London, that doesn't mean I never went for walks. I don't like racing up hills, that's all. It isn't necessary.'

He slowed as the hill became steeper, and Rachel decided, if she was forced to have his company all the way back to the farm, the best thing to do was to make conversation, as normally as possible, to try to let him think that, perhaps, after all, she hadn't realised exactly what was in the cave, or that he might have any connection with it

'Were you out in Sea Pie today?' she asked.

'No, I've been away inland with the van. No customers wanting to hire the boat at this time of year, and I only fish in the week.'

'Only, I thought I saw the Sea Pie, out at sea, rounding the headland beyond the bay.' Was it her imagination or did he stiffen, the fingers on her arm tightening for a moment? It had been the Sea Pie, she was sure of it now, so why was he lying about not being out in it?

Abruptly, Stephen stopped by the hedge,

near the bend in the road. 'We can reach the farm by the short cut here. Save continuing walking up the hill.'

Rachel shook her head. 'I'm wary of short cuts, ever since I lost myself in the sea mist when I first came. It was round here that I was wandering about in the fields, wasn't it?'

'There's no sea mist now. And you've got me with you. You won't get lost. I know these fields like the inside of my own cottage. The stile's right by here. Over you go.'

When she still hesitated, he said impatiently, 'It's much further by road. Look, the farm is just the other side of a couple of fields. You'll be there in a quarter of an hour. By road it will be three times as long.'

That was true, though most times she had driven the road way so it hadn't seemed so far. She saw the outline of the stile, the gap in the hedge and the bar across the space. It was almost completely dark here, with the trees overhanging the road. Probably it would seem not quite so dark once they were in the open field, and Stephen certainly knew the way. She was feeling tired, after the stresses of the day, and hungry, too. It would be a relief not to have to continue for another half mile up the steep hill.

He gave her a little push forward and she

climbed over the stile. Stephen vaulted it easily close behind her, and took her arm again. This time she could hardly object, for the ground was uneven and tussocky, and it was, after all, darker in the field than she had expected.

Stephen seemed to know exactly which direction to take, and continued hurrying her along at speed. She gave up trying to keep up a conversation, having barely enough breath as it was. She let him guide her in what appeared to be a direct line across the field, certain that if she was by herself, she would have completely lost her bearings by now. There was only the dim, blacker outline of trees and hedges on the far side that stood out as any kind of landmark. She noticed one tree in particular, a deformed, strange shape leaning at an angle. She thought she recognised it as the dead tree where she'd pushed through the hedge that earlier time. Stephen seemed to be making for a gap in the hedge a little further along from it.

She stopped suddenly. 'Surely, this isn't right? I remember coming this way when I was lost, then I met you and you told me I was miles from High Topp farm.'

'No, you're confused. This is the right way. Trust me. I told you, I know every inch of these fields. I was born in the village, remember?' He drew her through the gap in the hedge and, less willingly now, she followed him.

'Stephen.' In an effort to slow his pace, she began to chat again. 'I've been wanting to say this for some time. You must have realised — Jennifer is very fond of you. You don't treat her particularly well, do you?'

'Jennifer? How should I treat her?' He sounded amused.

'You and she are so much alike, both so very — Cornish. You'd make a good couple.'

Stephen gave a short laugh. 'We'd make a good couple, you think? What's that supposed to mean?'

'I know she cares for you very much. I don't think she's truly serious about Alan, though she goes out with him. But that's only because she doesn't see much of you. I know it's none of my business — '

'Too right it isn't. I think you've done enough meddling without bringing Jennifer into it,' Stephen said harshly. 'She lives her own life and I live mine. That's how we both like it. What has she been saying about me, then?'

'Nothing. Nothing at all. It was just that I could tell, from the way she acts when you come to the farm — '

'Mind your own business,' Stephen said roughly.

'I'm sorry. I didn't mean to interfere.' Rachel was seeing a side to Stephen she hadn't known before, rough, rude, almost on the edge of violent, and she didn't like it at all. She looked round her and saw the sharp angles of a building looming up in front of her. She knew at once what it was.

'Stephen, we *have* come the wrong way! This is the disused mine where I met you that other time. It's miles away from the farm; we can't reach High Topp over the fields from here.'

'No, we haven't come the wrong way,' Stephen said, pausing by the padlocked gate. 'I need to collect something from here. I use this place as a store, see?' He produced a key from his pocket and unfastened the padlock.

'I wish you'd said earlier! This isn't a short cut at all, coming this way. It would have been perfectly safe and much quicker if I'd stayed on the road,' Rachel said crossly.

'You've never seen a Cornish tin mine before, have you?' Stephen asked, unperturbed. 'Care to come in and take a look now?'

'What, in the dark?' She wondered what on earth she could do, now. Last time, Stephen had taken her across the field to the road, and driven her to the farm. If she left him here, she doubted if she would find her way back alone, yet she certainly didn't want to wait for him while he collected whatever it was from the mine, and then have a long way to walk back, whichever direction he decided to take.

'Come on, take a look.' He grabbed her hand and pulled her inside the gate.

'Not in the dark! Uncle George said it was dangerous, and, besides, there's a notice warning people to keep out.'

'You didn't take any notice of warnings to keep out of Penhaligon's Rock!' he snarled. He started to drag her forcibly across the rough ground from the gate towards the ruined wheelhouse, stark against the sky.

'Stephen, let me go!' She fought him, but he was far too strong for her. In one easy movement he picked her up and slung her across his shoulder, as easily as if she had been a sack of grain.

'I'm sorry, Rachel, but I can't let you go back to the farm. You shouldn't have been so curious about the rock. If you hadn't meddled in things which didn't concern you you'd have been safe. But now, you know too much.'

She struggled desperately as she realised — too late — that she was in great danger. Stephen was a smuggler, a modern day

291

Penhaligon, but with a cache of contraband far more dangerous than brandy and tobacco. He'd stop at nothing now to ensure her silence. That body in the cave could well have been someone like herself or Mike who had discovered the cave and its contents by chance. A Customs officer, perhaps, or maybe someone who, like her, didn't realise what he'd stumbled upon until it was too late. Stephen might well have murdered him!

He held her virtually upside down, her wrists gripped easily in one hand, while he unlocked the heavy steel door that gave access to the wheelhouse. Once inside, he tipped her head over heels on to the concrete floor.

The breath was knocked from her body, but she strove to keep her mind clear and avoid panicking. One thought gave her hope. Michael would be going to the police any minute now, and there was no way Stephen would be able to stop him. Her job now would be to reassure him, try to make him think she didn't know as much as he feared, or, at least, that she hadn't understood the implications of anything she might have seen on Penhaligon's Rock.

When she had her breath back, she said 'Stephen, why are you doing this? I only went on the rock. You're probably right — the skeleton was old — might even have been Penhaligon himself. Not worth mentioning it to anyone, is it? After all, no one else is ever going out there, are they? Everyone believes there's no way on to it and the rocks all round are too dangerous — '

'How did you know about the landing stage?'

'I met someone. She told us — me — she used to row out there years and years ago, when she was young.'

'Who?'

It occurred to her that if she mentioned Mrs Dudley by name, the old lady could be in danger. 'It was someone who was selling up. She's left the area now,' she said hastily. 'I won't go on to the rock again, I can assure you. There's nothing to see and it's all covered in gull's droppings. I know now I wouldn't want to sunbathe on the top — '

She was babbling, trying to reassure him, but it wasn't working. Stephen stood over her, menacing.

'Shut up,' he said.

She was silent, wondering what he was intending to do with her.

'I'm sorry to have to do this to you, Rachel,' he said, in an almost friendly, conversational tone, 'but you shouldn't have been so damned nosey. I did warn you. I liked you, Rachel. Things could have been different if you hadn't got yourself involved with that London chap, Conway. That was a foolish mistake. You'd have done much better to have stuck with me.' He shrugged and turned away. 'It's all too late now. I'm sorry but here's where you are going to have to stay. I can't allow you to see anyone.'

'No!' she cried out. 'Don't leave me in here, Stephen! At least, leave me some light.'

'Too risky. Goodbye, Rachel. You should have stayed in London.' She heard him step towards the door and scrambled up to run after him, but all she heard was the crash of the steel door shutting after him, and the sound of the key grating in the lock.

'Stephen!'

Her voice echoed round the walls but she was sure he couldn't hear her. Neither would anyone else be able to hear her; the mine, she knew, was in the middle of fields and far away from any other buildings. With the warning of danger on the padlocked gate, it was unlikely that anyone would come this way. The mine was on High Topp land but the only creatures likely to come anywhere near, would be George Prescott's cows.

She sat on the hard, concrete floor for a few moments to calm her pounding heart. There must, surely, be another way out of here, though the existence of the heavy steel door made it seem unlikely. She wished now she had picked up the carrier bag containing the remains of their picnic, instead of leaving it in the boat for Michael to drop in the rubbish bin at the boatyard. There was still a packet of biscuits they hadn't eaten, and, more importantly, the matches. She could at least have seen what kind of a place this was.

At last, she stood up, found the steel door and ran her hands over it. As she had feared, it was quite smooth, not even so much as a door handle on this side. From the door she began feeling her way round the walls, seeking for something, another door, even a blocked up window; something that might conceivably give her a chance of escape. The walls were rough brickwork and there was nothing, no break of any kind, in them, no door or window that she could find.

The building appeared to be circular, and when she arrived back at what she recognised as the steel door again, she moved away from the walls, venturing into the centre. On one side, there seemed to be a huge iron contraption, stretching up, way over her head. She ran her hands over it, feeling metal bars and something with cogs which shifted an ich or so at her touch, but no more. Loose flakes fell from it on to her face, and she guessed that, whatever it was, it was rusty with age. Alongside it was a rail at waist height. Rachel slid her hands along the top of it, following it. Perhaps there were steps near here, leading down to a lower floor, maybe with an exit Stephen had forgotten. The rail curved, then stopped. She put out a tentative foot, feeling in front of her. Yes, this felt as if it was the top of a flight of steps; her foot touched the edge of the floor. Surprising, though, that the rail did not continue downwards beside the steps. She took another step forward and there was nothing in front of her. She pitched forward into something that seemed like a large well, falling down and down. It flashed through her mind that this must be the mine shaft, and likely to be hundreds of feet deep. She wasn't going to survive a fall of that distance, and, in any case, no one was ever going to find her. Her body would lie at the bottom and gradually decay like the corpse in Penhaligon's cave.

Rachel was not aware of reaching the bottom. The world had blacked out completely before she stopped falling.

11

It was completely dark by the time Michael brought the boat up the river, back to the boatyard. The yard itself was in darkness and he nearly missed it, until he was hailed from the shore.

'Mr Conway? That you bringing my boat back at last?' The boatyard owner, not best pleased at being kept waiting longer than he had bargained for, grabbed the side of the boat as soon as Michael came in near enough, and made fast with a deft flick of his wrist.

'You been out a long time,' the man grumbled. 'Wasn't reckoning on you keeping it out after dark. That's dangerous, for them as doesn't know the water.' He peered into the boat. 'Where's the young lady? You haven't gone and drowned her, have you?'

'No, she wanted to disembark at the harbour in St Morwenna's bay. It was a little out of our way, and I had some trouble finding the mouth of the river. There are no house lights at that part of the coast.'

'I see.' Clearly, the man imagined they'd had a quarrel and Rachel had stormed off, demanding to be put ashore as soon as possible.

'She's left her car in the car park,' the man continued, his voice doubtful with suspicion.

'She'll come and collect it tomorrow morning,' Michael said, clambering wearily on to the boatyard jetty. 'It'll be all right to leave it here overnight, won't it? Or perhaps I can bring her back later this evening to collect it. She had some urgent business in the village.'

The boatman gave him a look which said clearly he didn't believe a word of it, but he had his boat back safe and unharmed and that was all he was concerned about. Let these idiot townies who wanted to go out on a cold, blustery day and stay out in the dark, sort out their own problems. He hoped the young lady was all right, but they hadn't looked like a couple who would do one another harm.

Michael sat in the driver's seat and wondered if he should drive back to St Morwenna's bay and collect Rachel to pick up her car. She must have seen Mrs Blamey by now and would probably be back at High Topp farm. There didn't seem much point in driving back there; possibly that uncle of hers would give her a lift later to collect her car. The main thing for him to do would be to report their finding of the body at the first police station he came to, on the way back to Truro.

Ten minutes later he passed through the first village large enough to have its own police station. There was the familiar blue sign, but outside a bungalow which was clearly the policeman's own home. He pulled up and went up to the front door. The place was in darkness, but there was an outside security light, illuminating a framed notice beside the door. Michael learnt from this that at weekends, anyone requiring the service of the police should call the number given, presumably the nearest police station on duty.

It was getting late, he was cold and very hungry, having not eaten since breakfast, apart from Rachel's soup. He was tempted to leave reporting the body until the next day. After all, there was no real urgency and the police could do nothing until daylight. He got back into his car and drove on towards Truro.

Driving along the winding, country lanes, he found he was missing Rachel. He wanted to talk to her, mull over the events of the day. He'd come to Cornwall because he had had enough of dealing with violence and death and he'd hoped he'd seen his last dead body when he left the ambulance service. This one today wasn't quite the same thing; not a freshly dead, mangled body by the roadside, but it had been a body and it surprised him how much the sight of it had disturbed him. All right when he had to act calmly because Rachel was there, but now, thinking it over by himself, he realised that they had come upon something more sinister than he had at first thought. Those sacks — they had to be drugs and the amount was large. Someone had been killed — almost certainly the man had died by violence of some sort, and by the same people who were involved with bringing in the drugs haul.

He shuddered. He and Rachel had been in danger while they'd been on the rock. Suppose the smuggler had come back and found them? He remembered again the way their boat had been fastened to the iron ring in the rock. It hadn't been tied as he had left it. Someone had come while they were in the cave, he was sure of it.

He was half a mile from the turning on to the main road, barely a mile from home, when, from nowhere, it seemed, a small van came racing past on the otherwise deserted road, passing him so closely that it dipped the side of the bonnet, knocking him sideways. He fought to control the car, but it was a light model and spun round to the left with some force. He saw the hedge at the side of the road coming towards him, wrenched at the steering wheel and felt the car lurch into the ditch. He was thrown forward, his safety belt preventing him from flying through the windscreen, but not from striking his head hard against the steering wheel.

Dazed, he sat in his seat, not believing what had happened. This was a narrow lane, impossible to pass except at designated passing places. No one in their right minds would try to push past, however much of a hurry they were in.

After a minute, it registered that he must get out of the car. He scrambled out, went round to the front and looked at the damage. The front wheels were far into the ditch, no possibility of getting them out without a tractor or a crane of some sort. Fortunately, he wasn't blocking the road, but there was nothing for it but to walk the rest of the way home and telephone to a garage. He took the warning triangle from the boot, propped it in the road some yards back, then began walking towards the main road and Truro.

He had time to think while he walked. That van — he'd seen a flash of white as it passed, but no lettering. And the way it had been driven — no one but a maniac, or someone who had deliberately intended to force him off the road, would have acted like that. Was that what it had been, deliberate? He found it hard to accept. There was no reason, unless it had some connection with the contents of the cave on Penhaligon's Rock, if someone knew they had been there and wanted to frighten them off, or silence them.

Them? Did the driver know about Rachel? Had he assumed they were both in the car? If not, then Rachel was in danger, too.

He made the rest of the journey at as brisk a pace as he could. He wanted to be in the safety of his home, with a telephone to hand,

There was a note left for him on the mat; a hastily hand written message but bearing the logo of a local estate agent:

'We have shown round a prospective buyer in your absence this morning, Sunday. He has made an offer which we consider well worth your consideration, since it is above the asking price. Please contact our office first thing on Monday to confirm and agree further instructions.'

It was the first cheerful news of the day. He felt a lightening of his spirits. Mrs Dudley's cottage would be theirs, after all. Rachel would be delighted. First, he must telephone the garage and get them to collect his car, then he would ring Rachel, make sure she was all right, and tell her the news. Thoughts of contacting the police station faded from his mind.

The bell rang for some time before a rather flustered Freda Prescott answered.

'Oh, Michael, it's you! Sorry it took so long to come, but we've a sick heifer in the barn and I was out there with George and the vet. Rachel? I thought she was still with you, but she may well have come in while we were busy outside. I didn't hear the car, though.'

'She didn't have the car. She left it at the boatyard. She would have walked up from the harbour at St Morwenna's bay.'

'Then I'd not have heard her. She must have gone straight upstairs. I'll call her, shall I?'

'Not if she's gone to bed. I have some good news for her but it'll keep until tomorrow. Really, I only wanted to check if she was back yet, but we've had an eventful day so I'm not surprised if she went to bed as soon as she came in.' He was surprised, though. It seemed early for someone like Rachel, but then, if the rest of the household were out in the barn, concerned about a sick animal, there wouldn't be much else to do for the remainder of the evening.

'We're early bedders here,' Freda said, a little apologetically. 'We'd have been practically settled for the night ourselves by now ourselves if it hadn't been for the heifer. Goodnight to you, Michael. I'll tell Rachel in the morning that you rang.'

'Tell her I'll be late in at the shop,' he said, before Freda rang off. 'I have to see the estate agent and — some other people first.' Better not to mention the police; Rachel might not want to tell Freda and George where they'd been and what they'd found, just yet.

It was half past nine; too late to do more than find himself something to eat and then go up to bed himself. Michael lay awake for a long time, wondering what he should tell the police; how to explain why they had gone, against all local advice, to Penhaligon's Rock and whether to mention the incident with the van. It might have no connection with the drugs haul or the body in the cave, and yet, it seemed too much of a coincidence.

Next morning he went first to the estate agent, who had more good news. A man with a wife and young family, coming to work in the town, urgently needed somewhere for them to live. 'He's willing to pay a premium if he can move in as soon as possible. He starts work here in a week and wants to have his family settled by then.'

'He can move in tomorrow if he can organise the paperwork by then,' Michael said recklessly. 'I have a house I'm intending to buy, but at worst I could sleep over my shop until I can move in there.'

'I'm sure we can persuade him to make all speed with the contract,' the estate agent said smoothly. The busy time for house sales was largely over now, he had the leisure to give this sale his full attention. Both clients wanted a speedy settlement; he would see they had one.

By the time Michael left the estate agent's office, he had not only sold his own home, but agreed the purchase of Mrs Dudley's, telephoning her from there. Rachel would be delighted; Mrs Dudley had said they could move in as soon as they wished; with hardly any furniture to move to her new flat, she could move out as soon as the formalities were settled.

On the pavement outside, Michael hesitated. He ought to go now to the police station, in fact, he thought he should have gone there first of all but he hadn't wanted to risk being kept waiting when he needed to clinch the deal with his estate agent. Now, he still hesitated. He wanted to tell Rachel the news about Mrs Dudley's cottage before anything else. The police would probably keep him, wanting to take a statement and it was only right to see to his business first. He turned in the direction of the shop.

Rachel had her own set of keys. Even if she had had to come in by bus, she ought to have the place open by now, very likely she'd have the kettle on for coffee.

He was surprised to find the shopdoor locked and the shutters still down. 'Sleepy head!' he muttered, letting himself in and preparing the place for customers. Rachel must have gone to collect her car from the boatyard first, but how would she have got there? Silly girl, he thought. He would have driven her there after work, that would be the sensible solution.

By lunchtime Rachel had still not put in an appearance and he didn't want to shut the place while he went to the police station. He rang the number of High Topp farm, but when no one had answered after the first half dozen rings, he replaced the receiver. Rachel must be on her way, and the Prescotts out in the barn, ministering to their sick cow. He couldn't delay the visit to the police any longer, so he left a note for her in the office, locked up the shop and walked back into town.

The interview with the police took, as he had suspected, far more time than he wanted to spare. After explaining his business, Michael was passed on to another police officer and had to repeat his story. It was only when he mentioned the body that the officer began to take more than a routine interest.

'A body, you say? Do you mean a human body?'

'Yes.' What did the man think he'd meant?

'You're sure of that? It wasn't just a bundle of clothes, or some rubbish? It was at the back of the cave, you said? In the dark?'

Michael sighed. 'I've worked for the ambulance service. I know a dead body when I see one,' he said patiently.

They took rather more notice after that, taking him into an interview room and having a sergeant take notes while the police officer questioned him, but the questions seemed endless. He answered them as well as he could. 'The body was badly decomposed but there was enough of the face left to establish it was that of a bearded man, probably forty to fifty years old, wearing a navy jersey, denim dungarees and seamen's boots. I've no forensic training, but from the state of the body I'd say it had been there some years.'

'You had a good look at the body, then? Touch anything?'

'I've been trained not to. But I was also trained to be observant. I had a good look because I was curious. There have been local stories of fishermen lost at sea and their bodies never recovered. I wondered if this

307

chap could have been one of them.' Too late, he realised he didn't want to start a hare by suggesting the body could be that of Stephen's father or Walter Blamey. That had been Rachel's idea, jumping to conclusions with absolutely no evidence to support it.

'Hmmph! Sailor lost at sea swept on to the top of Penhaligon's Rock?' The policeman sounded scornful. 'I know that place. Used to live in a village five miles inland from that bay. Always understood the rock was inaccessible. Boatmen give it a wide berth; they say the rocks round it are dangerous and there's a strong current. Locals say it's strictly for the birds and you'd need a helicopter if you wanted to land on it. So how did you manage? And why did you go out to it? Hardly the time of year for a picnic, I'd have thought.'

Michael explained how Rachel had been fascinated by the rock, ever since her arrival in Cornwall, and had wanted to reach the top just because it had seemed so inaccessible. This idea appeared incomprehensible to the sergeant, who clearly expected everyone to have a good, rational reason for everything they did, or the action was highly suspect.

'Likes living dangerously, this Miss Hayward?' he asked. 'Where is she now? Not here with you to add her bit to the story?'

Someone else who thinks I might have drowned her, Michael thought. Aloud, he said 'Miss Hayward is at her home, High Topp farm, near St Morwenna's bay. Or, at least, I suppose by now she'll be at my shop, Conway Antiques, looking after customers who I should be seeing. And wondering where I am.'

'Just a few more questions, Mr Conway,' the police officer said apologetically, recognising Michael's growing exasperation. 'How did you manage to reach the top of Penhaligon's Rock?'

He hadn't wanted to go into the details about Mrs Dudley's chance remark, but there was no help for it. As he told them, he sensed both the policemen's interest quicken.

'You say there's a gap in the rocks, leading to a natural harbour with a jetty and steps leading to the top? Well, I never! I've lived all my life in that part of the county and I've never heard anything like that! And this elderly lady, this — Mrs Dudley — told you she and her sister rowed out there frequently when she was young? When would that have been? Fifty, sixty years ago?' The sergeant was fascinated. 'Can you see this cave from the sea?' he asked.

'Shouldn't think so. There's a kind of rock pillar in front of the entrance. All you'd see

309

from a distance, if you could see anything at all, would be a fault in the rock, just a crevice.'

'And these sacks you saw there? How big? What did they look as if they had in them? Did you open any of them? Move them or touch them at all?'

Now the policemen were exchanging glances and Michael knew they were at last going to take him seriously.

'We'll be on to the coastguards about this,' the police officer said. 'Thank you for your information and co-operation, Mr Conway. Where can we contact you if we need to speak to you again soon?'

Michael gave them his home and shop telephone numbers, and was dismissed. He was relieved to be out of the interview room at last, and to hear the beginning of the officer's urgent call to the coastguard service. He wanted to hurry back to the shop and tell Rachel all about it, and, even more important as far as she'd be concerned, give her the news about Mrs Dudley's cottage.

The shop was exactly as he'd left it, closed and his note to Rachel lying where he'd put it on the desk in the back. Feeling uneasy now, he picked up the telephone and rang High Topp farm.

'Mrs Prescott? How's the sick heifer? And

how's my girlfriend? Is Rachel feeling all right?' he asked.

'Heifer's better, thank you, Michael. But what do you mean about Rachel? She's at the shop with you, isn't she?'

'Hasn't shown up here yet. I suppose she's late because she'd have had to come in by bus. What time did she leave?'

'There aren't any early buses from here after September,' Freda said. 'Only on market days. But Rachel wasn't here at breakfast. I thought she'd left early. The thing is, we've been out in the barn most of the time; I haven't paid attention to anything else but the poor beast, since yesterday.'

'Perhaps she's still having a lie in. We had a rather stressful day, yesterday.' And perhaps Rachel had had a hard time of it with Ida Blamey, he thought. 'I'll come round to the farm now,' he said. 'Not much point in keeping the shop open any longer. Tell her I'll drive her round to the boatyard to pick up her car.' He was frowning as he rang off; it wasn't like Rachel not to come in to work and not telephone to let him know. His uneasiness grew as he pulled down the shutters, locked up and went across the waste ground towards his van.

Freda met him at the back door. 'Rachel's not here. Her bed's made and her room looks as tidy as it did yesterday. I don't think she could have been here last night, unless she left very early in the morning, before we were up ourselves. She wasn't planning to attend one of your house sales, was she?'

'Not without transport. She left her car at Blake's boatyard yesterday afternoon. It's about five miles from here, she'd hardly have walked there to fetch it, would she?'

'I haven't seen Rachel since she left to meet you yesterday afternoon,' Freda said. 'Neither has George. But we've been so concerned about the wretched heifer we've hardly been in the house. Where would she have gone? Without transport, she could hardly have gone far!'

Jennifer looked over her shoulder from where she was peeling vegetables at the kitchen sink. 'I didn't see her at all this morning,' she said slowly. 'And when I washed up the breakfast crocks there wasn't a plate or cup for her. She must have gone out without even a cup of tea or a bite to eat. That's not like her.'

Freda was staring at Michael with wide, anxious eyes and the same thought came into both their minds together.

'Didn't she come home at all last night?' Freda asked. 'But she was with you, and you said she didn't have her car. You would have brought her back here in that case, surely?'

'It was a bit more complicated than that.' Michael felt the puzzled, almost accusing eyes on him. If Rachel had come to harm, when she was supposed to be with him —

But that was ridiculous. He'd left her at the harbour, less than a mile from the farm.

'She said she wanted to see Mrs Blamey,' he said. 'I left her by the harbour steps, no further than across the road from the shop. I went on to take a boat back that we'd hired.' No need to go into more detail about that.

'Ida Blamey doesn't open her shop on Sundays,' Freda said. 'Whatever would Rachel want to be buying at that hour?'

'It wasn't to shop. She wanted to see her about something else — of course! That's where she'll be!' Ida might have been taken ill; more upset by the news than they expected, particularly if she believed the body might be Walter's. 'I'll go down to the shop right away.'

'Rachel at Ida Blamey's all night?' Freda looked like wanting answers to some awkward questions. Michael wanted to get away, and clearly Mrs Blamey was the person to ask, particularly if it was possible Rachel was still with her. He ran back to the van, leaving Freda staring blankly after him.

The general stores looked as usual. He

pushed open the door, expecting to find either Ida or Rachel, or both of them, in the shop. There was no one. He hammered on the door leading to the back of the premises. After a while, Mrs Blamey appeared, looking flustered.

'Where's Rachel?' Michael demanded, his voice sharp in his anxiety.

'Rachel? Rachel Hayward? How should I know? I haven't seen the lass since Saturday night. She'll be up at the farm with her folks, no doubt.' Ida glared at him; if he wasn't a customer, he had no call to disturb her.

'Rachel came to see you yesterday evening,' Michael persisted. 'I left her by the harbour steps, across the road from here. You must have seen her.'

'She didn't come here. I was alone upstairs. I'd have heard if she had knocked.' Whether she would have opened the door was another matter, but that was not this man's business.

'She wanted to see you urgently. She had only to cross the road. She must have come. It would have been between seven and eight o'clock, I suppose.'

'I can assure you she didn't come here. I was by myself upstairs in my flat all yesterday evening.' Mrs Blamey made to turn back into the private part of the building, then paused. 'Happen she went to see Stephen,' she said, with a sly look. 'She may have told you she was coming to see me, but then, I know she's very friendly with him and she may have thought it better not to say anything.'

Michael gave an exclamation of exasperation. He knew Rachel would not have deceived him, but it was just possible that, if she hadn't been able to make Mrs Blamey come to the door, she might have gone to Stephen's cottage to ask him to break the news to her. In fact, the more he thought of it, from what Rachel had told him about the pair of them, it was beginning to sound likely that Rachel had changed her mind and decided to ask Stephen to tell Ida for her, or at least to come with her to break the news to the elderly Cornishwoman. With a muttered 'thank you' he turned on his heel and strode out of the shop.

He knew which was Stephen's cottage, a couple of doors along, beyond the passage running beside the shop. The front door opened right on to the street and Michael hammered on it loudly, but to no avail. He went down the passageway which led to the backs of the row of shops and cottages, to see if he could see Stephen's van parked anywhere, but it was not there. He crossed to the harbour wall and tried to pick out Sea Pie among the boats at anchor. Most of them had been laid up for the winter, with awnings covering the cockpits, so it was easy to spot the few still being used, but there was no distinctive blue — sailed boat among them.

He didn't know where to enquire next. All this was very unlike Rachel and he was seriously worried. If she was all right, the sensible thing for her to do by now would be for her to collect her car from the boatyard. It was impossible to do much in this county without one's own transport and she'd need it to reach the shop or anywhere else she might have thought of going. Rachel was an independent girl, she might well have walked to the boatyard rather than ask someone, such as her uncle, to give her a lift. Perhaps she would have left a message with the boatmen. He climbed back into his van and took the road towards the boatyard.

When Michael arrived, he saw at once that Rachel had not been to collect her car. It was still in the same position where she had left it on Sunday. The boatyard men, from being mildly suspicious, turned sympathetic when they realised Michael was genuinely concerned about Rachel.

'She has the keys with her. She'll have to come and collect it soon; she needs that car,' he told them.

'Oh, aye. Can't get anywhere this time of

year without your own transport,' the boatmen agreed. 'Shall I tell her to give you a call, like, when she comes?'

It was as much as he could do, but to make sure Rachel got the message, he wrote 'Rachel — call me immediately! Michael,' on a page from his diary, tore it out and tucked it under the windscreen wipers.

For want of any better ideas, he returned to the farm. By now, Freda was torn between worrying over Rachel and her anxiety over the calf, who had not made as complete a recovery as at first had been thought. The vet had been called out again, and was with George in the barn. George was phlegmatic, sure that, wherever she was, Rachel was able to look after herself and would turn up with a reasonable explanation in due course. He was far more concerned with the fate of his ailing heifer and disinclined to think of anything else.

Michael telephoned the shop and his home from the farm, and had no reply from either. He rang Mrs Dudley in case Rachel had taken it into her head to visit her, but there was no news there, either. He didn't mention their visit to Penhaligon's Rock, playing down Rachel's disappearance and saying casually that he wondered if she had called in to see her.

'No, Mr Conway, I haven't seen her, not since you last called to see me together. I'm busy packing to move to my flat and do you know, I'm quite excited about it?' Mrs Dudley was disposed to be chatty, but he cut her off with the excuse that he had more calls to make, and came back into the farm kitchen. The truth was, he had run out of ideas of where to look. Rachel seemed to have completely disappeared off the face of the earth.

He also felt guilty. He should never have left her at the harbour. He should have come with her to see Mrs Blamey, or insisted that they took the boat back together and then drove back to St Morwenna's bay. He knew Rachel would have argued; either they'd be late bringing the boat back or late before calling on Ida Blamey. It made no difference; he felt somehow that Rachel's disappearance was his responsibility.

'You look as if you could do with a coffee.' Jennifer was in the kitchen and reached for the kettle as soon as she saw him. 'It's not like Rachel to up and disappear like this, without leaving any message. You two didn't have a row, did you?'

'Far from it. We were planning to buy a house together. We had made all kinds of plans for the future,' Michael said morosely.

Jennifer brought two cups of coffee to the table and sat down opposite him. He was glad she was the only one here at present; Freda's twittery anxiety and George's lack of concern for anything but his animal, were both driving him to exasperation.

'I'm glad things are working out here for her,' Jennifer said, sipping her coffee. 'I was rather a pig to her when she first came. I thought she'd be a stuck-up townie, but she proved she could pull her weight when it came to work. I'll own she was much better at the B & B business than I ever was,'

'That's what we are planning to do in the new house, as well as running the antiques business,' Michael said. 'I wanted to tell her, the house purchase is going ahead. We have so many plans. We were talking about them yesterday but I didn't know then that I'd had an offer for my own house. She would never have disappeared willingly. I'm worried something must have happened to her, but what could have, between here and the village?'

'Have you told the police?'

'No, but I'm going to have to. I've already seen them once today.'

'You've seen the police? Why, what for, if not about Rachel?' Jennifer's dark eyes regarded Michael with a puzzled look.

He hesitated; perhaps he ought not to say anything, but it would all be public news soon; the police were intending to set out in the coastguards' launch as soon as possible.

'We went out on a boat trip yesterday,' he told Jennifer. 'Rachel's had this obsession ever since she came here. She wanted to have a picnic on the top of Penhaligon's Rock. I know it's hardly the right time of year — '

'But you can't get on to the rock! The sides are sheer, and there's sharp rocks all round! And the tides are fearfully dangerous!' Jennifer's eyes rounded in horror.

'So everyone was always telling her. But we had met someone, an old lady, and by chance she happened to mention that she and her sister used to row out and land on the rock when they were young. She made it sound quite easy — '

The colour had drained from Jennifer's face. 'Oh, my God!' she whispered. 'You didn't try?'

'Yes, we did. And the old lady was right. There's a narrow gap in the rocks, just as she told us, and a tiny jetty with steps cut, leading to the top. You'd never know, you'd never even see it unless you knew where to look for it.'

'You didn't land on the rock?' Jennifer's hand, holding her cup, shook so much she spilt coffee on the table.

'Yes, we landed. It was disappointing, pretty awful, really. Gulls everywhere. But while we were there we found a cave — '

'Cave?' Jennifer stuttered.

'A fault in the rock which had been artificially enlarged. Must have dated from the time old pirate Penhaligon was using the rock for his wrecking activities. But it had been used for other purposes since. Quite recently, I should think. There were things in the cave, things which had to be reported to the police.'

'What things?'

'Some sacks. I'm virtually certain they were part of a drugs haul. Looked like they had heroin or something similar in them. And there was something else, too. There was a body, buried under some rocks at the back of the cave. Rachel was convinced if had to be either Mrs Blamey's husband or Stephen's father, who were both lost at sea. I know it sounds unlikely, but she'd heard how their bodies were never recovered, and that's unusual, round this coast. The corpse looked to have been dead about five or six years, about the time they were lost, she said. She was so convinced, she wanted to prepare Mrs Blamey straight away, before the police came to see her. She thought it might be a great shock to her; a shock anyway whoever it turned out to be. The man was dressed like a fisherman; if he was local Ida probably would have known him.'

'Rachel thought the body belonged to Ida's husband? And so she went to see her?'

'Yes. I landed her by the harbour steps. She only had to cross the road to the shop, but Ida Blamey swears she never spoke to her, never had a visit from her at all. It's ridiculous; Rachel must have gone to the shop. Where else could she have gone?'

Jennifer was on her feet, white and shaking. She grabbed Michael by his sleeve and pulled at him.

'Stephen!' she said in a choking voice. 'Come on, quickly! We must go to Stephen's cottage!'

Michael was about to say that he had already been there, without success, but Jennifer's manner made him decide to go along with whatever was in her mind. After all, she knew Stephen better than anyone.

'Turn your van round in the yard while I fetch something from upstairs!' Jennifer commanded. She ran out of the room and he did as she bade him, hardly ready before she rushed out of the farmhouse and flung herself into the passenger seat beside him.

'Harbour!' she gasped. 'Stephen's house!'

Five minutes later he pulled up outside the

tiny cottage. 'I've been here already,' he said. 'Stephen wasn't in.'

'I have his keys. I can check if he really isn't here. Or if Rachel's here.'

Jennifer slid out of the van and ran up to the front door. She pulled a bunch of keys from her pocket, unlocked the door and flung it open. Michael followed her inside, the door leading directly on to the main living room. It looked very bare; an armchair drawn up to the dead ashes of a fire, a worn rug covering a stone flagged floor and in the corner a scrubbed wooden table and two chairs. Jennifer took everything in in one sweeping glance, then turned to run up the uncarpeted staircase leading from behind the front door. Michael heard her clattering around on bare boards upstairs and thought, with mild surprise, that she seemed to know her way around the cottage very well. Rachel had told him how Jennifer had seemed to be very possessive where Stephen was concerned, though he didn't appear to show much interest in return. But surely, he must feel something for the girl, else why had he let her have the keys to his home?

'He's gone.' Jennifer came rushing back down the stairs. 'All his clothes and personal things have gone. He's cleared out.'

'What? And you think Rachel might have

323

gone with him?' There was a cold stone in the place where Michael's heart had been, as he recalled Ida Blamey's insinuation.

'Not willingly. She couldn't stand him. But if she's been snooping round the rock then he'd have needed to keep her quiet.'

'What do you mean, keep her quiet?' Michael was remembering the white van which had forced him off the road last night. Stephen had a van, and he thought it might have been white. But had Rachel been a passenger in it?

Jennifer faced him, her face white and frightened. 'I mean, Stephen's involved with things. Things against the law, smuggling and such. If he knows the police are going to Penhaligon's Rock then he'll have disappeared. What I don't understand is, why take Rachel with him if he knew you had seen the cave too, and what was in it? Unless he planned to hold her hostage.'

'Where would he go? You must know. You seem to know him very well.'

'Oh, I know him very well indeed! I've always known what he was getting himself into. We'd better see if his van is still here.'

'It wasn't round the back. I looked earlier,' Michael said.

'He keeps in it the Anchorage car park.'

'Then it probably is still there. His boat

isn't in the harbour. He must have left in that.'

'Not necessarily. Someone else uses Sea Pie sometimes.' Jennifer ran out of the cottage and down the street to the ancient pub. Michael followed close behind her.

The Anchorage's car park was empty.

'He's really gone, then.' Jennifer stood stock still, looking as if she had finally run out of steam. She put out a tentative hand and touched Michael's arm. 'Don't worry about Rachel. I'm sure he wouldn't do her any harm. And it's always seemed to me, she's one tough, resourceful woman; she wouldn't let him take her anywhere she didn't want to go.'

'Then where is she?'

Jennifer stared back down the road. Thoughtfully, she said, 'You said you left her at the harbour steps? Sometime between seven and eight o'clock?'

'Yes, it must have been about that time. It was nearly completely dark. I had trouble finding my way back to the boatyard, up river.'

'And you actually saw her crossing the road towards the shop?'

'No. I didn't wait. I was anxious to be away. Soon as she was on the steps I pushed off. I didn't look back, I was too busy avoiding the boats moored here. I should have come with her, I know I should. But she only had to cross the road. How could she have not have reached the shop and seen Mrs Blamey?'

'Not if Stephen had seen her first. He might have done. And she would have told him where she'd been, perhaps even asked him to come with her to speak to Ida. He'd have known then that he'd need to get away, and fast. But he wouldn't have been able to pack his things and take her with him. He must have tricked her somehow; persuaded her to go somewhere where she wouldn't be able to raise the alarm, to give him more time. But where? Oh, my God, no!' Jennifer's hands flew to her cheeks and she stared up the road, a look of horror on her face.

'What is it?' Michael asked.

'The old tin mine. I know he uses it to store some of his stuff. It's on the Prescott's farm land but he has access. It's a terribly dangerous place, there's an open shaft in the wheelhouse — surely he'd never — oh, come on, quickly, we must get over there and find out!'

12

Jennifer rushed for Michael's van and he leapt into the driving seat beside her. 'Show me the way!' he demanded, starting the engine.

'Nearest we can get by road is along the road leading out of the village. You'll have to park half way up the hill and cut across the fields. Stop just before the bend — you'll see a stile in the hedge.'

It wasn't a good place to leave any vehicle, let alone a van, but Michael was past caring. He pulled over by the stile and they both scrambled out. Jennifer led the way across the fields and he hurried after her, trusting she knew the way.

'Shouldn't we drive back to the farm and call the police?' he asked.

Jennifer shook her head. 'Not yet. Mrs Prescott would be worried sick if she overheard you calling the police. Let's make sure Rachel isn't here first. We'd be wasting time to go back to High Topp before we've checked here.'

Michael saw the ruined buildings as they crested a rise in the ground. The wire fence surrounding the mine was intact, but Jennifer ran at once towards the gate.

'The padlock has gone! And he always keeps it locked! Stephen must have been here recently.'

'Rachel! Rachel, where are you?' Michael shouted. There was no reply.

'Where could he hide her here? These buildings are nothing but crumbling shells,' he said.

'There's the wheelhouse, where the shaft leads down into the mine. That's mostly intact, and it's been sealed off.' Jennifer was hurrying forward and Michael had difficulty keeping up with her as she slipped between the walls of buildings. 'No one ever comes here, it's too dangerous with the open shaft still there. They blocked off the wheelhouse but Stephen has a key. He uses it to store things; the Prescotts think he just keeps fishing nets and things like that, but that's not all he keeps here. If he's put her somewhere here, she could be here for months, years even, and not be found.'

Michael looked round frantically. 'Where's the wheelhouse, then? Where could he have put her?'

'Over here.' Jennifer led the way across the mine and stopped in front of a brick building, still largely intact. Michael stared at it. 'Is this the only way in to it? That's a steel door! We can't break that down!'

'Prescotts put that up because holiday people love to mosey round old places like this and they were worried they wouldn't take any notice about the Danger — Keep Out sign on the gate. They don't, either.'

'Look, you had Stephen's keys. Would one for this door be with them?'

'I had his house key. I go and clean up for him occasionally. I don't have any others of his.' Jennifer stared at the solid door. Then, she pointed to the ground nearby. 'Look, those marks. Two grooves, like something being dragged — two feet gouging out a track to the door. She must be in there.'

'Rachel! Rachel, can you hear me? For God's sake, say something!' Michael shouted.

The silence was unnerving. He looked around and found a plank, half buried in the weeds growing nearby. Desperately, he used it to try to lever the door from its lintel, but succeeded only in snapping the plank, rotten with damp.

'It's no good. We'll have to go back to the farm,' he said. 'Has Mr Prescott a key, do you know, or should we try breaking it down with a crowbar?'

'Only Stephen had a key for this door,' Jennifer said. 'And you'll need the Cliff

Rescue Service to break down that door. I suppose you'll want to call the police, too, but Stephen will be long gone by now.'

Michael stared at her, realisation dawning. 'You wanted him to get away, didn't you? You checked his house first to make sure he had gone, before you thought of rescuing Rachel.'

'I didn't think he'd do her any real harm,' Jennifer said. Her voice shook a little, but then she added, defiantly 'but yes, I wanted Stephen to get away first. Of course I did.'

By now, Michael was not sure of his bearings but he decided it must be quicker to go back to his van and drive to High Topp farm by road. He raced back over the tussocky grass, leaving Jennifer behind and not caring whether she could keep up or not.

It was lucky that the first person he found when he drove into the yard of the farm, was George Prescott. George's calm manner and practical sense asserted itself at once.

'Freda's out feeding the hens. Best if she don't hear what's afoot until she has to,' he said, when Michael had explained what he feared about the mine. 'You go in and call the emergency services. Tell the police what's needed. I'll collect what we have here; ropes, crowbar and such. Take it on the tractor; it'll get across the fields quicker'n anything. Tell 'em to meet us at the mine. They'll know where it is; all of 'em are listed in their records.'

Michael went straight through the kitchen into the hall, helping himself to the telephone. The police were at first sceptical about the likelihood of anyone being shut in the mine, without any firm evidence, but were prepared to come and check inside the wheelhouse. Michael was too concerned about Rachel to confuse the issue by reporting Stephen's disappearance. The man had gone; whatever connection he had with Rachel's disappearance could be gone into once Rachel was found.

He drove back to the stile in the hedge, not knowing any other way to the mine through the Prescott fields. He found George and a couple of farmhands already there. The fence had been pushed aside to make room for the tractor to be driven inside. They had already set up ropes in an attempt to pull down the steel door.

'If we can't do it this way, I'd drive the tractor into the wall and knock a hole,' George said, 'except our lass might well be lying behind it. Got to go carefully; we don't know what we may find inside.'

They had not managed to shift the door before an official looking van trundled across the field towards them. A policeman in combat gear jumped down and examined the door.

'Won't get yourselves very far with ropes on a door like that,' he commented. 'But don't worry; we'll soon have it moved aside. What's inside?'

'The mine's winding gear and the shaft — and, we think, my niece,' George said. 'There's evidence someone was recently dragged across the rough ground from the gate to this door, and the man who has the only key has made off, sudden-like.'

The uniformed men went to work with steel ropes and professional skill. Barely a quarter of an hour later, the steel door was lying on the ground and they were all clustered round the gaping hole where it had been.

'My God — he's flung her down the shaft!' Michael cried out, staring in horror at the pit in the centre of the floor, and the empty space surrounding it. He moved forward to the rail that went part way round the edge, and looked down. The shaft was probably some hundreds of feet deep, but was blocked by the roof of the lift cage, ten feet below. And, lying on the top of the cage in a motionless heap, was Rachel.

'We'll need ropes and a stretcher to reach her,' the policeman said. 'The ambulance is on its way. We'll send an experienced cliff rescue climber down first to make sure all's safe.'

'No! I'll go down myself. Your men can lower me,' Michael said.

'I couldn't allow that, Sir. My men are experienced — '

'I'm a trained paramedic. Lower me now; I can assess the situation while we're waiting for the ambulance. Look, I can do it. I have been trained for situations like this.'

The policeman muttered his disapproval but called for ropes and a lowering cradle to be set up. While he waited, Michael looked down at the pathetic heap below, lying so horribly still. The nightmare was repeating itself; he was back to that day when he had approached the body laid out by the side of the roadway. He'd been in the car behind, had seen the crash, knew it had been Carol in the car that took the full brunt of the smash. He'd walked up to that body, not knowing what he was going to find. Again, the scenario was about to be repeated; he was going to be lowered down to Rachel and he didn't know what he was going to find when he reached her. This time, though, it was he who was responsible. Instead of watching helplessly while ambulancemen fought for Carol's life, it would be him, and the first thing that he did for her, which might determine whether Rachel lived or died. That was, if she was not already dead.

'We're ready, Sir. If you insist on going yourself. But there is a competent ambulance crew here, used to cliff rescues.'

He looked towards the door. Two men in dayglo orange plastic jackets stood, holding a stretcher.

'I was a paramedic in London for ten years,' he said. 'And I have a bit of experience of climbing with ropes.'

One of the ambulancemen nodded. 'We're not trained paramedics. Ambulance service doesn't run to that much training for half the crews. You'll be all right, Sir. They'll lower you in a strap seat and you can direct us with the stretcher.' He looked over the edge of the shaft. 'That's the roof of the lift cage she's on. Must be wedged in the shaft, not much more than ten feet down, I'd say. There's a chance she's okay, but be careful when you land on it. Don't want your weight to dislodge it and send it to the bottom.'

Michael flashed him a grin and a thumbs up sign, showing a confidence he didn't feel. They began to lower him over the edge but it seemed an age before he was on his knees beside her, barely daring to move in case he dislodged the lift cage. He felt for a pulse and his voice sounded hoarse and echoed in the shaft as he called up. 'She's alive! Pulse is faint but it's there! I'm checking her injuries.'

He slid his hands round her neck, then down her back and to his intense relief Rachel stirred as he touched her.

'Michael — ' It was no more than a whisper.

'Darling! You're safe now. We'll get you up in a stretcher just as soon as I've checked for injuries.'

'I think I might have broken my shoulder. I think I must have fallen on it and it hurts like hell. I must have passed out. How long have I been here? Oh, I'm so cold!'

He bound her arm to immobilise her shoulder and covered her with a blanket that was quickly lowered down to him. The stretcher followed and he laid Rachel on to it, following the instructions from the cliff rescue servicemen above. One of them had wanted to come down and assist, but did not want to risk any extra weight on the lift roof. George was already expressing concern that the rusting winding gear that had held it in place would not support much weight now.

It took the combined skills of the cliff rescue team to ease the stretcher, with Rachel strapped to it, out of the shaft. Michael followed swiftly, discarded the harness and

335

caught up with the stretcher bearers by the time they were loading it into the ambulance.

'I'll try to go steady, the field is pretty bumpy,' the driver apologised, as they set off.

Jennifer climbed in beside Michael, looking at him questioningly.

'Looks like a broken shoulder and concussion. And the beginnings of hypothermia,' he told her. 'We've been so lucky. It could have been so very much worse.'

When Rachel opened her eyes again the place seemed to be full of light, everything white where she had expected the blackness of the mine shaft. Someone took her hand.

'Michael?' she asked hopefully, not really believing it could be possible.

'I'm here, darling. You're safe now.'

She saw his face, in front of what seemed to be an enormous bank of flowers. She stared at them, blankly. Flowers in a mine?

'Mrs Dudley sent them,' Michael said, following her eyes. 'I've things to tell you. Good things, about the house. But not until you're feeling up to hearing about them. They will keep.'

'I fell. It was down a deep shaft. I don't remember reaching the bottom. It must have been miles deep. So how — ?' She looked at her surroundings; a white, clearly a hospital, bed; a small, white painted room and the scent from masses of glorious flowers. The best thing of all was that Michael was there beside her, holding her hand. She frowned in an effort to remember. 'Tell me what happened,' she asked.

'You hurt your arm. Fractured collarbone, the doctor diagnosed. And you have some concussion. Nothing that won't heal completely in time. Don't struggle to remember anything now. It'll all come back to you eventually.'

'But I do remember,' Rachel said. 'Stephen shut me in the wheelhouse at the mine. But he didn't push me down the shaft; I fell, in the dark. But the shaft must be hundreds of feet deep. How did I — ?' She stared at Michael, a bewildered look on her face.

'The lift cage was wedged in the shaft, about ten feet below. You fell on to the roof of it.' He couldn't tell her then, what he had seen by daylight himself the following day, how easy it would have been for her to miss the lift cage and fall down the gap between the wall of the shaft and the cage itself. There would have been nothing to stop her falling hundreds of feet and ending up below the cage, almost impossible to reach, and almost certainly dead. Stephen might not have intended to harm her, but he must have known the danger of the shaft and that she was likely to fall down it in the dark. Michael closed his eyes, not wanting Rachel to see the horror reflected in them. He was glad Stephen had disappeared, otherwise there might well be another body in the shaft, and he wouldn't be rescuing that one.

Later that day, Jennifer came shyly into the little room off the main ward. She hesitated by the door, looking questioningly at Michael.

'How is she? I don't suppose she'll want to see me.'

Rachel opened her eyes. 'Of course I do,' she said. 'I'm feeling much better now. Why should I not want to see you?'

'Because Stephen was responsible, wasn't he?'

Rachel gave a gentle shake of her head, all she could manage without a sharp twinge of pain.

'He didn't try to kill me. I fell. But he did shut me in there. I'm sorry, Jennifer. I know how you feel about him. You've always been in love with him, haven't you?'

'In love with him?' Jennifer shook her head. 'I care a great deal about Stephen, but hardly in love. He's my brother, after all. Didn't you know that?'

'Your brother? But how could that be?

338

You're name's Pascoe, not Tresillian.'

'Half brother. Same mother, different fathers. And that's just as well, in my opinion. Stephen's father was a crook; went into smuggling drugs in a big way. Stephen has gone a fair way towards following in his father's footsteps. I've worried about him for years, but what could I do? He would never listen to me or take any notice of anything I said.'

'You seemed so — you seemed as if you were jealous of me, the times it looked as if I was being too friendly with Stephen. The times I went out with him in his boat,' Rachel said.

'Not jealous,' Jennifer said gently. 'But I didn't want you getting close to him. Either you'd have found out about his smuggling and shopped him to the police, or you'd have been drawn into it yourself. I wasn't sure at first which way was more likely but either way there would have been trouble. He was very attracted to you and I didn't want you to be mixed up with him, for the Prescotts' sake. They've been good to me. But for your own sake, too. I liked you, though I know I didn't exactly show it. You have so much energy for work, and you've been so successful. I envied you, I suppose. It was like a window opening on the real world, having you at the farm.'

Rachel stretched out her good arm and clasped Jennifer's hand. 'Thanks,' she said. 'I'm sorry we had to be the ones to uncover Stephen's activities to the police. But there's more, that you may not know. We found a body in the cave on Penhaligon's Rock.'

Jennifer nodded. 'It had to come out, eventually. They couldn't hide him for ever, But it wasn't Stephen who was responsible for his death, or for putting him there. That I do know.'

'You knew about there being a body hidden on the rock?' Michael asked.

'Yes. Stephen told me what happened. I'll tell you both everything I know now, but afterwards I shall deny I knew anything at all. Do you understand? There will be trouble enough and repercussions in the village for people who have done nothing wrong, as it is.'

'Tell us,' Rachel begged. 'After that bang on my head I shall probably forget everything afterwards, anyway.'

'The body has been on the rock about six years. At that time, Stan Tresillian and Walter Blamey were involved in a drugs smuggling racket with a gang from the continent. They met with a Dutch sailing boat out at sea, received a consignment of the stuff and hid it in the cave on the rock until it could be shipped ashore and sent on to the dealers, mostly in London and other big cities. Cornwall is a good place for landing smuggled goods, always has been. And no one expects a boat from Holland to come this far to unload. It's always drugs these days, that's where the money is.'

'I'd never have thought of Stephen as a drugs runner,' Michael said. 'His home was pretty spartan. What does he do with his money?'

'Stephen isn't where the real money is. He meets the boat and collects the consignments. He stores the goods either in the cave or at the mine. What he is paid for that keeps him, no more. Have you any idea how bad the fishing and boat hire business is? He only does that as a cover, so it looks as if he is earning a living from it.'

'Whose body is it in the cave?' Rachel asked. 'Is it Stephen's father or Walter Blamey?'

'I don't know what the man's name is, but I know it's neither of them. Stephen wasn't so much involved in those days, though he'd sometimes go out and crew for them. The story as I heard it from him, was that there was some argument with the Dutch skipper about one of the consignments, and the man followed them on to the rock. There was a fight and the man was knifed. Stanley and Walter hid the body but then they had the problem of what to do with the man's boat. Stanley took it out to sea with the idea of abandoning it near the Dutch coast. No one knows what actually happened, but he must have got into difficulties and the boat capsized. Stanley was drowned, but it's likely that if his body was found, he was identified as the Dutch skipper. Walter decided to disappear and lie low. He's not dead, but everyone believes he is. Only Stephen and Ida Blamey know different.'

'He still visits her, late at night?' Michael asked.

'How do you know that? He does, but no one has seen him. I never have.'

'We have,' said Rachel. 'We saw someone going down the passageway beside the shop, one evening when we were parked near the harbour wall. We thought it was someone about to break into the shop, so we followed him. Then we heard Mrs Blamey speak to him and we thought it must be a secret boyfriend.'

Jennifer smiled faintly. 'Not Ida. Unless you think a drowned husband might come back as a secret lover. I don't know where Walter lives but I suspect he is still involved with Stephen in the smuggling. They'll both be lying low somewhere and there are plenty of places for them to go.'

'There's something I don't understand,' Michael said. 'The Sea Pie wasn't in harbour when I looked for it, but Stephen's van had gone, too. He couldn't have taken both. How did he get away?'

'Walter uses Sea Pie. It hasn't been in harbour for the last few days.'

'Of course!' Rachel exclaimed. 'I was sure I'd seen the Sea Pie when we were on Penhaligon's Rock, but Stephen said he hadn't been out. I didn't believe him, I was so sure I'd seen the boat.'

'Then you probably did, with Walter on board.'

'And Walter came to the rock while we were there,' Michael said. 'He tampered with our boat. I knew something was different about the way it was tied up when we came to leave.'

'It had to have been Walter. Stephen didn't know where we'd been until I told him.' Rachel made a face. 'I should have kept my mouth shut. Then maybe I wouldn't be here in hospital with a broken collarbone.'

'But Walter knew. They'd have had to silence you,' Jennifer said. 'But did Stephen really believe you'd been out there by yourself? He must have realised that shutting you in the mine wouldn't be enough. How could he be sure that Michael wouldn't go to the police?'

'He tried to make sure,' Michael said quietly. There was a touch of grimness in his tone. 'He — or someone in a white van like his — tried to force me off the road on the way home. I suppose he didn't intend to kill me, merely cause an accident which would delay me for long enough for him to get away as far as possible.'

'He'll have met Walter along the coast somewhere that night,' Jennifer said. 'They'll be miles away in Sea Pie by now.'

'Not for long,' Michael said. 'The police will catch up with them for sure. I'm sorry, Jennifer, but I fear your brother won't enjoy freedom for much longer.'

'I know.' Jennifer sighed. 'Please believe me when I say that I was never involved with Stephen's drug smuggling. I think it's a filthy business. But I couldn't help knowing things. He is my brother and I couldn't shop him.'

Michael looked at her thoughtfully. Then he said, 'You took me to Stephen's cottage, looking for him, yet you must have known he was gone. You wasted valuable time, when you must have suspected where Rachel was hidden.'

'I didn't know! I swear it! I really did think

he might have left her tied up in the cottage at first, then, later, it dawned on me that it would have been easier to persuade her to take the short cut through the fields to the farm, and take her past the mine. But I needed to be sure he'd gone before I could help you rescue her. Stephen was my brother, after all.'

Michael looked as if he would have liked to strangle her, but Rachel put out her hand to him. 'Please, Michael. Let's forget how much Jennifer knew about Stephen. She did try to protect me from him. It wasn't her fault I misunderstood her reasons because nobody told me he was her brother. And I imagine the police will catch up with both him and Walter this time. Let's talk about something more pleasant. Did I dream it or did you really tell me that you've sold your house and can go ahead and buy Mrs Dudley's?'

'I'll leave you now, if you're going to be planning your own futures,' Jennifer said, rising. 'Only I wanted you to know what happened. Some of it may not come out even when it's all made public. I'm not fool enough to think Stephen and Walter will manage to stay free for much longer. But I don't intend to be around when the police start asking everyone what they knew. Goodbye, Rachel. I don't know if we'll see each other again, but good luck with the B & B venture, and the antiques business. You deserve to succeed.'

She had gone before Rachel had time to reply.

'I think,' Michael said gently, 'she was a great deal more involved than she wanted us to think. Not actually involved with smuggling drugs, but she knew exactly what Stephen was up to. She'll disappear too, no doubt, and very probably Ida Blamey will go with her.'

'An empty village! St Morwenna's Bay really will become a ghost town,' Rachel sighed.

'Up to us to put it back on the map when we start up in business next summer,' Michael said. 'Let the tourists know there's more going on in a sleepy Cornish village than they'd ever imagine! Hurry up and get well soon, my love. We've a tour of the country's house sales and auctions to attend, a house to get ready and even a wedding to fit in somewhere before the summer season begins. How does that sound to you?'